Advance

MW01251257

I sat down with *Home of Her Heart* and didn't put the pages down until the end. I couldn't bear to leave Luisa and her life. Tara Goldstein has woven a multi-generational story featuring Luisa, a young woman who has a thirst for the truth, an appetite for love, and a spirit driven by both blood and her chosen family. Tara transports the reader to other continents, different times in history, linking seventeen-year-old Luisa with her adoptive one-hundred-and-two-year-old grandmother Lottie. Luisa's and Lottie's stories remind us of how war and conflict affect children and how their young spirits can find hope for new lives. I was transported into these women's stories.

–Mary Ellen MacLean, Playwright/Creator/Actor/Director

Luisa just wants to know why. Why was she adopted from Colombia to become the daughter of Canadian parents? In her quest for answers, she travels across the Americas, across generations, and deep into the secrets of families and nations. Set in the borderlands of *Latinidad*, Jewishness, queerness, and poverty, there are creative families, profound love, and evocative art. Goldstein offers us a page turner where taboos are challenged head on and adults have to answer for themselves. Crushes and kisses steal the show, and social justice reigns!

–Karleen Pendleton Jiménez, author of *The Street Belongs to Us*

I really appreciate the inclusive and empathetic lens Tara Goldstein shares in this story. It means a lot of us adoptees to be represented with complexity—including the anger, grief, and sadness that we often feel unable to share.

–Martha Hen, writer and editor

The story Tara Goldstein tells here so skillfully is warmly humorous at times, with a real sense of heart, some well-drawn characters, and a powerful message at its core. Her protagonist Luisa journeys down a very difficult road toward growth, and Goldstein doesn't romanticize or oversimplify the complex problems that can stem from international adoption.

–Blair Hurley, author of *The Devoted* and *Minor Prophets*

Heartfelt exploration across two continents and a century of facing the painful impact of childhood loss and having the courage to heal.

–Diane Samuels, author of *Kindertransport* and *Waltz With Me* and creator of daily writing prompts @writingbright

TARA GOLDSTEIN

HOME OF
HER HEART

Home of Her Heart
Copyright © 2023 by Tara Goldstein

Tellwell Talent
www.tellwell.ca

ISBN
978-0-2288-8752-2 (Hardcover)
978-0-2288-8751-5 (Paperback)
978-0-2288-8753-9 (eBook)

To Rose Goldstein with love.

> Our time together was too short. But in the time we did have together, no one could have made me feel more special than you.

To Audrey Lowitz with love.

> Our years of care and friendship will always be with me.

To Margot Huycke with love.

> Our life together has made so much possible.

Shver iz dos lebn in goles.
Life in exile is difficult.
(Yiddish proverb)

AUTHOR'S NOTE

*H*ome of Her Heart is a story about the experiences of queer families who have adopted children transnationally. From 2008 to 2014, I researched a variety of personal narratives from different parts of the world through written work, documentary films, and interviews I conducted with members of transnational/transracial adoptive queer families living in Toronto. The reflections of adoptees were particularly moving.

The Canadian family portrayed in *Home of Her Heart* is a fictional family, the construction of which is informed by my research and reflection. The family is composed of a White, Jewish, lesbian mother named Harriet, her White, non-binary partner Marty, Harriet's daughters Luisa and Ana, who were adopted from Bogotá, Colombia, and Harriet's birth daughter Clare. While Luisa identifies as Colombian and has a strong desire to return to Bogotá, her younger sister Ana does not. Harriet, Luisa, and Ana's different understandings and experiences of adoption reflect the different experiences adoptees shared in interviews and writing. Luisa's adoptive grandmother Nana Lottie is also a fictional character. Her story of being a part of Kindertransport, a program that transported Jewish children and youth out of Nazi Germany in 1933 to live with foster families in England, reflects stories Kindertransport adults have also shared in interviews and writing. Readers interested in reading and listening to adoption and fostering stories can consult the "Further Reading" list at the end of the novel.

Adoptees have written about transnational adoption as "the intimate face" of colonization, racism, militarism, imperialism, and globalization.[1] Many have described their experiences of racism, isolation, abuse, depression, addiction, and alienation through adoption, and they reveal the ways transnational adoption results in emotional and spiritual costs. They also call for long-term solutions that address the root causes of racialized children being removed from their families or surrendered for adoption. At the same time, adoptees have also written about the strategies, supports, and care practices they have created for living beside the trauma. While both Luisa and Nana Lottie experience racism, isolation, and alienation, they also find ways to thrive in places that are far away from the homes of the families they loved and grew up in.

Home of Her Heart is the third writing project I have undertaken to share the experiences of queer families that have adopted children transnationally. The first project was a play called *Harriet's House*, which featured the character of Harriet and focused on how she navigated the challenges of being a White, lesbian, Jewish mother raising two racialized adopted children from Bogotá. I followed up *Harriet's House* with a second play called *Ana's Shadow*, which explored the different ways Luisa and Ana experienced life in Toronto and the different memories they had about their lives in Bogotá. While both plays engaged with the complexities of transnational adoption and raised issues adoptees themselves have written about, I wanted to do a deeper dive into the complicated family and societal politics of transnational/transracial adoption and fostering. Writing a story about two young women, one leaving her home in Germany and the other returning to her home in Colombia, has given me the opportunity to do so. I hope reading the novel will encourage discussions about these politics.

---

1   Jane Jeong Trenka, Julie Chinyere Oparah, and Sun Yung Shin, eds. *Outsiders Within: Writing on Transracial Adoption* (Cambridge: South End Press, 2006).

CHAPTER 1

Luisa held her breath. The Colombian border control officer peered at her passport. Looked up at her, then down at her photo again. Her heart was racing. If he asked why Luisa was alone, she might be in trouble. She was only seventeen. Maybe too young to be travelling without permission from her parents.

"Are you here by yourself?"

He spoke quickly, and it took Luisa a moment to translate his Spanish into English. The question she'd been dreading.

"Yes, I mean, *si*."

Luisa couldn't believe she'd answered him in English. The language that had been her nemesis was now the first thing out of her mouth.

The officer stared at Luisa for several long seconds and then continued in Spanish. So did she.

"Where are you from?"

It was a complicated question. Louise kept it simple.

"Toronto."

"What's the purpose of your visit?"

"I'm volunteering at El Orfanato Para Niños y Niñas in Bogotá."

"What are you going to do there?"

"I'm not sure yet."

The officer gave her another long look and then glanced down again at her passport.

"Luisa Gómez Rodríguez Silver." He took his time saying Silver, drawing out each syllable.

"Yes."

"Canadian?"

"Yes."

"Born in Canada?"

"No. Born in Bogotá. Silver is my adopted name. Gómez is my birth father's name. Rodríguez is my mother's."

"Your adopted family is Canadian?"

"Yes."

"How old were you when you were adopted?"

"Ten."

"Does your family know you're here?"

"My adopted family?"

He frowned, immediately suspicious. "Yes, your adopted family in Canada."

Luisa nodded earnestly and lied. "Of course."

"And someone from the orphanage is expecting you?"

She lied again. "Yes."

"How long are you staying?"

"Six months."

"You don't have a visa. You need a visa if you stay longer than ninety days."

"I know."

It was a sore point. Before Luisa had been adopted, she had been a citizen of Colombia. "Colombia with an *o* not a *u*," Luisa would tell people. "Canadians usually spell it wrong." At one time she could have stayed in the country as long as she wanted. Forever. But not anymore. Now she needed a visa. She was a Canadian tourist.

"But I can apply for it from Bogotá, right?" Luisa asked. "I don't have to leave the country?"

The second the question was out of Luisa's mouth, she regretted asking it. Maybe she'd revealed too much.

"That's correct," the officer said, stamping her passport with a thud.

Luisa allowed herself a quiet, deep breath. "Thanks."

She headed to the baggage pick-up area. It was packed with excited, anxious people, waiting to spot their luggage on the carousel so they could haul their bags off and head out the exit. Luisa was anxious too, and when her suitcase with the bright red ribbon she'd tied around the handle was finally tossed onto the conveyer belt, she cried out with relief, "That one's mine," and pushed her way to the front of the crowd to grab it.

As she joined the passengers waiting to exit, Luisa reminded herself of her next steps: find an ATM, get some pesos, and take a taxi to the orphanage. But when she walked through the glass doors to the arrivals area, she saw a woman holding up a big sign with her name on it.

Luisa's heart started pounding. She hadn't told anyone she was coming. Who'd been sent to pick her up?

The woman lowered her sign so Luisa could see her face. She laughed. It was Sister Francesca, one of the sisters who'd taken care of her and her younger sister Ana when they lived at the orphanage. Sister Francesca's hair had some gray in it, but other than that she looked exactly the same. Big and round. Still wearing the wireframe glasses she had on the day Luisa left. Seven years ago.

"*Hermana* Francesca!" Luisa called out in Spanish.

She broke out in a huge smile. "Luisa! I didn't know if you'd recognize me."

"Of course I recognized you!" She reached around the sign to give Sister Francesca a hug. She felt exactly the same. Soft.

Luisa had always liked Sister Francesca, and Sister Francesca had always liked Luisa. She hadn't been the easiest kid to like when she was living in the orphanage. When Luisa and Ana first arrived, Luisa was only seven and very angry. The smallest little thing set her off. Like someone whispering about her. She had spent a lot of time in the kitchen doing extra chores for saying something mean to one of the other kids. Sister Francesca was in charge of the kitchen. She'd give Luisa potatoes to peel and talk to her. They didn't talk about what Luisa had done to land herself in Sister Francesca's kitchen. She'd talk about her life as a young girl and tell Luisa stories about the sisters who had been her teachers. She loved them so much that she left home at fifteen to join their community, the Sisters of Hope. Luisa once asked Sister Francesca if she'd been scared to leave home so young. She said no. God was calling her. Luisa couldn't imagine choosing a life of service to God. He had too many rules.

"Well, I almost didn't recognize you!" Sister Francesca said. "You're all grown up. I'm so happy to see you, *pequeña*." Luisa loved Sister Francesca's nickname for her. It meant little one.

"I'm happy to see you too." Luisa reached over to give her another hug. "But how did you know I was here?"

"Your mother called Sister Lorena—she's the new director—and asked if someone could come pick you up at the airport."

Luisa dropped her arms and took a few steps back. "Harriet's not my mother," she said. It came out too sharp.

Sister Francesca nodded her head, looking upset. "I know, *pequeña,* I'm sorry."

Luisa took her hand. "No, I'm sorry. I know you know." She took a deep breath and tried again. "Is Harriet angry at me?"

"More worried than angry. You're very young to be travelling by yourself."

"No, I'm not! I've been on my own since I was seven." Still too sharp, she thought.

"I know, but you shouldn't have left without your parents' permission, *pequeña*."

Luisa decided not to argue.

"I want to stay a while and work in the orphanage. Do you think Sister Lorena will let me?"

"You've come back to live with us again?"

"I'll help you peel potatoes."

"You hate peeling potatoes."

"I'll peel a thousand potatoes if Sister Lorena lets me stay!"

"What's wrong?"

"Nothing."

"Are you in some kind of trouble?"

"No!"

"Then why are you here?"

"It's a long story."

Sister Francesca looked at her watch and decided not to push it.

"Okay, you can tell me later, let's go."

"Wait, I don't have any Colombian money. I need to get some pesos."

"Make it fast. Sister Lorena doesn't like to be kept waiting."

On the taxi ride to the orphanage, Luisa sat behind the driver so she could look out the window to catch her first glimpse of Bogotá. There wasn't a lot to see from the highway until they passed the National University of Colombia. But the taxi was moving so quickly Luisa didn't get a chance to get a good look at it.

Sister Francesca wasn't interested in looking out the window. She wanted to talk about Luisa's sister Ana who was fourteen, three years younger than Luisa. Although they were birth sisters, Ana and Luisa didn't look alike. Luisa had long, black, curly hair. Ana's was straight. She was tall and thin, Luisa was shorter and curvier. Luisa's skin was deep caramel brown. Ana's was much lighter. When they moved to Toronto, Ana's gorgeous straight black hair and light skin made it easier for her to fit into their new school, which was almost totally White. She didn't stand out. Luisa did. Ana was able to make friends. Luisa wasn't.

"Does Ana still play hockey?" asked Sister Francesca.

"Three times a week."

"And guitar?"

"Every day. She's writing her own songs now."

"Beautiful! And Clare?"

Clare was Luisa's adoptive sister. She was eleven.

"She's taking Spanish classes after school so when the family comes to visit, she'll be able to talk to everyone."

"Wonderful."

It was easy for Luisa to talk to Sister Francesca. Although they hadn't seen each other for seven years, every month Luisa had written her a letter in Spanish about life in Toronto, and Sister Francesca had written back with news about El Orfanato. Life in Toronto would have been even harder without Sister Francesca's letters, which kept Luisa connected to the one place that felt like home.

As they got closer to the city, traffic slowed right down and the taxi crawled along the highway for what seemed forever. Sister Francesca kept looking at her watch. When they finally arrived in the mountainous, rural district of Ciudad Bolívar, Luisa looked out the window in both awe and shock. In awe because the Andes created a sea of green that was stunning. But in shock because there were so few paved roads. The taxi bumped along one main dirt road passing by one old neglected brown brick building after another. Buildings were crammed up against each other and every one seemed to be falling apart. Luisa wondered what kind of shape the orphanage was in.

When they finally arrived, Luisa was relieved. None of the windows were broken and boarded up with cardboard, and there was no garbage surrounding the house. It looked exactly like she had remembered it. Well-cared for. Luisa paid the taxi driver and hustled after Sister Francesca who was racing to Sister Lorena's office. When they got there, the office door was open, but Sister Lorena wasn't there. Sister Francesca told Luisa to wait.

"I'll see you later," she said.

"Pray for me." Luisa wasn't joking. She'd come back to El Orfanato without asking Sister Lorena for permission. She might not be as happy to see Luisa as Luisa was to see her.

Luisa rolled her suitcase into a corner of the office, sat down on the wooden chair in front of Sister Lorena's big, old desk and looked around. She'd only been in the office once before; the day Sister Francesca showed Luisa and Ana a map of the world so they could see where their new home in Canada was. The map was on the wall beside the door. It was full of coloured pins marking the cities where all the kids adopted from the orphanage lived. A whole bunch of pins circled Toronto. It was very far away from Bogotá. When Sister Francesca placed two new pins on the map, Luisa stared at the pins, holding Ana's hand, knowing their lives would never be the same. Neither of them wanted to leave El Orfanato. After three years of living there, it felt like home.

The map beside the door was still there. There were now a lot more pins surrounding Toronto. Dozens of kids had been adopted in the last seven years. Sister Lorena appeared at the door, and Luisa immediately stood up.

"Luisa Silver?" She didn't sound glad to see her.

Luisa answered in Spanish. "*Si. Hola, Hermana Lorena.*"

"If you don't mind, I'd like us to speak in English."

"Oh. Okay."

"Please sit down."

Sister Lorena spoke English perfectly. Without an accent. Luisa thought Sister Lorena probably correctly assumed Luisa's English was now better than her Spanish. Sister Lorena looked Luisa over. So Luisa looked her over too. Discreetly. Sister Lorena had short black hair, a long nose, and dark black eyes. She was more handsome than pretty.

Sister Lorena sat down, folded her hands on the desk. She looked right into Luisa's eyes, stern.

"Your mother's very worried. I just called to let her know you arrived here safely."

Luisa wanted to tell her Harriet wasn't her mother but didn't. Her gaze was too intimidating.

"Thank you, Sister."

"I asked if she wanted me to send you home."

"What?!"

Sister Lorena raised her eyebrows. Luisa's response was too impertinent.

"I'm sorry, Sister."

She nodded, acknowledging the apology.

"I asked her if you had finished high school—"

"I have, Sister! I've been fast-tracking since grade ten. I'm done now, and I'd like to live here for a while and help out."

Sister Lorena held Luisa's gaze. It wasn't a mean look, but it was very intense. Luisa had to look away.

"Why have you come back?" she finally asked.

Luisa knew she had to be careful about what she said. She needed to find just the right words.

"I have a lot of questions, Sister."

"What kinds of questions?"

"I want to find out why my mother—my birth mother—died. All I know is that she was sick with pneumonia. But people don't die of pneumonia. Not when they're young. And I need to know what happened to my father. Why he wasn't there to take care of us. Why he abandoned us."

Luisa's voice cracked, and her eyes filled up. The last thing she wanted was to cry in front of Sister Lorena. Sister Lorena handed Luisa a box of tissues.

"I was hoping you could help me."

"The orphanage isn't permitted to share any information with you unless we get official permission from the government. To get permission, you need to work with a lawyer. Lawyers are expensive."

"Oh." Luisa's mouth opened in surprise. "I didn't know I'd have to hire a lawyer. Do you think it's possible to look for someone from my mother's or father's family and ask them to tell me what happened?"

Sister Lorena crossed her arms over her chest. "When you left Toronto what was your plan?"

"I thought I could work in the orphanage in exchange for room and board. I'm very good in the kitchen."

"But you never wrote to ask if we had room for you. If your plan would work for us."

Blood rushed to Luisa's face. "No, Sister. I didn't. I'm sorry."

"So, you made an impulsive decision."

"I guess I did. And . . ."

"And?"

"I was afraid if I asked, you might say no."

Sister Lorena paused. Luisa forced herself to sit perfectly still, lowered her eyes and folded her hands in her lap. Finally, Sister Lorena spoke. Luisa looked up.

"This is a very busy place, and there are rules. Lots of them. You left home without your parents' permission and showed up at our door without an invitation. I'm not sure I can trust you to follow the rules."

She winced, now worried Sister Lorena was going to send her back to Toronto.

"However, Sister Francesca speaks highly of you, and your mother says you're an excellent student. I need someone to teach the children English. I know you don't have any kind of formal training, but do you think you could teach the little ones some English songs and games?"

Luisa allowed herself a moment of hope. Maybe Sister Lorena was going to take a chance on her.

"Sure, of course. I could do that."

"I want the older children to learn some English too."

She stood up, so Luisa did too.

"Do you have a phone?"

"Yes, Sister."

"Call your parents. Apologize and ask them if you can stay. If they say no, I'll send you back. If they say yes, ask them to text me. Your mother has my number. I'll make my final decision after I hear from her."

It was like Luisa was ten years old again, hearing for the first time that she and Ana would be leaving El Orfanato to go live in Toronto.

"Thank you, Sister." ·

"You'll need to phone them from here. The Wi-Fi only works in my office. When it works at all. The connection here isn't very strong. When you're done you can go and help Sister Francesca with dinner. Leave your suitcase here."

"Yes, Sister."

She nodded and left the room quickly, all business. Luisa could see she was a problem Sister Lorena didn't have time to deal with.

She walked over to the window. The blue wooden bench next to the front door of the orphanage was still there. The bench where the adoptive parents waited for their new children to say final goodbyes to their friends and the sisters. Luisa's adoptive parents, Harriet and Jonathan, had sat on that bench seven years ago waiting for her and Ana to come out. Luisa took a good look at the bench. The paint had faded and chipped.

Luisa took out her phone and called Harriet. She answered on the first ring.

"Hello?"

"Hi."

"Thank God. Are you okay?"

"I'm fine. Sister Francesca met me at the airport."

"Marty and I've been worried sick. So have your sisters!"

Marty was Harriet's partner. When Harriet and Marty got together after she and Jonathan were divorced, Luisa had been surprised. She hadn't known Harriet was bisexual. Neither had Ana or Clare. But when they thought about it, they realized that lots of Harriet's friends were queer so maybe it shouldn't have been a surprise. Lucky for all three of them, Marty, whose pronouns were they/them, was easy to like. They played women's hockey in a rec league, and when Ana asked Marty to coach her hockey team they immediately said yes. When Harriet first started seeing Marty,

Marty identified as a lesbian, but now they identified as non-binary. About a year after Harriet and Marty got together, Marty moved in.

"I'm sorry everyone was worried," Luisa said.

"I can't believe you left without telling me! When did you buy the ticket?" Luisa could hear she was struggling to keep calm.

"Right after you cancelled our trip."

"Which trip?"

"Which trip?! The family trip to Bogotá! The one you've been promising we'd take for the past seven years. The trip we were finally going to take this summer."

"Your sister won a scholarship to music camp! She couldn't do both."

"But the rest of us could've gone."

"Without Ana? No way. We can all go next summer. There's no big rush."

"Not for you."

"What's that supposed to mean?"

Luisa couldn't believe she had to ask.

"It means I've been waiting seven years to come back. I just couldn't wait anymore."

Sister Lorena had been right. Buying the ticket had been impulsive. The day after Harriet cancelled their trip, Luisa had read up about Día de los Reyes Magos, Three Kings Day. The day the three wise men brought gifts of gold, frankincense, and myrrh to baby Jesus. In Colombia people celebrate Three Kings Day with a parade. Suddenly she had a memory of walking in a parade holding her *mamá*'s hand. While most people have memories of their childhood, Luisa had very few. Memories of her *mamá* were precious, and this was a new one. She could hear drums beating and horns blowing. They were loud. Maybe they'd been walking right behind the musicians.

Luisa had googled Air Canada to see how much it would cost to fly to Bogotá in time for Día de los Reyes Magos. $707 for a cheap one-way ticket. She had $3,500 in her bank account and a credit card. She didn't have to wait for everyone else. She could go herself. All she had to do was type in the credit card number and buy the ticket. It took eight and half minutes.

"But why? Why couldn't you wait anymore?" Harriet was a little calmer now and sounded like she really wanted to know.

"I don't know. I felt . . ." Luisa searched for the right word. "Compelled."

"To do what?"

"Find out why Ana and I were sent to the orphanage."

Harriet was silent. "Your *mamá* was sick," she finally said. Her tone was gentle. "She had pneumonia."

"I know. But people don't die of pneumonia. Why didn't she see a doctor? And where was our father? Everything would've been different if . . . I need to find out what happened."

Harriet was silent again.

"Did anyone ever tell you why he couldn't take care of us when our *mamá* died?"

"No."

"Why did he abandon us?"

"You think he abandoned you?" Luisa could hear the surprise in Harriet's voice.

"Well, he wasn't around to take care of us when *mamá* got sick and then died, so yes, I think he abandoned us. And I want to find out why."

"But what if you can't find out? Or you find out and it's a terrible story?"

"I have to find out. Even if it's terrible."

"You'll be all alone in Bogotá with no one—"

"I can handle it."

Harriet was silent for a few seconds.

"Really, I can handle it."

"Why didn't you tell me how important it was for you to go back?"

"I don't know. I didn't think you'd understand."

Harriet sighed. A sad sigh. Luisa wanted to sigh too. This was just the latest in a long list of things she had never told Harriet because she didn't think she'd understand.

"How long do you want to stay?"

"Six months."

"Six months! That's a long time to be away from home."

"Toronto's not my home. It's *your* home. My home's here. You can't take a girl of ten from her home in Bogotá and expect her to forget where she comes from."

"I never asked you to forget!"

Luisa didn't answer. It was true Harriet had never told her to forget where she had come from. And it was also true that Harriet had always encouraged her to keep up her Spanish. But Luisa knew it'd be easier for Harriet if she did forget. Like Ana who wouldn't take Spanish at school because it was offered at the same time as music.

They'd come to an impasse. The silence was becoming unbearable. But Luisa wasn't going to break it first.

"Are you even allowed to stay for six months?" Harriet finally asked.

"If I get a visa, and . . ."

"And?"

Luisa hated to say it, but she had no choice. "If I have your permission to stay."

"What about university? Applications are due in three weeks."

"I can't think about that right now."

"If you want my permission to stay, you have to promise to apply to three universities before the deadline. And you have to promise you'll try one of them out. For a year."

"But what if I don't find out everything I need to know right away?"

"You can go back. After you finish your first year."

"But—"

"Listen to me. University's a privilege. How many children at El Orfanato get to go to university? One. Maybe two. You get to go. You're going to go. You're going to try it. One year."

Luisa wanted to hang up on her. "I have no idea what I want to study."

"You'll figure it out."

Luisa didn't answer.

"Okay?" Harriet asked.

It wasn't okay. But if Luisa wanted to stay, she had to agree.

"Yes," she said, reluctant.

"Three universities. One year. Promise?"

If Luisa promised, she'd have to go through with it. She always kept her promises. Harriet knew that.

"Promise."

"Good."

"So you'll text Sister Lorena and tell her it's okay for me stay?"

"Yes," answered Harriet, resigned.

"Do I have to get Jonathan's permission too?"

Jonathan now lived in Vancouver. Luisa wasn't sure if he even knew she was in Bogotá.

"I called him right after I talked to Sister Lorena," said Harriet. "He's okay with you staying if I'm okay with you staying."

"Okay, that's good. Really good. *Gracias.*"

Whenever Luisa spoke to Harriet in Spanish, Harriet knew what she was saying came from a place deep inside. Spanish was the language of her heart.

"I want you to call or text me once a week."

"The Wi-Fi only works in Sister Lorena's office. And I can't go in without her permission."

"I'm sure you can find a café with Wi-Fi nearby."

Luisa knew that she'd never find the café with lattes and Wi-Fi that Harriet imagined existed at the end of the street. But it was too hard to explain all that quickly. So instead, she just said, "I'll try."

"Try hard, okay? And be careful."

"I will."

"Good, your sisters want to talk to you. I love you."

Harriet paused for a second waiting for Luisa to say, "I love you too." Luisa almost did, but then didn't. Harriet put Ana on the phone.

"Hello?" said Ana.

"*Hola. ¿Cómo estás?*" asked Luisa.

"What's wrong with you?" answered Ana. "How could you just leave like that? Without telling us?"

Recently, Ana had refused to speak Spanish to Luisa. It used to be their special language. The one they used when they told each other secrets. But that was before they had begun to drift apart.

"*Lo siento,*" said Luisa.

"I hope you're sorry. Do you have any idea how worried I've been?"

Luisa gave up and switched to English. "I'm fine."

"I threw up twice waiting for you to call." Luisa knew Ana often threw up when she was anxious so decided not to feel guilty about it. "Bogotá's dangerous! It's full of drugs and guns and criminals."

"Toronto's full of drugs and guns and criminals too."

"Not where we live."

"I'll be safe at the orphanage."

"When are you coming back?"

"In the summer. You'll be at camp."

"You're staying there until the summer?! Why?!"

"I need to find out why we were sent here. Why there was no one in our *familia* to take care of us."

Ana didn't answer.

"Are you there?" asked Luisa.

There was still no answer.

"Do what you have to do," Ana finally said.

That really annoyed Luisa. "Don't worry, I will. Let me talk to Clare."

Ana dropped the phone on the granite kitchen counter. It made a loud smack. Clare picked it up immediately.

"*Hola*, Luisa!"

"*Hola*, Clara."

"*¿Cómo estás?*"

Unlike Ana, Clare loved speaking Spanish. And she loved it when Luisa called her Clara, the Spanish version of Clare.

"*Muy bien. ¿Y tú?*"

"*Bien*, but I miss you."

Luisa switched to English. "I miss you too. But you need to be happy for me. I've wanted to come back to Bogotá for a long time."

"I know. Text me, okay? And send pictures."

"I'll try."

"*Muy bien. Te quiero.*"

"I love you too." This time it was easy for Luisa to say "I love you too" because she really did love Clare.

Drenched in sweat, she hung up and wiped her hands on her jeans. Harriet said she could stay. Now it was up to Sister Lorena.

CHAPTER 2

A few minutes later Luisa walked into the kitchen and found Sister Francesca chopping vegetables. Sister Francesca looked up from the cutting board when Luisa walked in and smiled. Luisa smiled back. At least one sister at the orphanage was glad she'd come to stay, she thought.

"So?" Sister Francesca asked.

"She's thinking about it."

"Good. While you're waiting for her to make up her mind, you can finish peeling and cutting the carrots for the soup. But wash your hands first."

Luisa laughed. Sister Francesca always said that before putting her to work.

"Okay, but first, I have a present for you. This is for you."

"For me?"

Luisa handed her the gift she'd been holding behind her back. It was a navy blue cardigan Sister Francesca could wear over her habit. While lots of nuns in Colombia wore black habits with white coifs under their black veils, the Sisters of Hope at El Orfanato wore navy blue.

Sister Francesca unwrapped the package quickly.

"It's beautiful! And it matches my habit perfectly!"

Luisa grinned. "It took me weeks until I found just the right navy blue. It's a hundred percent wool so it'll keep you nice and warm. In your last letter you said you've been feeling the cold this winter."

"Thank you, *pequeña*!" She gave Luisa a big hug. "It's lovely! I'll wear it to church on Sunday. Now go wash your hands."

Luisa washed her hands and found a carrot peeler. It was the same peeler she'd used seven years ago. Old and beat up. Everything in the kitchen was old and beat up. The scratches on the long wooden counter were long and deep. The wooden cupboards didn't close properly. The plates, glasses, cutlery, pots, and pans were all chipped, cracked, and dented. But the food that came out of Sister Francesca's kitchen was always fresh, always delicious. She was an amazing cook.

"Okay, I'm ready."

Sister Francesca handed Luisa five bunches of carrots that looked a little old and limp.

"Don't worry," she said. "They'll taste fine once I cook them."

"I know."

Luisa had just finished peeling the second to last bunch when Sister Lorena walked in pulling Luisa's suitcase behind her. Luisa tried to read her face to see what she'd decided. It was unreadable.

"I received a text from your mother," said Sister Lorena. "You have your parents' permission to stay, but I'm still thinking it over. For tonight you can stay in Claudia's room."

Luisa nodded. "Thank you, Sister." She tried for a tone that was appropriately grateful. "I appreciate it."

"You're welcome. *Buenas noches.*"

As soon as Sister Lorena was out the door, Luisa asked Sister Francesca, "What do you think?"

"Hard to say."

"She doesn't like me. I can tell. And I can't say I'm crazy about her either."

"She's the director, *pequeña*. If she lets you stay, you'll have to respect her decisions. We all do."

Luisa gave her a moment to see if she'd say anything else. She didn't.

"So where's Claudia's room?"

"Next to the dining room."

"What's she like?"

"Claudia? She's a wonderful girl. Thoughtful, caring, a hard worker. She's also very smart. She's studying nursing at the National University."

"How old is she?"

"Seventeen."

"I thought everyone had to leave when they turned sixteen."

"Sister Lorena arranged for Claudia to work in exchange for room and board. It was the only way she could accept the scholarship."

"The Global Family Scholarship?"

Sister Francesca nodded. "She's the latest one to receive it."

When Harriet and Jonathan adopted Luisa and Ana, they made a donation to Global Family, the adoption agency they'd worked with, to start a university scholarship fund for the children who hadn't been adopted. Fundraising for the scholarship was one of Harriet's big projects. Marty, Luisa, Ana, Clare were all expected to lead at least one event a year. Marty and Ana always ran a hockey tournament in April. Clare and Luisa tried to do something different every year. Her favorite event was the painting party they hosted. They supplied the canvases, paints, and brushes, and people paid to spend the evening painting and eating and drinking wine and beer.

"What year is she in?" Luisa asked.

"Two. She's doing her nursing practicum at the university hospital. Cut the carrots into—"

"Small pieces. I remember. But she's only seventeen. How can she be in her second year of university? I'm seventeen, and just finished high school!"

"I told you she was smart."

"I'm smart too. My marks are all in the high eighties and nineties. And I didn't even speak English when I started!"

"I know. I remember. It must have been difficult at the beginning."

"Very. No one wanted to be friends with Ana and me. Every recess and lunch we sat by ourselves and watched the other kids play. Until one day, one of the girls waved at Ana and told her to come play tag with them. After that Ana played tag with the girls in her class every recess and every lunch. I sat watching and drawing in the sketchbook Harriet gave me. Pictures of me, Ana, and the girls at El Orfanato. The Toronto girls in my class used to huddle up in a tight group nearby and watch me draw. They'd raise their hands to cover their mouths and whisper and spread stories and lies about my *mamá* and my father. It reminded me of when some of the girls here used to whisper about me. I hated all that whispering!"

"I remember."

"The worst lie they told was that my father was in jail for selling drugs and my mother died of a drug addiction. That's why Ana and I had been adopted."

Sister Francesca was shocked. "*Pequeña*! You never told me about any of this in your letters!"

"I didn't want you to worry. And even if I'd told you, there was nothing you could've done. You lived so far away."

Sister Francesca nodded, tears in her eyes. Her tears made Luisa's fill up too.

"What I couldn't understand was why everyone was so mean to me but not to Ana. We had the same parents, but no one started rumors about her. Finally, I realized it was because I was Brown. Ana was too, but she was so light she passed for White."

Sister Francesca shook her head, confused. "I don't understand."

"At school, it was easier to make friends if you looked White."

She shook her head again, sad for Luisa. "But the second year at school was better, no?"

"Yes and no. At the end of the first year, my teacher said I had to repeat grade five."

"What?! But you were such a good student here! What happened?"

"I refused to answer the teacher's questions. She thought I didn't know the answers. But that wasn't why. It was because everyone laughed at my accent. And the mistakes I made. The only person I could talk to was

Clare. She was only three and a half and didn't care if I made mistakes. She made mistakes too."

Sister Francesca laughed to ease the tension. A quiet laugh. Luisa wanted to laugh with her but couldn't.

"Harriet told me not to worry. All I needed was a little more time to practice. And she was right. My English's perfect now. No accent. If you didn't know I was born in Colombia, you would think I was born in Toronto."

"I'm proud of you, *pequeña*."

Lisa's heart did a little flip.

"Not just because your English is so good now but because you didn't give up when it was so hard to learn it and when it was so hard to make friends. But I'm sure you have lots of friends now."

"Not really. But it doesn't matter."

"Of course it matters. You need friends. Everyone needs friends," she said with warmth in her voice.

"Well, I have a few friends from my Saturday Spanish class. They're from South America too."

"How often do you see them?"

"Only on Saturdays. But it's fine. It's enough. Now that I'm back, maybe I'll become friends with the older girls."

"What about the other children who used to live here? Do you ever see them?"

"Some of them. We get together twice a year. Once at Colombia Night and once at the Global Family summer picnic."

"What's Colombia Night?"

"I never told you about Colombia Night?"

She shook her head.

"It's a party. We have it every November at Harriet's house. It's epic. I make empanadas and everyone dances. I've made an amazing playlist. Salsa, reggaetón, Colombian rock." Luisa didn't know how to say epic in Spanish, so she said it in English.

"What's epic?"

"It means big, huge. Also amazing, fabulous."

"Do you sing?"

"No, just dance."

"You should sing!"

Sister Francesca loved to sing and was a beautiful guitar player.

"So, all the children from El Orfanato go to Colombia Night?"

"Well, not all of them."

"Why not?"

"Some parents think it's better for their kids to forget about the past. Some kids think so too. They don't want to come."

Sister Francesca shook her head. "But it's important to know where you come from! Your language, your culture."

"I know."

"What about church? Do you and Ana go to church?"

Luisa had been waiting for the question.

"You know Harriet and Jonathan are Jewish, right?"

She hadn't. "They're Jewish?"

Luisa nodded. "So's Clare."

"So, you don't go to church? You're Jewish too?"

"No, no," Luisa reassured her. "Ana and I are still Catholic. We celebrate the Jewish holidays with them, and they celebrate Christmas with us. We go to the Christmas Eve service at San Lorenzo."

"Is it a Catholic church?"

"No, Anglican. But the service is in Spanish as well as English and the congregation comes from all over Latin America."

"Why don't you and Ana go every Sunday?"

"It's too far. It takes about an hour to drive there."

Sister Francesca frowned.

Luisa tried to explain. "We have to drive all the way there on Saturdays to get to my Spanish class. That's where the class is. At the church. It's too far to go all the way back the next day."

"There aren't any Catholic churches with Spanish services closer to your house?"

"I don't know. I never asked. Harriet and Jonathan aren't religious. They celebrate the holidays at home. Not at synagogue."

Sister Francesca sighed, disappointed. She tried to hide it by gathering the carrots Luisa had finished cutting and putting them into the soup.

Luisa started cutting up the last bunch. "If you like, I can come to church with you on Sundays while I'm here."

Sister Francesca lit up. "That's a wonderful idea."

Luisa had no idea what going to church in Bogotá would be like. When she was little, they didn't go to Mass, they went to Sunday school. One of the younger sisters told them Bible stories and they'd draw pictures about the stories. Bible class was where Luisa learned to love art. She once drew a really detailed picture of Noah's ark with all kinds of angry looking animals inside. They hated leaving their home.

"Tomorrow's Día de los Reyes Magos, right? Are the kids marching in a parade?"

"We're marching with Father Álvarez."

"Who's Father Álvarez?"

"You don't remember Father Álvarez? He was the priest at your *mamá*'s church. He brought you and Ana here."

Luisa's jaw dropped. "What?! Really?! Then maybe he knows what happened! Why my *mamá* didn't recover from pneumonia. Why my father wasn't around to take care of us when she died."

Sister Francesca reached out for Luisa's hand. "So that's why you've come back. To find out what happened."

"Yes."

She shook her head.

"What?"

"Father Álvarez may not be able to help you. There are rules about sharing confidential information."

"I know. I need permission from the government. But maybe he could introduce me to someone in my *mamá's* or father's family."

"Maybe. But again—"

"I know, I know. There are a lot of rules." Luisa didn't hide her frustration.

"I know it's difficult, *pequeña*. But the rules are meant to protect you. Children come to live here because their families can't take care of them. Their families have suffered. From illness, from addiction. From all kinds of horrible violence. You're here alone in Bogotá—"

Luisa shook her head and dropped her hand. "I'm not here alone! You're here."

Sister Francesca sighed again, and this time it made Luisa angry. She slammed the knife on the wooden counter.

"You don't understand! I need to understand why Ana and I were put up for adoption. Living in Toronto has been really hard. You have no idea how hard it's been."

Sister Francesca took the knife out of Luisa's hand and gave her a hug. The kind of hug people give to someone who's too emotional and needs to calm down. Trapped in the tight hug, Luisa thought if Sister Francesca had sat in on her grade five class listening to the kids guess how much Harriet and Jonathan paid to adopt her and Ana, maybe she'd understand. She took a deep breath. Sister Francesca let her go.

"Can I come with you to the parade tomorrow?"

"Of course."

"I brought some candy from Toronto for the children."

"That's very nice of you!"

"Will you introduce me to Father Álvarez after the parade?"

"Yes, but you have to promise you'll be respectful and polite. And if he tells you he can't help you, I expect you to accept his answer with grace. Can you do that?"

Another promise. Luisa knew this one would be harder for her to keep.

"I'll try," she said. "I'll really try."

CHAPTER 3

At dinner, Luisa sat at the older girls' table and met Claudia. She'd just come back from the hospital and was wearing her nurse's uniform. Her hair was tied up in a tight bun, which gave her a severe look, but even so Claudia was very beautiful. She had big eyes, full lips, and high cheekbones. Smart, hard-working, *and* beautiful, thought Luisa.

"Hi. I'm Luisa," she said.

"Nice to meet you," Claudia answered, reserved.

"Nice to meet you, too. I hope you don't mind me sharing your room."

"Of course not." It was hard for Luisa to tell if she meant it.

"How long are you staying?" Claudia asked.

"I'm not sure yet, but I'll try to be as neat and quiet as I can."

Luisa promised this knowing it wouldn't be easy. She shared a bedroom with Ana who was always complaining she was messy. Ana wanted their room to be neat and orderly, but Luisa didn't care. If she didn't have enough time to make her bed before going to school, she didn't make it. Ana hated coming home after school to Luisa's unmade bed. So she made it for her. Ana also put away the clothes Luisa tossed on the floor and straightened out their closet. Luisa never asked her to. She just did it. Messy made Ana anxious.

"Good," Claudia said. "I need quiet. I need to study after dinner."

"Sister Francesca told me you won the Global Family Scholarship. Congratulations!"

Claudia smiled.

Encouraged, Luisa continued. "My adoptive parents Harriet and Jonathan were the ones who started the university scholarship. Last year I organized a bowling night to raise money for the fund. And donated some of my weekly allowance and babysitting money."

Claudia's smile faded. "That's very generous," she said, polite. Too polite, Luisa thought.

The girl sitting beside Claudia gave her a hostile look. Luisa tried to figure out what she'd said to deserve such a mean stare and realized she'd made a big mistake. Another one. None of the girls sitting at the table got an allowance, and none of them were paid for taking care of the younger children. She blushed. Claudia changed the subject.

"Sophia's applying for the scholarship this year." She looked at the girl who'd given Luisa the nasty look with affection. "She wants to be a pharmacist."

"That's terrific." Luisa smiled at Sophia, but she didn't smile back.

"You don't remember me, do you?" she asked.

Luisa looked at her carefully. Sophia had a round face and wore red-framed glasses. Her hair was dark brown and reached her shoulders. She wore a hair band to keep it off her face. She was cute but not beautiful like Claudia.

"No, I don't. I'm sorry."

"Are you?" Sophia was annoyed. "We slept in the same room. There were only seven of us in the room."

Luisa looked at her again and tried to remember the names of the girls in the room she and Ana had slept in. She could only remember four.

"When did you come?"

"A few weeks before you were adopted."

Something clicked. "Yes, I remember now!" Luisa said. "You didn't wear glasses then, right?"

"No."

"And Ana and I didn't have a lot of time to get to know you because we left right after you arrived."

Sophia refused to give Luisa a break. "We ate together at the same table three times a day."

Luisa moved on. "It's great you're applying for the scholarship."

"We'll see if I get it."

"You'll get it," Claudia assured her. "You're a straight-A student and have a ninety-five percent in chemistry!"

"Ninety-five percent! That's amazing," Luisa said.

"Amazing enough to get the scholarship?" asked Sophia.

"Are all your marks that high?"

"Not as high as ninety-five, but they're all in the nineties."

"Then I can't imagine why you wouldn't get it."

"What are your marks like?" Sophia leaned in and lifted her chin to look at Luisa from the bottom of her glasses.

"Pretty good. But I didn't get ninety-five percent in chemistry."

"What did you get?"

"Eighty-five. But Marty had to help me."

"Who's Marty?"

"They're my adoptive mother's partner."

"Partner?"

"Girlfriend." Luisa wasn't sure that was how Marty would describe themself but didn't know how else to explain their relationship with Harriet.

"Your mother has a girlfriend? What happened to your father?"

"They got divorced."

Sophia stared at Luisa, shaking her head in disapproval, rubbing the silver cross around her neck between her fingers.

"What happened?" asked Claudia.

"Jonathan was offered a job in Vancouver at the University of British Columbia. He wanted—"

"You call your father Jonathan?" Sophia interrupted.

"Yes."

"What do you call your mother?"

"Harriet."

She shook her head again.

"Anyway, Jonathan wanted the whole family to move to Vancouver, but Harriet didn't want to move. She said Ana and I'd already made one big move from Bogotá to Toronto. She didn't want us to have to move again. And she didn't want to live so far away from her mother, Nana Lottie. So, Jonathan moved to Vancouver without us."

The conversations Harriet and Jonathan had had about moving had been intense. Jonathan was sure that the family would adjust to life in Vancouver quickly and argued Nana Lottie was well taken care of at her retirement residence. Harriet argued back and said that after all her mother had been through, losing both her parents in the Shoah, there was no way she was going to move to the other side of the country when she was the only family Nana Lottie had left.

"Is Vancouver far from Toronto?" asked Claudia.

"Very far. Over four thousand kilometers away."

"Really?" She was surprised. Luisa had been surprised too when she found out how big Canada was. Nine times bigger than Colombia.

"You must have been upset to have Jonathan move so far away," Claudia said.

Luisa was thrilled she was interested. Maybe, she thought, they could be friends.

"I was very upset," she said. "I really liked Jonathan. He used to wake up early every Saturday to drive me across the city for my Spanish class. But I was on Harriet's side. We all were. Ana loved the girls on her hockey team. Clare's best friend lived next door. I wanted to keep going to my Spanish classes. We kept trying to get Jonathan to change his mind. But he didn't. The job in Vancouver was his dream job."

"I'm sorry," said Claudia.

Luisa nodded. "Me too."

"Does your mother's girlfriend live with you?" asked Sophia. Talking about Marty was more interesting than talking about Jonathan.

Luisa answered like it was no big deal. "Uh, huh."

"Are they married?"

"No."

"Because it's illegal?"

"No, in Canada, same-sex marriage's legal."

"Here too," said Claudia.

"Really?" said Luisa. "I was wondering if it was."

"It is."

"But the Church won't marry gay people," said Sophia. "Homosexuality is a sin."

Luisa could feel the anger making its way up to her mouth, but before she could say anything that she'd be sorry for later, Claudia calmly and lightly changed the subject.

"So, what are you going to do here?" she asked.

"I was planning to help Sister Francesca in the kitchen, but Sister Lorena wants me to teach English."

Sophia couldn't believe it. "But you're not a real teacher! Have you even finished high school?"

"Of course I finished high school!" Luisa replied flushed with heat, unable to hold in the anger any longer. "I'm applying to university this year, just like you."

Claudia tried to smooth things over. "What are you going to study?"

"I'm not sure yet. Maybe Spanish and Latin American studies."

"If you want to learn about Latin America, you should study here," said Claudia.

"I don't think my Spanish is good enough to study here."

"Actually, I think your Spanish is pretty good."

Luisa felt a rush of gratitude. "Really? I worked really hard not to lose it."

"But you have a really strong accent," said Sophia. "You don't sound Colombian."

It stung, and Sophia knew it.

"Time to clean up," said Claudia.

They both got up. Luisa could've offered to help but didn't. She needed some space from Sophia. Instead, she followed them into the kitchen, picked up her suitcase and rolled it into Claudia's room to unpack.

It was the plainest room she'd ever seen. Two beds, a desk, a chair, and a desk lamp. Nothing on the walls, no rug on the floor. There was a gray-black blanket covering the extra bed. When she lifted it up there were no sheets underneath. Luisa opened the closet. It smelled musty. Like the basement in Harriet's house. She pulled off a set of sheets and a pillow from the top shelf. They were damp. Luisa sighed and made the bed. January was supposed to be the dry season in Bogotá. The blanket was very thin and worn out in a few places. If Sister Lorena let her stay, she'd need to buy a new one. Her guidebook said it got cold at night. Luisa took her cell phone out of her knapsack to see if Ana had texted. No service. No Wi-Fi. She was about to turn it off when Claudia walked in. She took a long look at the phone. Luisa quickly put it back in her knapsack, pulled out the sketch book she'd packed, and started a drawing of Sister Francesca meeting her at the airport. Then her head began to ache. Suddenly she felt nauseous. She rushed out of the room, up the stairs into the girls' bathroom on the second floor. As soon as she got into the first stall she threw up. Again, again, and again.

Luisa returned to Claudia's room to get her toothbrush so she could brush her teeth and get rid of the taste of vomit.

"Are you okay?" Claudia asked. "You look a little pale."

"I just threw up."

"Your lips are blue."

"What?"

"Let me see your fingernails."

Luisa held out her hands.

"They're purple. You have altitude sickness."

"Altitude sickness!"

"Lots of tourists get it," she said.

"But I'm not a tourist! I lived here for ten years before moving to Toronto."

Claudia shrugged.

"What should I do?"

"Do you have any anti-nausea pills?"

Fortunately, Luisa had remembered Harriet's rule: Never travel without a medicine kit.

"Yes."

"Take two. They'll settle your stomach and help you sleep."

"Okay, thanks."

"If you want, I can get you some acetazolamide at the hospital tomorrow."

"What's that?"

"Pills for altitude sickness."

"Thank you. That's very nice of you."

"Make sure you drink lots and lots of water in the next few days. You should probably drink bottled water. And try to breathe deeply every few minutes. You need more oxygen."

"Okay."

Luisa gathered up her pajamas, toiletry bag, medicine kit and returned to the bathroom. She changed, swallowed two anti-nausea pills, brushed her teeth, and tried to take two deep breaths. It wasn't easy.

Before going back to Claudia's room, Luisa knocked on Sister Francesca's bedroom door. She took one look at Luisa's pale face and blue lips and went back to the kitchen to make her a cup of coca tea.

Coca tea is made from raw coca leaves. Sister Francesca took out three leaves, put them in a cup of boiling water and let them steep until the water turned yellow. Luisa leaned over to smell it.

"It smells funny."

"Drink it anyway."

She took a tiny sip. "It's bitter."

"You'll get used to it."

Luisa didn't, but by the time she finished the tea, she felt better. She thought it was the anti-nausea pills, but Sister Francesca was sure it was the tea.

When Luisa got back to Claudia's room, Claudia had turned off the main light so Luisa could go to sleep. She was reading by the light of the lamp on her desk.

"Is that enough light?" Luisa asked.

"Yes, it's fine."

"Okay. Well, good night."

"Good night," Claudia replied not raising her eyes from her book.

Luisa got into bed and touched her stomach. It was still tender, but the nausea had disappeared. As she snuggled under the sheet and blanket, she closed her eyes and allowed herself a moment of triumph. She had pulled it off. She'd made it back to Bogotá.

CHAPTER 4

Luisa didn't sleep well. The entire night she worried she'd be too sick to go to the parade and Sister Lorena would use her altitude sickness as a reason to send her back to Toronto. When she woke up the next day, Claudia was gone. Luisa hadn't heard her get up. Claudia's bed was neatly made, the sheets and blanket tucked in tightly under the mattress just like the sisters had taught them. Feeling nauseous again, Luisa made up her own bed just as neatly then dragged herself to the kitchen to find Sister Francesca. She had a cup of coca tea waiting for her.

"Do want any breakfast?"

"No thanks, I'd better not. I might throw up."

After breakfast, the children gathered outside to wait for the bus that would take everyone to Father Álvarez's church. Luisa packed up the bags of caramels, tootsie rolls, jelly beans, and gummies she had brought from Toronto. Then she went outside to join the lineup of children climbing onto the bus. Sister Francesca had saved the seat beside her for her. Luisa slipped into it, happy to be sitting close to Sister Francesca after all the years they'd been separated.

As they were driving to the church, Luisa tried to keep track of where they were going. But the driver made so many turns she soon gave up. She felt queasy again and popped another anti-nausea pill.

"How often do you go to Father Álvarez's church?" Luisa asked Sister Francesca.

"Just on Día de los Reyes Magos. To join his parade."

"What's he like?"

"He's a Jesuit," she said, expecting Luisa to know what that meant.

Luisa didn't but was too embarrassed to ask.

"He graduated from La Pontificia Universidad Javeriana. It's one of the oldest universities in Colombia. Very prestigious."

"So how did he end up in Ciudad Bolívar?"

Luisa couldn't imagine why someone who'd graduated from such a prestigious university would work in the poorest district of the country.

"He came while he was training to be a priest and found his calling. Most of the children here don't finish high school. They go to work. Father Álvarez knows all the families and the children at his church, and he talks to their teachers to find out which ones are good students. Then he finds a way to help them finish school. The people here love him because he cares so much about education. He's been their priest for over thirty years."

"How long has he been working with the orphanage?"

"I don't know. A long time."

The bus began to slow down and then stopped. Luisa looked out the window. Father Álvarez's church was smaller than she'd expected. It was a modest building made of brown and gray stones. On the top of the roof was a cross carved out of white stone.

Everyone got off the bus and joined the crowd of people lined up at the front of the church. When Luisa had googled Día de los Reyes Magos, she found pictures of parades with hundreds of people marching behind dozens of large glittering floats. Just like the Pride parade in Toronto. But the parade at Father Álvarez's church was small. There were only about seventy people lined up, including the kids from the orphanage. It didn't matter. When the drummer and horn player joined Father Álvarez at the front of the line, everyone cheered in excitement and anticipation.

Father Álvarez was in his early sixties, so light-skinned, Luisa thought, he looked White. He was tall, good-looking, and walked with the confidence of someone who believed he had a special place in the world. Three of the older kids from the orphanage were dressed up as the three kings. Their capes were bright yellow, blue, and red, just like the Colombian flag. They lined up behind the musicians. Everyone cheered again.

Sister Lorena joined Father Álvarez at the front of the line and handed him a Colombian flag. It seemed to Luisa that Sister Lorena thought Father Álvarez was special too. He raised it high over his head for everyone to see. The crowd cheered once more. The parade was about to begin. The drummer began a steady beat, and everyone began marching up the street. The horn player joined the drummer with a majestic melody announcing their arrival to the neighbourhood.

Luisa marched beside Sister Francesca enthralled by the sound of the drum and the horn. She had the feeling she'd been in this kind of parade before. In front of her marched a little girl who was seven or eight. She was holding the hand of a younger girl around four or five. Ten years ago, they could've been Ana and me, thought Luisa.

The older girl was wearing her hair tied back with a red ribbon, and Luisa felt a sharp pang of sadness. Her *mamá* had bought her a ribbon just like it for her first day of school. After Luisa had finished breakfast, she remained in her chair at the kitchen table while her *mamá* slowly brushed her hair and pulled it into a ponytail. The first time Luisa's *mamá* tried to tie it back with an elastic, a strand escaped, and she had to start all over again, her hands brushing against Luisa's neck as she scooped up her thick hair. The second time the ponytail was perfect, and she tied the ribbon around it.

The day Ana and Luisa were taken to the orphanage, Luisa was wearing the red ribbon. By then it had started to fade and fray a bit. Sister Francesca told Luisa if she wanted it to last longer, she should only wear it to church on Sundays. So that's what Luisa did. She packed it up in a small box Sister Francesca had found for her and only wore it when she got dressed for church.

When Luisa and Ana left for Toronto, the small box with the ribbon was somehow left behind. Whoever had helped them pack, didn't pack the ribbon. When Luisa arrived in Toronto and realized it wasn't in her suitcase, she was extremely upset. Harriet called the orphanage and gave Luisa the phone so she could ask Sister Francesca to look for it. Sister Francesca looked everywhere but couldn't find it. It was lost forever. Harriet offered to buy Luisa a new one, but she didn't want a new one. She wanted the ribbon her *mamá* had bought her. To shake off the memory, Luisa began talking to the girl wearing the ribbon.

"Hi, I'm Luisa. I'm visiting the orphanage. I used to live there."

"Were you adopted?" asked the older girl.

"Yes."

"Where do you live now?"

"Toronto."

"Toronto!" she said, excited. "Just like Valentina."

"Valentina López? I know her! I met her at a party at my house."

"Valentina was at your house?!"

"Yes, with some of the other kids who were adopted from the orphanage."

"They go to parties at your house?"

"Yes, once a year. For Colombia Night."

"Does Valentina like it in Toronto?" she asked, hopeful.

"I think so," Luisa replied as encouraging as she could manage.

Truthfully, she wasn't sure how much Valentina liked Toronto. When Luisa had tried chatting with Valentina at Colombia Night, she'd answered all her questions with "Yes," "No," or "I don't know." It didn't matter if Luisa spoke in English or in Spanish. The only thing she'd say was "Yes," "No," or "I don't know." Luisa wasn't sure if Valentina was just shy or if she'd withdrawn from her new world the way Luisa had.

"Can she speak English now?" the older girl asked.

"A little bit. But it takes time." A lot time, Luisa thought.

"I wish I could learn English. So when Paola and I are adopted I can speak to our new parents right away."

"Paola's your sister?"

"Yes."

"What's your name?"

"Carolina."

"Well, Carolina, maybe I can teach you English."

"Are you a real teacher?"

"No, but I speak English."

She smiled. "Tonight, can you come into our room and tell us a story about Toronto? In Spanish, not English. We don't understand English yet."

"Sure. Maybe we should invite the boys too? So they don't feel left out?"

"Okay. If you promise to tell us a story every night."

Luisa laughed. "It's a deal."

The parade made its way up the street for two blocks until they reached a busy intersection. Father Álvarez led everyone across the street to a park where dozens of families were celebrating Día de los Reyes Magos with a picnic lunch. Although they'd only been walking for five minutes, Luisa was very tired and having trouble breathing. There was a lot of noise. Cars honked their horns, people shouted hello and cheered as they passed by. It hurt her head.

As they entered the park, a group of children waved and called out to the people in the parade. They waved and answered back. It was chaotic and rowdy. After they'd marched around the entire park, Father Álvarez took everyone back to the church. On the way, Luisa ducked into a store and bought several bottles of water. She drank an entire bottle while waiting for the cashier to give her change. Almost immediately she felt better. She joined the stragglers at the end of the parade. Sister Lorena was waiting for them at the front door of the church. As soon as Luisa and the last few children arrived, she led them to the bus where the others were waiting for them.

"Do we have time for me to meet Father Álvarez?" Luisa asked Sister Francesca, afraid the answer would be no.

"Yes, here he comes now."

Luisa followed her gaze. Father Álvarez was coming right towards them.

"Hello Father. This is Luisa Gómez Rodríguez Silver. She's come from Canada to visit. Do you remember her? She's Inés's daughter."

"Of course, I remember Luisa." His response was warm. "Welcome back." Luisa was amazed and happy he remembered her.

"Thank you, Father. If you have time for me, I'd like to come speak to you about my birth family. Is that possible?"

"Perhaps." Luisa thought his warmth seemed to chill a bit. "How old are you?"

"Seventeen, but I'll be eighteen in a week and a half."

"Well, come see me then."

Luisa was about to ask why she couldn't just talk to him right then and there, but Sister Francesca gripped her arm.

"Thank you, Father."

Sister Francesca kept her grip on Luisa's arm. "Time to go."

"Goodbye, Father. I'll see you soon."

He nodded and went on to talk to someone else. Sister Francesca hurried Luisa along so they wouldn't keep the others waiting any longer. But Luisa kept looking back to catch a glimpse of Father Álvarez. He had remembered her. That meant he'd remember her *mamá* and father too, she thought.

Luisa and Sister Francesca were the last ones to climb onto the bus. Sister Francesca offered Luisa the window seat. As they were about to pass the park, the bus stopped at a red light. At the park entrance, Luisa noticed a young girl selling empanadas from a food stall. Suddenly she felt goose bumps on her arms. She'd seen that food stall before. Or one just like it. Something was happening. Now that she was back in Bogotá, her body was remembering things her mind couldn't.

When the bus arrived back at the orphanage, Luisa got up quickly so she could be the first one out and hand out candy to the children as they got off the bus. The children were excited. Especially the younger ones.

After the candy was gone, Luisa took out her phone and took a picture of the orphanage for Clare.

"El Orfanato is an old three-story house built at the top of a hill. A steep hill." she texted Clare. "24 kids live here plus Sister Francesca and Sister Angelica. Sister Lorena lives nearby with two other Sisters of Hope. Sister Angelica takes care of the babies and toddlers. Sister Francesca takes care of everyone else."

Clare texted back immediately. "Is Sister Lorena going to let you stay?"

"Not sure yet," Luisa texted back. "Fingers crossed."

"Fingers crossed," Clare replied.

The day after the parade, Luisa start teaching the children English. Sister Lorena sat in on each of her classes, which were held in a small meeting room next to Sister Lorena's office. Luisa was on trial. In each class, she introduced herself in Spanish and told them about her adoptive family in Toronto. She talked about Harriet, Jonathan, Ana, and Clare, but didn't mention Marty. Luisa felt bad about leaving Marty out, but after hearing what Sophia had to say about her family, she decided not to talk about Harriet and Marty at the orphanage.

The pre-school kids and younger kids were easy to work with, but after a long day at school, the last thing the high school kids wanted to do was sit in the dining room and learn English. There were seven of them, four girls and three boys. Luisa had already met all the girls—Sophia, Mariana, Adriana, and Alejandra. The boys were Sergio, Christian, and Julian. Sophia looked at her watch every five minutes. The watch she'd received from Global Family last Christmas. All the high school kids got watches. It had been Luisa's idea. Every time Sophia looked at her watch, Luisa wished she'd thought of something else to send. Like new blankets.

On the second day, the high school kids asked if they could watch television on Luisa's tablet. The television at the orphanage didn't work anymore, and Sister Lorena didn't have the money to buy a new one. Luisa wasn't sure how they found out she'd brought a tablet with her but was ecstatic that there was something the high school kids wanted to do in her class.

"What kinds of shows do you like to watch?"

"Sports."

"Telenovelas."

"Reality shows."

"Do you like any English shows?"

They didn't know any.

"What's your favourite show?" asked Sergio.

"I don't have one, but my sister Clare really likes *The Amazing Race*. It's a reality show where teams compete in a race around Canada and other places in the world with just a little bit of money."

That caught their interest.

"I vote we watch *The Amazing Race*," said Adriana. "Who wants to watch *The Amazing Race*? Raise your hands."

Everyone raised their hands except Sophia.

"Can you get it on your tablet?"

"I don't know. I'll try. But we'll have to watch it in Sister Lorena's office. Do you think she'll give us permission?"

"Probably not," said Sergio.

"What if I teach you a little bit about Canada first? If Sister Lorena thinks the show will help you learn about Canada, she might say yes. Okay?" Luisa said *Okay* in English.

"Okay!" they all repeated in English. Except for Sophia. She just looked at her watch.

Sister Lorena walked into the meeting room while Luisa was teaching everyone the names of the Canadian provinces, territories, and capital cities. At the end of the class, they had a competition. Everyone had to name the capital city of the province or territory Luisa called out. If they got the answer right, they remained in the game, but if they got the answer wrong, they were out. Luisa was shocked when Sophia won the game. She didn't think she'd been listening.

When the dinner bell rang and class was over, Sister Lorena told Luisa she could stay at the orphanage and teach English until her visa ran out in July. Luisa felt like jumping up and down. Instead, she gave Sister Lorena a big smile.

"Thanks so much, Sister."

Sister Lorena smiled back. When she smiled, she looked a lot less intimidating.

"I expect you to follow the same rules as all the other children. No one leaves the building without telling Sister Francesca or Sister Angelica where they're going and when they're coming back. And no one goes out alone at night. Is that clear?"

"Yes, Sister."

"Good. After dinner, I'll tell everyone you're staying for a while."

"What about *The Amazing Race*?"

"If you promise not to touch anything, you can watch it in my office."

"Thank you, Sister. You won't even know we've been there."

"I hope not. You can bring in the chairs from this room and then return them once you're done."

She paused and gave Luisa another one of her intense stares. "I have high expectations of you, Luisa. Please don't disappoint me."

Luisa shook her head forcefully. "Don't worry, Sister. I won't."

CHAPTER 5

The rest of week went by quickly, and before Luisa knew it, it was Saturday, the day the children did their chores. The older girls all went shopping at the market with Sister Francesca. Luisa asked Sister Francesca if she could join them so she could get to know the girls. To get to the market from the orphanage, they had to walk down a steep and narrow crumbling sidewalk next to a very busy road. The shopping carts from the orphanage were old and the wheels were wobbly. They were hard to hold onto. Halfway down the hill, Luisa's cart hit a deep crack in the sidewalk and rattled away from her. She had to chase it all the way down the rest of hill to capture it. Luisa thought Sister Francesca and the girls would die laughing.

When they arrived at the market, Luisa let Sister Francesca and the girls walk ahead and tried to find a place to text Harriet. She stopped at the first stall that wasn't jam packed with customers and asked the man selling vegetables where she could find a place with Wi-Fi. He was a little taller than her and stocky. He looked her up and down and then stared at her breasts.

"What are you looking at?" she asked feeling her face flush.

He shrugged and grinned. Luisa buttoned up her jacket so he'd have less to look at. He laughed, shook his head, and narrowed his eyes. It was unnerving. Luisa turned around and walked away.

"Bye, bye *gringa*," he said, teasing.

Gringa meant foreigner. It wasn't a compliment.

The market was crammed full of people rushing by Luisa to get to their favourite stalls before the best fruits and vegetables were gone. Luisa looked around for Sister Francesca and the girls but couldn't find them. She began walking, checking out every stall to see if they were there. A man with a big basket pushed past her. She lost her balance and fell hard to the ground. Embarrassed she got up and assessed the damage. Her jeans were torn, and her knee was bleeding. The scrape was quite bad and began to sting. Luisa realized there was no way she'd ever find Sister Francesca and the girls in the crazy crowd. She needed to find her way back to the main entrance and wait for them there.

Too afraid to open her *gringa* mouth and ask for directions, Luisa retraced her steps. She passed stall after stall after stall. People were laughing, joking, and bargaining as they filled their carts and baskets and bags. She listened carefully, trying to understand what they were saying and caught some of it. A woman wanted to know if the pears were sweet. Another thought the avocadoes too hard. But there was a lot she missed. When she was young, Luisa thought, she had understood everything. She spoke Spanish perfectly. Without an accent. Not anymore.

Eventually Luisa found the entrance. Twenty minutes later Sister Francesca showed up without the girls.

"What happened? Where did you go?" She was upset.

"I stopped at one of the stalls to ask about—"

"You shouldn't have stopped. At the market, everyone stays together. No one goes off on their own without permission. Those are the rules. You said you understood."

"I'm sorry, I didn't realize—"

"What happened to your knee? It's bleeding." Now Sister Francesca was even more upset.

"I know, I tripped and fell."

"Here." She pulled out a clean handkerchief from the pocket of her habit. "Clean it up."

Luisa took the bandana, wet it with some water from her water bottle and tried to clean the wound.

"Where are the girls?" Luisa asked.

"Doing the shopping while I looked for you." She glanced at her watch. "Dinner's going to be late," she said, distressed.

"I'm sorry. I'll help you prepare dinner. Maybe we can make up for lost time."

Although dinner was only fifteen minutes late, Sister Francesca was antsy right up to the moment the last dirty pot was washed, dried, and put away. Luisa thought she seemed tired from rushing to get dinner on the table and was surprised when she told her to go gather all the children and bring them to the reception room. She had promised them she'd play her guitar after dinner so they could sing. It was a Saturday night tradition at El Orfanato. Luisa had forgotten.

Luisa remembered Sister Francesca's favourite song was "Soy Colombiano," I am Colombian. It was written by Raphael Godoy who had been forced to leave Colombia and live in Venezuela because of his work in the trade union movement. In "Soy Colombiano," Godoy talks about how proud he is to be Colombian. The minute Sister Francesca played the opening chords, Luisa's heart soared. She remembered singing the song when she'd lived at the orphanage. Another memory retrieved. The longer she stayed at the orphanage, the more she'd remember. And when she collected enough memories, she thought, maybe she'd feel like she really, truly belonged in Bogotá. Despite all her years away. Despite her English accent.

Its melody was dramatic, totally over the top, but Luisa could see Sister Francesca was very moved by the song and sang it with deep emotion. While she didn't remember most of the words, Luisa did remember the last two lines and sang along. "Ay! How proud I am to be a good Colombian. Ay! How proud I am to be a good Colombian." At that moment, that's what Luisa wanted more than anything. To be seen as a good Colombian. To feel like a good Colombian. Even though she'd been away for so long.

On Luisa's first Sunday afternoon in Bogotá, after getting Sister Francesca's permission to leave the orphanage, she took the bus to La Candelaria, the place where the Spanish had lived when they arrived in Colombia. Some of Bogotá's oldest churches had been built there. It was also where all the university students and local musicians hung out.

Taking the bus turned out to be a mistake. Luisa had never been on a bus that was so crowded. The smell of body odor was so strong she had to bury her nose in the sleeve of her jacket so she wouldn't throw up. Then a guy moved in behind her and started rubbing himself against her. She couldn't see him, but she felt his weight against her back. She immediately tried to move away. But when she leaned a little to the right, he moved right along with her. She was trapped. Luisa pulled the cord in front of her to signal she wanted to get off. The bus didn't stop.

She yelled, "Stop the bus! Help!"

The bus still didn't stop. She pulled the cord again, again, and again, until the driver finally slammed on the brakes, throwing everyone on top of each other. Luisa pushed her way through the crowd shouting, "I want to get off, I want to get off!" in her accented Spanish, clutching her knapsack. When she finally reached the back door of the bus, the driver started driving off.

"No, no! I want to get to off!"

The driver didn't hear her. She yanked the cord again. He slammed on the brakes one more time, and she tumbled out. Luisa had no idea where she was.

She looked around and saw a bench. She sat down and started to cry. A woman carrying a baby and holding the hand of a little girl stopped to see if she needed help. Luisa was crying so hard she couldn't answer. The woman and her little girl sat down beside her, and when Luisa had calmed down a little bit, the woman asked her what had happened. She shook her head in disgust and told Luisa from now on she should take a taxi instead of the bus.

Luisa nodded. No one had told her it wasn't safe to take the bus, she thought. Not Sister Francesca. Not Claudia. She had to hear it from a stranger. If her *mamá* had been alive, she would've warned her. She would've taught her how to take care of herself. Luisa reached into the bottom pocket of her knapsack and took out a small Canadian flag pin. She'd gone to the dollar store just before she left and bought a whole bunch of them. Luisa asked the little girl if she'd like one. She smiled shyly and said yes. Her mother pinned it on her jacket, got up off the bench, patted Luisa on the arm, and told her to take care of herself. Then she gathered up her daughter and walked away.

Luisa looked at her watch. It was still early. She didn't have to go back to the orphanage for another few hours. She still had a whole afternoon to explore La Candelaria. Across the street was a big hotel with a line of taxis waiting for customers. She pulled out a bandana from her knapsack, wiped her face, and blew her nose. Then she reached for her wallet in the small middle pocket where she always kept it. It wasn't there. Maybe it was in another pocket. She couldn't dump all her stuff out on the bench in front of everyone so she got up, crossed the street, and went into the hotel. Luisa sat down in a quiet corner of the lobby. Her hands were shaking, but she managed to take everything out of her knapsack to see if she could find her wallet. It wasn't there. While she was on the bus, someone must have opened the zipper of her knapsack and taken it. She was missing 200,000 pesos. Ninety-two Canadian dollars. Luckily, she'd left her credit card and bank card back at the orphanage, and her phone was safely tucked into the inside pocket of her jacket. If it'd been in her knapsack, it might've been stolen too. But Luisa had no money to take a taxi to La Candelaria or back to the orphanage. She would have to call Sister Francesca on her one afternoon off and ask her what to do.

As Luisa reached for her phone in her pocket, she felt a small change purse in the corner. She opened it up and found 75,000 pesos inside. She'd forgotten that she'd put it there. For an emergency. Just like Harriet had taught her. She had enough to get to La Candelaria and then back to the orphanage.

Luisa hailed a taxi and asked the driver to drop her off at the Plazoleta del Chorro de Quevedo. She walked along cobble-stoned streets, holding her knapsack on one shoulder and gripping it tightly under her arm. She wanted to take pictures of the vibrant pink, blue, and green buildings but didn't want to put her bag on her back again. It wasn't safe. She'd have to come back another time to take pictures.

There was street art everywhere. Almost every wall in La Candelaria was covered with a brightly coloured mural or graffiti. It was incredible, and for the first time since Luisa had gotten off the bus, she began to relax. As she walked back to the plaza to find a café to have a coffee, she found a store with a beautiful red alpaca blanket in the window. The same colour as her blanket back in Toronto. For a moment, Luisa felt a sharp pang of homesickness. She buried it. Her eighteenth birthday was just a week away. She needed to look forward, not backward. Next Saturday, she'd come back and buy the blanket. Claudia's room was freezing at night.

Next door to the wool shop was a café with an outdoor patio. Luisa found a seat and ordered a café con leche, coffee with lots of milk. A group of students sat down at the table next to her, and she spent the next half hour listening to them joke around and laugh. She couldn't understand everything they were saying, but they were having so much fun she knew she wanted to join them.

In the taxi on the way back to the orphanage, Luisa tried to think of a way to start a conversation with Claudia. They'd been sharing her room for five days, and Claudia had rejected almost every friendly overture Luisa had made. So had all the other older girls. Sophia had probably turned them all against her, she thought. If Claudia warmed up, maybe the other girls would too.

The older girls idolized Claudia. Not only was she smart, she was also caring and empathetic. Every night at dinner Claudia asked each one of the girls at the table how their day at school had gone. When they answered she gave them her undivided attention. The girls' eyes would shine as they told her of something good that had happened, and they'd smile their biggest smiles when she told them how happy she was for them. When something hadn't gone as well as they'd hoped, Claudia would take their hands, squeeze them lightly, and tell them not to worry, tomorrow would be a better day. It was a joy to watch her.

The problem with trying to become friends with Claudia was that she was very, very busy. She spent all day working at the hospital and then after dinner had to finish her kitchen chores and do all her course work. She didn't have much time to chat. But that night, as Luisa was getting ready for bed, she had an idea.

"Claudia, what if I took your place in the kitchen after dinner?"

She looked up from her book.

"You'd have another hour to study after dinner."

"You'd do that for me?" she asked, surprised.

"Sure."

"Why?"

"You need the time."

Claudia nodded. "If you clean up, I could start an hour earlier and get another hour of sleep. Last night I didn't get to bed until midnight and was up at four."

"Why so early?"

"I had a biochemistry test today. There's one every week, and I haven't been doing well. I need to do better."

"I could help you study. When I had trouble in chemistry, Marty gave me a stack of blank cards. On one side, I wrote out a list of questions I thought would be on the next quiz. On the other, I wrote out all the right answers. Then the night before the quiz, Marty read out the question on each of the cards and I answered them. Marty told me if my answer was right or wrong. When I'd finished all the questions, I had to re-answer the ones I'd missed."

Claudia nodded. "That's a great idea. Can we try it next week?"

"Sure."

"Thanks."

She smiled. Not a little smile. A real smile.

"When are you seeing Father Álvarez?" she asked.

Luisa realized it was the first time Claudia had begun a personal conversation since they had met. She tried not to sound too eager.

"Next Sunday. The day I turn eighteen."

"What are you going to ask him?"

"How my *mamá* died of pneumonia and why my father wasn't there to take care of us."

"Do you think your father's still alive?"

"I have no idea."

"Well, I hope Father Álvarez can help you," she said, sincere.

"Me too."

"Maybe after you find out what you need to know you'll feel more settled. You can go back to Toronto with a lighter heart." Luisa didn't realize how obvious her pain was.

"But I don't want to go back to Toronto," Luisa said, forceful. "I told Harriet I'd try university for a year, but I don't want to leave. I want to stay here."

"At the orphanage?" Claudia asked, in disbelief. "And do what? Teach children English for no money? Clean floors and wash the dishes every night?"

Claudia was mad. Really mad. It surprised Luisa. She didn't understand why.

"Everyone in this orphanage wants to go to university. But they can't because they don't have a family with money to send them."

She sounded exactly like Harriet, Luisa thought.

"Do you know what Adriana and Mariana and Alejandra are going to do when they leave here? Clean rich people's houses. You don't have to clean houses. You can study anything you want, for however long it takes.

You can be a doctor if you want to. I can't. There's only enough scholarship money to be a nurse."

"I know," Luisa said, chastised. "But I can't help how I feel. I don't have any friends in Toronto. I don't belong there." She started to cry.

Claudia softened immediately, taking her hand just like she took the other girls' hands. Luisa's heart jumped.

"I'm sorry it's been hard. But you need to recognize how lucky you are. There's no future for you here. You need to go back."

Luisa nodded and swallowed what she wanted to say. There wasn't a future in Toronto either.

"Your *mamá* died of pneumonia. People who can afford to see a doctor usually survive pneumonia. If I were you, I'd go back and do whatever I needed to do to get into medical school, become a doctor, and then come back here and open a health centre for families in Ciudad Bolívar. That's what I'd do if I were you."

Claudia had planned it all out for Luisa. She nodded to acknowledge she'd heard what Claudia had said. But at that moment going back to Toronto for another seven years, maybe longer, was the last thing Luisa wanted to do.

CHAPTER 6

The day Luisa turned eighteen she went to Mass with Sister Francesca. While it felt cozy sitting next to Sister Francesca in church, Mass didn't do much for Luisa. She thought she'd like it a lot more than she did. Luisa knew that going to church was really important to lots of Colombian families, but she couldn't understand the Latin prayers, and most of the time she had trouble understanding what the priest was saying in Spanish. He spoke too quickly. Then, while standing in the long line to take communion, Luisa wondered if the priest would give Harriet and Marty communion if they'd been Catholic. She doubted it.

When everyone from El Orfanato returned to the orphanage after Mass, Sister Francesca had a surprise for Luisa. A traditional Colombian birthday cake called *ponqué*, which tasted like pound cake. When Sister Francesca brought it out, everyone clapped and sang "Cumpleaños Feliz." Luisa got a little teary. She hadn't expected to spend her eighteenth birthday in Bogotá with Sister Francesca and the kids at El Orfanato. Sister Francesca handed Luisa two birthday packages. One from her family in Toronto and one from Nana Lottie, Luisa's adoptive grandmother. Growing up in Harriet and Jonathan's house, Luisa had spent a lot of time with Nana Lottie. Her retirement residence was close by, and she came to dinner every Friday night. Nana Lottie was also always the first one to arrive to Colombia Night so she could help set up. Nana Lottie loved Colombia Night, and at the age of 102 she was still the liveliest, most upbeat person Luisa knew. She was also the one person in Luisa's life who always knew what to say to make Luisa feel good about herself.

The package from the family was full of candy, fudge, and comic books for the kids. There was also a gift for Luisa. She passed everything out and opened her present: a pair of her favorite jeans. Not too expensive, not too flashy. Something she could wear without showing off. They were perfect. Luisa saved the package from Nana Lottie to open after her visit to Father Álvarez. As soon as lunch was over, she got ready. She put on her new jeans and matched it up with a plain white shirt and black blazer. Then she put her hair up in a bun like Claudia, so she'd look older and more reserved. When she looked in the mirror, Luisa almost didn't recognize herself. She looked conservative. Like a girl who had never left El Orfanato.

She took a taxi to the church, found her way to the office, and introduced herself to Father Álvarez's secretary.

"I've come to see Father Álvarez."

"Is he expecting you?" she asked, puzzled.

"No, but he told me he'd talk to me about my birth family when I turned eighteen. I'm eighteen today."

"Oh." She raised her eyebrows. "He doesn't usually take appointments on Sunday."

Luisa couldn't believe she needed an appointment to see a priest.

"But since it's your birthday. I'll see if he has time to talk to you."

"Thanks. I really appreciate it." Luisa put a grateful smile. "I've come a long way to see him."

"I knew you weren't from here! It's your accent. You're American, right?"

Luisa shook her head, doing her best to keep the smile.

"No, I live in Canada."

"Oh, sorry."

The secretary knocked on the closed door behind her and slipped inside. While she waited, Luisa looked around. The walls were filled with children's drawings of Bible stories. Noah's ark was popular. In all of them, the kids had drawn happy animals glad to be travelling to a new land. Those poor animals, thought Luisa. They had no idea what was coming. Finally, the secretary came back out and told Luisa to go in.

Father Álvarez stood up from the chair behind his desk. He looked even taller in his office than he had at the parade. He shook Luisa's hand and smiled. A reserved smile. The kind of smile, Luisa thought, people put on to distance themselves from the person they're smiling at. But then Father Álvarez started to laugh.

"You look so much like Beatriz," he said.

"Beatriz?" asked Luisa.

"You don't remember Beatriz?" he asked, surprised.

Luisa shook her head.

"She's your aunt! Your mother's sister."

Luisa could feel a sharp intake of breath.

"I have an aunt named Beatriz?" she asked.

"Yes."

"I can't believe it! I don't remember her at all!"

"Well," said Father Álvarez, "You were quite young when your mother died."

"Not that young. Seven."

Father Álvarez looked sorry he'd said anything about Beatriz.

"Please sit down," he said.

"Thanks," said Luisa as she took a seat on the other side of the desk.

He waited until Luisa was fully seated before sitting down himself.

"How's your sister Ana?"

Luisa tried for a friendly smile. "She's fine."

"How old is she in now?"

"Fourteen."

"How's she doing in school? Is she a good student?"

"Yes, we both are."

Father Álvarez nodded with approval. "Good, do you go to church?"

"I've been going with Sister Francesca."

"And in Toronto?"

"At Christmas."

He frowned.

"What about university?"

"I'm starting next September."

Father Álvarez smiled again. "Excellent."

Luisa was getting impatient but forced herself to keep a smile on her face and answer each question politely. She knew if she wanted answers, she had to give Father Álvarez some first.

"Have you found your vocation yet?" he asked.

The question took Luisa off guard. "My vocation?"

"Your purpose in life."

The only purpose in life Luisa had was to find someone who could tell her how her *mamá* had died of pneumonia and where her father had been when she and Ana needed him. Luisa didn't want to waste any more time talking about herself when she could be talking about her family. But she knew that Sister Francesca would want her to show Father Álvarez the respect she thought he deserved. So she answered as humbly as she could manage.

"No, Father, not yet."

"Well, maybe you'll find it here."

"Maybe."

Finally Father Álvarez asked the question Luisa had been waiting for. "So, what do you want to know?"

She took a deep breath.

"Sister Francesca told me you were the one who took Ana and me to El Orfanato. Why were we sent there?"

He leaned back in his chair, creating more distance between them.

"It was only going to be for a while, until your mother got better. There was no one who could take care of you while she was sick. Your grandparents worked all day selling empanadas. Beatriz was in school.

After school, she took over the food stall so they could go home and make more for the next day."

Luisa had stopped breathing and forced herself to take a breath. It was the first time she'd ever heard that she and Ana were supposed to stay in the orphanage for only a short time. It was the first time she'd ever heard her grandparents had sold empanadas and had owned a food stall just like the one she'd seen in the park near Father Álvarez's church. Maybe Ana and I have been there, she thought. That would explain the goose bumps on the way home from the parade. But Luisa knew she couldn't spend time talking about the food stall or her grandparents just yet. She needed to talk about her *mamá* and her father first. She started by asking for facts.

"We were told she died of pneumonia. Is that true?"

"Yes."

"But how did that happen? People don't die of pneumonia."

Father Álvarez gave Luisa a funny look.

"People with pneumonia take antibiotics and get better," she said.

"If they can afford them."

It was Luisa's worst fear. Her *mamá* had died because she didn't have money to buy antibiotics. She began to feel dizzy. Like she might faint. She leaned forward and put her head between her knees like Harriet had shown her.

Father Álvarez immediately stood up.

"I'll get you some water," he said.

He left the office, and Luisa just sat there with her head between her knees. When the dizziness subsided, she sat up. Father Álvarez returned with a glass of water and leaned against his desk, just inches away from her. Imposing, she thought.

"Sip it slowly," he said.

Luisa nodded. "Thank you."

"You should go back to the orphanage and rest."

"No!" Luisa said loudly. "I mean," she continued lowering her voice, "I'd like to stay and hear everything you remember."

The concerned solicitude disappeared. Luisa could see Father Álvarez didn't want to tell her what he knew.

"Please, I need to know. You asked about my vocation. I don't have one. I promised my adopted mother I'd apply to university while I'm here, but I have no idea of what I want to study. I can't begin to think about my future until I understand my past. I'm stuck."

Luisa was shocked by her honesty. By how much she'd revealed. But her confession seemed to change Father Álvarez's mind. He returned to his desk, sat down, folded his hands together, and leaned them on the desk.

"Your grandmother said it started with a bad cough. The coughing got worse, and your mother stopped eating. She became very weak. Inés and Juan Andres had moved out of my parish, but your grandmother asked me to go see her. Inés was on her own and needed help. When I arrived, I found out she couldn't get out of bed. A neighbor who was taking care of her let me in. I told Inés I was going to take her to the hospital, but she wouldn't leave until I found someone to look after you and Ana. I told her I'd take you and Ana to El Orfanato and that the sisters would take care of you until she was better. We were all hoping and praying she'd get better."

"What happened at the hospital?"

"When we got to the hospital the emergency doctor gave her antibiotics. I paid for them. But the infection was too severe. They didn't work."

Luisa wanted to scream. But when she opened her mouth to speak, it came out as a whisper.

"How long was she in the hospital?"

"A week." Luisa thought of her *mamá* lying in the hospital all by herself without her daughters to comfort her. But she pushed the thought away. She'd have time to think about that later. She needed to find out as much as she could from Father Álvarez before he told her it was time to go.

"Then what happened?" she asked. "Why did Ana and I end up living at El Orfanato? Why didn't we go to live with our grandparents? They owned a food stall! They had a business. Ana and I could have helped them sell empanadas. Like Beatriz."

Father Álvarez nodded as if he had been anticipating the question. His answer was confident.

"You were both very young. Ana wasn't even in school yet. Your grandparents didn't think they could take care of you as well as the sisters." Something about his explanation didn't seem quite right, but Luisa let it go.

"I want to meet them."

"Your grandparents? I'm sorry, they're no longer with us."

"You mean they're dead?"

"Yes."

"What about Beatriz? Could I meet her?"

"I haven't seen Beatriz for a very long time. She moved away after your grandparents died."

Suddenly, Father Álvarez stood up. "I'm sorry, but I have a sick call to make."

The meeting was over. He wanted Luisa out of his office. But she didn't get up.

"Do you think you could find Beatriz for me?"

"Bogotá's a very large city."

"I know, but maybe Beatriz still goes to church. Maybe someone you know has met her. Knows how to contact her. Could you ask around for me?"

It wasn't a lot to ask, Luisa thought. It would seem small of Father Álvarez to say no, and she knew that he thought so too.

"Yes, I can ask around. Now I really must go."

"Just one more question. You said my *mamá* was on her own. Where was my father? No one seems to know. You're the only person I can ask."

Luisa hated having to beg him for information, but she didn't know what else to do.

Father Álvarez sat down again. He knew what she'd said was true. There was no one else she could ask.

"No one knows. He disappeared."

"Disappeared?! How did he disappear? People don't just disappear!"

"He went back to Medellín to visit his mother. She was sick."

"My father's mother lived in Medellín?"

"Yes. So did your father for a while. He grew up there but after high school came to Bogotá to find work. He was only supposed to stay in Medellín for a week, maybe two. But he never came back to Bogotá."

"He didn't call? He didn't write?"

"No."

"I keep trying to remember something, anything about him, but I can't. I can't remember what he looked like, anything he wore, what his voice sounded like. I can't remember anything. If I could only find out what happened to him, I'd know something."

Luisa's head started pounding. She'd been given so much information in such a short time. After seven years of not knowing anything, it was a lot to take in.

"I'm sorry. I can't help you. No one knows what happened to him."

"Was there an accident?"

"Maybe."

"Was he arrested?"

"Maybe."

"But you don't know?"

"No."

"Well, what do you think happened?"

"I think if there'd been an accident or he'd been arrested, your mother would've found out."

"What else could it have been, then?"

"You really want to know?"

She nodded with conviction.

"I think he got into some kind of trouble in Medellín, and he's dead."

Luisa wasn't so sure.

"Or maybe he just abandoned us," she said. Saying it aloud hurt.

"I don't think so," answered Father Álvarez. "He cared a lot about Inés. They seemed very happy together. I know this is hard to hear, but you said you wanted to know."

"Yes." Her voice was hoarse.

"I'm very sorry, but I'm going to leave now. The family's waiting for me. Camila will call you a taxi."

Father Álvarez got up and left the office, leaving Luisa alone with the bombshell he'd just dropped. Another family needed him. It didn't matter that Luisa needed him too. To help her find out what had happened to her father.

Camila came in, walked Luisa out of the church and waited with her until the taxi arrived.

"I'm very sorry for your loss," she said. Camilla had heard the entire thing.

"Thank you." Luisa knew it sounded as empty as she felt.

The taxi dropped Luisa off in front of the orphanage. Sister Francesca was waiting for her on the chipped blue bench. Luisa immediately ran over to her and threw herself into Sister Francesca's arms. She began to sob. Sister Francesca held on to Luisa tightly.

"She died because she didn't have enough money to buy antibiotics."

"I'm sorry, *pequeña*. So sorry."

"It's so unfair."

"I know."

"Why wasn't my father there to help us?"

"I don't know, *pequeña*."

"Father Álvarez thinks he's dead. Do you think that's true?"

"I don't know, *pequeña*. It's possible."

The dinner bell rang. Both of them jumped at the sound.

"Come and have some dinner."

"I can't eat right now. I need some time alone."

"Alright."

Sister Francesca walked Luisa to Claudia's room. As soon as Luisa heard her go into the kitchen, she put on her running shoes and slipped out the front door. She needed to go for a run and get rid of some of the tension she was feeling. Luisa ran down the hill, around the market, which spanned several blocks, and then to the convenience store where she could buy Wi-Fi by the hour. Luisa walked to the back of the store and turned on her phone. There were phone messages from Harriet, Marty, Ana, Clare, and Nana Lottie, all wishing her a happy birthday. Luisa had forgotten it was her birthday. She texted Harriet. Texting was easier than calling.

"My *mamá* didn't have enough money to buy antibiotics. When she finally got them, they didn't work. She wasn't strong enough to fight off the infection."

Harriet texted right back.

"But she was strong enough to make sure you and Ana would survive. Strong enough to send you somewhere you'd be cared for. Strong enough to make sure you'd live even if she didn't. Imagine the strength she had to do that. You have her strength. You have your mother's strength."

"What about your father?" Harriet asked.

"He went to Medellín and never came back. Nobody knows why. But *mamá* had a sister. Beatriz. Maybe she knows."

"A sister!"

"But Father Á doesn't know where she is."

"How are you doing?"

"Not good. Terrible."

"Do you want me to come?"

"To Bogotá?"

"Yes."

"No, it's okay."

"Sure?"

"Yeah. Gotta go. Can you tell Ana everything? Gently?"

"Of course."

"*Gracias.*"

"Call or text anytime. I love you."

Luisa signed off with xo.

Luisa's Wi-Fi time was almost over so she quickly texted Maureen, one of the support people who worked at Nana's residence, and asked her to say thank you to Nana for sending her a birthday package. Then Luisa paid for her Wi-Fi time and ran back up the hill. Sister Francesca was waiting for her on the blue bench. She'd been crying.

"What's wrong?"

"You've been gone for over an hour. I sent Sergio, Christian, and Julian out looking for you. I was about to call Sister Lorena and the police. You may not like the rules we have here, but you have to follow them. Nobody here goes out alone without permission. And never after dark. It's not safe."

Luisa had forgotten. "I'm sorry," she said. "I needed to text Harriet. The Wi-Fi here—"

"If it happens again Sister Lorena will ask you to leave. Do you understand?"

Luisa had never heard Sister Francesca sound so harsh.

"Yes. I'm sorry. What can I do to make it up to you?"

"I don't know."

"I can do more chores. I can help the boys next Saturday."

The boys cleaned all the bathrooms. The toilets, the showers, the floors. They were the worst chores at the orphanage. It didn't matter. Luisa knew she needed to do whatever she had to to get back into Sister Francesca's good graces.

Sister Francesca shook her head. "I'm very upset with you, *pequeña*. And very disappointed."

"I know. I'm very sorry." Luisa reached out and took her hand. "Please forgive me."

It took a while, but several days later Sister Francesca forgave Luisa. Sister Francesca believed in forgiveness. She also believed that people who held grudges only hurt themselves.

When Luisa finally got back to Claudia's room that night, Nana's birthday package was waiting for her on her bed. She opened it up and found a letter, a printed photo, and a small package wrapped in tissue paper. Luisa started with the photo. It was a picture of Nana Lottie, Luisa, Ana, and Clare standing in front of the gate to the CNE. Luisa noticed she had a bit of a stunned look on her face, which meant it was probably the first summer Nana had taken them there. She turned the photo over to see if Nana had written the date of the visit. She had. "Canadian National Exhibition, August 2011. Luisa, 10. Ana, 7. Clare, 3 going on 4." Luisa smiled. The first thing Clare had ever said to her on the day they met was "Hi. I'm three going on four."

In the photo, Nana was wearing a hot pink sleeveless linen dress with white sneakers. She was carefully made up, with light blue eye shadow, just a touch of mascara on her eyes, a touch of rouge on her cheeks, and pink lipstick, which was the exact colour of her dress. Nana was always a sharp dresser, Luisa thought, and she looked really excited to be taking her granddaughters to the Ex for the first time. It was the first of many trips to Toronto's CNE Luisa, Ana, and Clare took with Nana. They spent hours going on rides and eating hot dogs, popcorn, cotton candy, and candy apples—or as Nana would call them, toffee apples, the word they used in England.

Nana was a thrill seeker and loved riding the roller coaster. Nana was ninety-six when she took Luisa, Ana, and Clare to the Ex for the first time. Clare was still too young and small to get on, so she stayed behind with Harriet and watched Nana, Luisa and Ana climb into the front car.

Sitting beside Nana on her first roller coaster ride ever, Luisa felt the same thrill of excitement and danger Nana did as the car climbed up the track and then bolted its way down. When the car came to a stop, she was giddy with relief. The scariest part was over. She had survived. Nana was laughing her head off. The teenager helping them out of the car started laughing too.

"Let's go again," said Nana. And they did.

Luisa put the photo down and started reading the letter that was from Nana but not in her handwriting.

My dearest Luisa:

Happy birthday! I can't believe you're turning eighteen! It feels like yesterday that you were ten, going to the Ex for the first time. I hope the photo from that day brings back nice memories. I also hope your birthday at El Orfanato is special in its own way.

To celebrate your eighteenth birthday, I am sending you a story. It's a story told in a set of five letters that I wrote to you during your first summer in Toronto.

I don't know if you remember, but on the first day I met you, you told me—in Spanish, the language of your heart—Bogotá was your real home and that you were going back to Bogotá as soon as you could. I believed you. When I first came to Toronto after marrying Grandpa Harry, Toronto wasn't my real home either, and I remembered how hard I had to work to make it my home. But unlike you, I didn't have a real home to go back to. I hadn't thought about my childhood home in Munich for decades. But when you told me you wanted to go back to Bogotá, I started thinking about Munich and the day I left my home there. I decided to write out the story of how and why I left Munich to share with you when you were older. When it was time for you to go back to Bogotá. I was already ninety-six the summer you and Ana came to live with Harriet and Jonathan and wasn't sure how many years I'd have left to share my story. It turns out I've had more years than I thought! All these years I've kept these letters in a safe place, waiting for the right moment to share them with you. The right moment is now. I've re-read each of the letters and have added a little more to each of them. At 102, I need a little help with writing letters, so I've dictated what I wanted to say to Maureen. The writing you see in this letter and at the end of each of the other letters is hers.

The story I've written in these letters is a story I haven't shared with anyone. Not even Harriet. I won't lie. It's not going to be an easy story to read.

But I think it's a story that may be important for you to hear. Like Harriet, I'm worried your trip back to Bogotá might be painful as well as wonderful. Your country has a history of violence similar to the history my family lived through in Nazi Germany. I hope with all my heart your trip home is easy and joyful, but just in case it isn't, I thought reading my letters might help. Read them when the moment is right.

Sending you lots of love on your birthday,
Nana Lottie

Luisa read Nana's birthday message one more time and tried to imagine the Nana she knew who had laughed her head off on the roller coaster as a young girl who had had to leave her home in Munich when the Nazis came to power. She ran her finger across the rainbow ribbon around the package and then put the package into her suitcase under her bed. She wasn't ready to read them. The day had been hard enough.

CHAPTER 7

Dear Luisa:

I begin my story about leaving Germany with Kristallnacht, which means Night of Broken Glass in German. It was called Kristallnacht because that night the Nazis smashed the glass windows of Jewish businesses, schools, and synagogues. It was a frightening, horrific night for Jewish families in Germany. They were woken up in the middle of the night by Nazi stormtroopers banging on their apartment doors shouting, "You're all under arrest. Put on some clothes! Open the door! You're coming with us!"

They did as they were ordered and were marched to an assembly point where they were forced to stand in the cold and dark alongside other Jews from their neighbourhoods. Eventually the women and children were allowed to go home. But the men were herded into concentration camps until their families could ransom them out. These camps were not yet extermination camps, but some of the men were beaten up so badly they didn't live to see their families again. The Nazis murdered innocent civilians. Just like the military men murdered innocent civilians in Colombia during its civil war. When Harriet told me she was adopting two girls from an orphanage in Bogotá, I started reading up on the history in Colombia. I wanted to know as much as I could about the country you lived in before coming to live with Harriet. I wanted to know about the events that may have shaped your life. When I read about the civil war and the killing of innocent people, I went to shul to pray that your life and Ana's life had not been touched by the violence. My own life had been forever changed by Nazi violence, and I prayed that your lives had not.

That night, the night of Kristallnacht, my family was luckier than most. Even though we were Orthodox and very religious, we lived in a building that was occupied by non-Jews. The Nazis passed us by that night. We didn't suffer the terrifying banging on the front door. But when I went to school the next morning, our synagogue was burning. The violence from the night before had continued into the next day. Standing across the street, I stared in disbelief as the flames raced through the building. The smoke from the fire burned my eyes and my throat and made me cough. My friend Susanne and I waited anxiously for the fire trucks to arrive. When the sound of blaring sirens finally came from around the block, Susanne grabbed my hand and shouted, "It's going to be alright. The firemen will save the shul." But it wasn't alright. When the trucks stopped in front of the shul, the firemen didn't try to put out the fire in the synagogue. And they didn't try to stop the fire from burning down our Jewish school next door. The only thing they did was stop the fire from spreading to the non-Jewish houses nearby. Suddenly I understood. No one was going to save our shul. No one was going to save our school.

"I need to find my parents," I said to Susanne, dropping her hand and running straight to their shoe repair shop. It was their second business. They'd lost their first business a few years before when Hitler told people to stop buying from Jews. My parents had owned a small manufacturing company that made wool sweaters. The sweaters had sold very well because we lived near the Alps, and people wanted something warm to wear when they walked in the mountains. The shoe repair business was my mother's idea. She and my father took lessons from someone they knew at the synagogue who had just retired and closed his own business. His Jewish customers became our customers.

The smell of the smoke clung to my hair, my coat, my stockings. When I arrived at the shop, breathless from running, my parents weren't there. The windows had been smashed and three Nazi stormtroopers were taking money out of the cash register. We stared at each other from opposite sides of the broken windows. They were young, just a little older than I was. But their huge black boots and brown shirts tucked into brown pants with huge belt buckles gave them an authority that frightened me. That's what uniforms do. They frighten people and make them compliant, eager to follow orders.

"Go home!"

I took a few steps back but didn't leave.

"I'm looking for my parents. This is their store."

"They aren't here. The store's closed. Go home!"

I wanted to do exactly that, run home as fast as I could, but instead I heard myself asking, "My schoolbooks are in the desk. Can I come in and get them?"

I used to do my homework at the shop after school and had left some books in one of the side drawers of my father's desk. I don't know why, but they said I could, maybe because I was young. Just a schoolgirl. When I opened the drawer, I saw my father's address book with our customers' names in it and slipped it into my school bag along with the books.

Feeling bold, I asked the Nazis if I could also take the shoes that were ready to be picked up. "I'll deliver them to the people they belong to."

They let me take them, thinking our customers' old, repaired shoes had no value. The moment I left the store, they boarded up the windows and sealed up the front door. Just like that, the business was gone.

I ran home, stinking of fire and smoke, and handed my father the shoes I'd taken home. Later that day, he delivered them. I wanted to go with him, but he told me to stay with my mother and hide anything that was valuable. We didn't have much, but my mother and I found a hiding place in the back of one of the closets for my grandmother's silver candlesticks and my parents' wedding rings. When he came home, my father's face was white.

"What's wrong?" my mother asked in Yiddish.

"When I knocked on the Shulmans' door to deliver their shoes, no one answered. The door was half-open, so I walked in."

He stopped.

"What happened?" she asked, bracing for bad news.

"They killed themselves." His voice was shaking.

"Oy vey," said my mother, shaking her head back and forth. "Oy vey, oy vey, oy vey."

It was a shock. Until Kristallnacht, my father believed the Nazis would never target us.

"They don't mean us," he'd say again and again. "We're just ordinary people, small people, working people. They mean the rich Jews with the big firms and the big, big businesses. We don't have to leave."

"I don't know," my mother had countered. "Maybe we should leave."

"No, we're going to stay here and wait for it to blow over."

Writing about it now, of course, I'm surprised my father was so naïve. Unlike the German Jews who believed they were German first, Jews second, my parents were Polish Jews who had emigrated to Germany. My father knew all about being persecuted for being Jewish. But until Kristallnacht, he believed Hitler's anti-Jewish laws would eventually be repealed. The anti-Jewish hatred would disappear. After Kristallnacht, that changed. My parents started to look for a way out.

It was pure chance I found out about the Kindertransport. A few days after Kristallnacht, Susanne came to the house and said she had a secret to tell me. She was going to England. Susanne was born in Germany and was hit very hard when Hitler expelled her from her German school, forcing her to come to my Orthodox Jewish school. Both Susanne's parents and grandparents had been born in Germany, and she told me she couldn't understand why she'd been so viciously rejected when she didn't even feel Jewish. When I told my father Susanne was going to England, he immediately went to talk to Susanne's parents. They were very unhappy Susanne had told us she was leaving and asked us to keep it quiet. My father went straight to the Jewish welfare people and said he wanted a place for me on the Kindertransport. At first, they said no, but my father insisted. "If you don't give her a place," he said, "I'm going to tell all my friends about it." Finally, they gave him a place for me. I was very, very lucky. There weren't many children from Munich who had a place on the Kindertransport.

I still wonder what would have happened if I'd had brothers and sisters. Would I have gotten a place? Or would my parents have sent one of my siblings instead? If they had to choose which of their children would go, would it have been me? Fortunately, my parents didn't have to make that decision, but Susanne's parents did. When I asked her how her parents decided which of their daughters should be sent to England, she said her parents had heard the British government was giving out domestic worker visas to German Jews who had jobs waiting for them in England.

"When I get settled," she said, "I'm going to try to find them work. I'm not as shy as my sister. I don't mind knocking on strangers' doors to ask people if they have work for my parents."

I didn't know it was possible to get my parents out of Germany by finding them work as a housekeeper or gardener. Like Susanne, I vowed to do everything I could to find them positions in England.

In mid-December, a little more than a month after Kristallnacht, my parents received a letter saying I needed to be ready to leave in four days. Those four days were very busy. I was allowed to take one suitcase, which I had to be able to carry myself. Someone came to our house to inspect what I had packed. I wasn't allowed to take anything valuable. I remember I had a stamp collection, which had belonged to my grandfather in Poland. I didn't think it was very valuable and wanted to bring it with me but wasn't allowed. What I ended up taking was mostly clothing and a photo album my mother made for me. I remember we had a big discussion about me taking one of my mother's favourite woolen scarves. It was a light gray cashmere scarf, soft and cozy, that matched the dark gray coat she gave me. At first, she put it in the suitcase, but then she took it out saying, "I'll bring it when I see you again." A few moments later she put the scarf back in the suitcase. "It's going to be cold in England. You're going to need it." Then she took it out again. "No, I'll give you another scarf and keep this one until we join you in England."

In the end she gave it to me.

Although my mother tried everything she could think of to get the smell of smoke out of my coat—soap, vinegar, baking soda—she couldn't get rid of it, and we had to throw it away. To replace it, she gave one of her coats to take with me, a knee-length dark grey woolen coat. It was a little big on me, but that was fine my mother said. I'd have some room to grow into it.

Packing kept us calm. Numb. I don't remember either of us crying or showing any emotion at all while we decided together which sweater to take and which sweater not to take. When there was absolutely no space for anything else, my mother found room for four new towels.

"You never know when you might need them," she said.

After my suitcase was inspected, it was officially sealed with a sticker that said it had been examined and there was nothing valuable inside—no money, no jewellery, no stamps. In addition to my suitcase, I was allowed to take a knapsack, which didn't have enough room for all the books I wanted to take. I was an avid reader and had a lot of books. Choosing which ones to take with me and which to leave behind was too difficult. Whatever books I chose to take with me, I'd miss the ones that didn't come with me to England. I was so upset I had to leave my books behind that I burned them all in the oven in the kitchen. It was an old-fashioned oven that you fed with coal. I fed my books into the oven one by one and watched the flames destroy all the stories I had loved. Stories that showed me how people who were different than I was lived. Stories about how to think about the world. When the last one finished burning, my books, like my synagogue, like my school, no longer existed.

On the day I left, my parents took me to the train station but weren't allowed to accompany me to the platform. The week before, a mother of a young boy of seven had been so upset at having to say goodbye to her son she had fainted on the platform. So now parents and children had to say their goodbyes in the waiting room. Once again, I was lucky. I wasn't travelling alone. Susanne was on the same train I was. We waved to each other from different sides of the waiting room. While we had no idea if we would be placed in homes close to each other in England, at least we'd be able to keep each other company on the way.

Susanne and I were both sixteen going on seventeen, but many of the children were much younger. It was excruciating for parents to part with their children, and the scene in the waiting room was horrendous. Just inside the entrance to the waiting room, a mother and father were pulling on the arms of their daughter who looked about nine or ten. The girl's mother was trying to pull her out of the waiting room, and her father was trying to pull her inside.

"No. Please. Stop. I don't want her to go," said the mother. "It's better for us to die here together then for us to be separated."

An older man, maybe the mother's father, came over and pulled her away from her daughter.

"Go," he said to the girl's father while the mother sobbed. "Go now."

My parents and I turned away and found a quiet corner to wait in, our backs to the goodbyes in the waiting room. My mother took my hand in hers, then reached for my father's hand, and began to pray. She started in Hebrew, then switched to Yiddish.

"Blessed art thou, our Lord, our God, King of the Universe. Shver iz dos lebn in goles. Life in exile is difficult. Keep our daughter Lottie safe in a strange new country, give her strength and fortitude to live the best life she can in someone else's home, help her keep the Sabbath and follow your commandments. Amen."

"Amen," my father and I replied.

The children were being lined up at the entrance to the platform, suitcases in hands, knapsacks on backs. It was time to go. My mother gave me one last hug.

"You have been an exceptional daughter," she said. "Write as often as you can. We love you."

"I will. I love you too."

"It'll only be a few weeks," said my father holding me tighter than he ever had before. "Things will blow over and you'll come back again, or we'll come and join you."

It was a promise every parent in that waiting room was making to their child. It won't be long. We'll see you soon.

Luisa, I believe when your mamá *sent you and Ana to El Orfanato she was hoping and praying her separation from you would not be a long one. That she would see you again soon. Like my parents, she spent her days and nights waiting to be reunited with you. It is devastating to know none of them ever saw us again.*

Lots of love,
Nana Lottie

73

CHAPTER 8

There was nothing to do but be patient. While it was a comfort to Luisa to know Nana Lottie was right that *mamá* hoped to bring Ana and her home from El Orfanato once she recovered, waiting for Father Álvarez to track down Beatriz was driving her crazy.

She tried to keep busy. Taking over Claudia's work in the kitchen, quizzing her for her biochem tests, and telling the younger kids stories helped. But it wasn't enough. Luisa decided to look for an art class. Drawing and painting had kept her grounded all those years in Toronto. It could keep her grounded now. On Saturday morning after obediently asking Sister Francesca for permission, Luisa took a taxi to La Candelaria to find an art class.

It was Harriet who had encouraged Luisa to draw. The first day she and Jonathan came to meet Luisa and Ana, they brought a bag full of toys, puzzles, and art supplies for them to play with. Ana chose a puzzle of kids skating on a frozen lake. Luisa chose a small sketch book and coloured pencils. Harriet took out a bigger sketch book and began drawing a picture of her house. Luisa drew a picture of Ana and herself standing in front of the orphanage. When she was done, Harriet copied her picture of Ana and Luisa in front of her house. Luisa started crying. Sister Francesca, who'd been watching over all of them, took Luisa's hand and squeezed it. Harriet took Sister Francesca's hand and squeezed it too. But she didn't try to take Luisa's hand. She waited to see if Luisa would take her hand on her own. She didn't. The two of them sat holding Sister Francesca's hands until

Luisa opened up her sketchbook to a fresh page and drew a new picture. Jonathan was holding Harriet's hand, Harriet was holding Ana's hand, Ana was holding Luisa's hand, and Luisa was holding Sister Francesca's hand. Harriet nodded. She understood. She and Jonathan weren't part of Luisa's family yet.

After they arrived in Toronto, Harriet signed Luisa up in a neighbourhood art class and when it was over, signed her up for another. Luisa had taken art lessons every year she lived with Harriet and discovered she liked painting portraits best. Wild, wonderful portraits with exaggerated hands and feet. She modeled her work after Rubén Vera Hermoza, an artist from Peru who used brilliant vibrant colours to paint pictures of rural women holding baskets of avocadoes and potatoes. Hermoza painted the women in his pictures with huge hands and feet. To show how hard the women had to work to take care of their families, Luisa thought.

The taxi dropped Luisa off in the centre of La Candelaria, and she started gallery hopping. Most of the galleries were showing work by local artists: paintings, sculptures, multimedia installations. She paid special attention to the portraits, imagining the day she might be a local artist whose portraits were being exhibited in La Candelaria.

Before leaving each gallery, Luisa asked if they offered art classes. None of them did. She was about to give up when she found The Art Shop nestled between a tiny second-hand bookstore and a small café. The man standing behind the counter was wearing jeans and a white t-shirt. His hair was tied in a ponytail.

"Hi," he said.

"Hi. I'm looking for a drawing or painting class."

He pointed to group of people behind the counter.

"That one's just getting started."

"It meets on Saturday afternoon?"

"From two to four."

"Perfect."

He stuck out his hand. "I'm Diego."

"Luisa."

"Where are you from?"

In Toronto when people asked Luisa where she was from, it was usually because they didn't think she was born in Toronto. But she didn't think Diego meant to be mean, so she kept it light.

"What gave me away? My accent?"

He grinned. "Yeah."

"I'm from Toronto."

"Laura's from Toronto! She's the one teaching the class. Why don't you go in and meet everyone?"

"I don't have any supplies with me."

"That's okay. I'll set you up."

Luisa walked around the counter and got a feel for the space. The counter was the only thing separating the store from the studio. Laura had arranged four easels in a semicircle. Customers shopping in the store could see people painting behind the counter, but they couldn't see what they were working on. Smart, thought Luisa. There was a big skylight in the centre of the room that let in lots of natural light. Three women around Harriet's age had already set up at three of the easels. There was one easel left. Luisa went over and stood beside it.

Laura walked into the studio. Like Diego, she was wearing jeans and a t-shirt, but hers was orange. Laura gave them all a big hello, welcomed them to the class, and asked them to introduce themselves by talking about an artist who'd influenced their work. It could be a painter, but it could also be a sculptor, or a potter, or a writer, or a musician. Any kind of artist.

"I'll start us off," said Laura. "I'm Laura Martinez. I was born in Mexico, immigrated to Canada with my parents and my younger brother when I was fourteen."

Fourteen, thought Luisa. The same age as Ana is now.

"My partner Diego Ramírez and I set up The Art Shop just over two years ago. Diego's a sculptor from Bogotá, and we met at the Ontario

College of Art and Design in Toronto. I spend half the year in Toronto and half the year here teaching painting. Diego teaches sculpting.

"An artist who's had a major influence on my work is a writer named Gloria Anzaldúa who grew up on the Mexican-American border in Texas. She writes about what it means to live on the border, in the Borderlands. She says it means not living fully in Mexico and not living fully in the United States. It means living partially in both. She also says, 'To survive the Borderlands you must live without borders, be at a crossroads.' Like Anzaldúa, I don't believe in borders. I cross them."

Luisa stood beside her easel, transfixed.

When it was her turn to speak, she talked about being born in Bogotá, living in Toronto, and volunteering at the orphanage. But she didn't say anything about being adopted or why she'd come to Bogotá. Instead, she talked about Rubén Vera Hermoza and how he gave the women he painted enormous hands and feet.

When it was time to start painting, Luisa went back to the front of the store to buy some supplies. A sketchpad, some pencils, two canvases, palette knives, some oil paint, and a bunch of brushes. She also bought a gray cotton apron with two big pockets on the sides.

Luisa opened her sketchbook and began to block out an image of a woman with huge hands and feet. She also gave her huge breasts.

Laura came over to see how Luisa was doing.

"Who is she?" Laura asked Luisa in Spanish even though she could have spoken to her in English.

"Sister Francesca. One of the nuns at the orphanage."

"What's she holding?"

"A little girl."

"Who is she?"

Luisa hesitated, not sure she wanted to tell her. But then she took a risk. "She's me."

"So the orphanage you're volunteering in . . ."

"Was the one we lived in before moving to Toronto."

"I see. You're beginning a very important painting."

Luisa nodded. "Yes, it feels that way."

After the art class, Luisa went into the café next door and ordered a café con leche. The café had Wi-Fi, and she googled Gloria Anzaldúa. Her most famous book was the one Laura talked about. She wrote it in two kinds of English and six kinds of Spanish so when people read it, they'd have to look up the words they didn't know. Just like Anzaldúa did when she was learning English. As she read about Anzaldúa's difficulty learning English, Luisa nodded in agreement. It was comforting to know others had struggled too.

Later that day the children and sisters at El Orfanato celebrated Mariana's fifteenth birthday. Her *quinceañera*. Many families plan a celebration for their daughter's *quinceañera*. Families with money throw a big party where everyone dresses up, and there's lots of food, music, and dancing.

After dinner everyone headed over to the reception room, which was where adoptive parents met their would-be children for the first time. It was the nicest room in the house. It had a comfortable couch and a few armchairs placed around a beautiful red, yellow, and blue hand-woven rug. A large wooden toy box sat in the corner. The sisters had framed some of the drawings and paintings the kids had made, and they gave the room a warm, welcoming feel.

When the children entered the room, they were greeted by a salsa band Sister Francesca invited. The musicians got everyone dancing. In Toronto, Luisa had taken salsa lessons for two years, and she began to dance with Sister Francesca. Everyone was impressed by how well she danced. For a moment she felt like she belonged back in Bogotá.

After the performance, there was ice cream and cake and the sisters presented Mariana with a present. A silver cross necklace. The same necklace Sophia and Claudia wore. They'd each received one from the sisters when they turned fifteen. Mariana was very moved. She cried when Sister Lorena put the necklace around her neck. Luisa felt a little teary herself. It was hard celebrating your *quinceañera* without parents and a family. At least Mariana had a family at the orphanage.

Later that night when Luisa walked into the young girls' room for their bedtime story, everyone was talking about the party.

"Did you have a *quinceañera*?" Carolina asked her.

"Yes."

"Tell us the story of your *quinceañera*!"

Luisa looked at the boys. "Do you want to hear that story too?" They all did except for Santiago. He wanted to hear a story that was scary.

"What if I tell the story of my *quinceañera* tonight and a scary story tomorrow?"

"Okay," he said, resigned to waiting one more night for the story he really wanted to hear.

"Okay. The Story of Luisa's *Quinceañera*. When Luisa was about to turn fifteen, she really wanted to have a *quinceañera*. She remembered celebrating other girls' *quinceañeras* at El Orfanato. But in Canada turning fifteen isn't a big deal like it is in Colombia so she didn't expect a party. The Saturday night before her birthday Luisa went to her babysitting job like she did every Saturday night. But when she got there, the parents didn't want to go out because their daughter was sick. Luisa wondered why they hadn't called her to tell her not to come. It was strange. She went back home, and she opened the front door with her key. Everything was dark. Then suddenly all the lights came on, and a whole bunch of people yelled 'Surprise!' Someone had planned a surprise *quinceañera* for Luisa. Who do you think planned it?"

"Harriet!" shouted the kids.

"Yes! Harriet!" Harriet was gaining mythic status in Luisa's stories. She was always the one who knew what Luisa, Ana, and Clare needed and wanted.

"Tell us about the party," said Carolina.

"All the Globals were there."

"Who are the Globals?" asked Santiago.

"They're the families who've adopted children from Global Family."

"What's Global Family?"

"The adoption agency in Toronto that adopts children from our orphanage."

"They're looking for families for all of us," said Carolina, hopeful.

"But not everyone is adopted," said Paola. Her tone was matter of fact, repeating what Sister Francesca told the children whenever they asked her when it would be their turn to be adopted.

It was too sad and complicated a truth to talk about at bedtime, so Luisa quickly went back to the story.

"Harriet knew I wanted to learn how to salsa, so she hired three musicians and two salsa dancers to teach everyone how to salsa. We danced to live music, just like tonight."

"So, is that when you learned how to salsa?" asked Carolina.

"Yes. And I liked it so much, Harriet signed me up for classes."

Salsa dancing always lifted Luisa's spirits. Once she'd mastered some of the basic moves, her confidence soared, and she had a real sense of achievement. Luisa also felt sensual and sexy when she danced, and it began to show in how she walked and moved off the dance floor. It was after she'd started salsa dancing that Carlos, one of the boys in her Saturday Spanish class, started calling her *Hermosa*, pretty one.

"Was there ice cream and cake?" asked Santiago.

"Yes."

"Did you get a silver cross necklace like Mariana?" asked Paola.

"No. But I got a beautiful silver heart with my name on the front. With the date of my birthday on the back."

"Is that the heart you're wearing?"

"Yes."

"Can we see it?"

"Sure."

Luisa took it off and passed it around.

"It's beautiful."

Luisa smiled.

"What was the best part of your *quinceañera*?"

"The speech Harriet made before we cut the cake."

"What did she say?"

"She said the day Ana and I arrived in Toronto changed her life forever. She never thought she'd have so much fun or learn so much. She said she and Clare and Marty were blessed to have me and Ana in their lives." Luisa's voice caught in her throat.

"Who's Marty?" asked Carolina.

Luisa knew she'd messed up. Up until that moment she'd been careful never to mention Marty when she talked about her family in Toronto. But she was so involved in the story that she was telling she forgot to be careful.

"Harriet's best friend," she said. It wasn't so much a lie as a half-truth. Marty was Harriet's best friend as well as her partner. Luisa waited to see if Carolina would ask anything else. She didn't.

"That was a beautiful speech," said Carolina. Then in English, "Epic!"

"Epic," everyone shouted.

Luisa laughed. "It was totally epic. Okay, it's time for bed. Who has my silver heart?"

Paola gave the heart back to Luisa, and she put it around her neck.

"Is Ana going to have a *quinceañera*?" asked Carolina.

"No. She wants a sweet sixteen." Luisa said *sweet sixteen* in English.

"What's that?"

"It's a party that girls in Toronto have when they turn sixteen."

"They have a party at sixteen, not fifteen?"

"That's right."

"So, Ana's a Canadian girl!" said Santiago.

"Yeah." Luisa wasn't happy about it, but it was true.

"But not you! You're a Colombian girl!"

Luisa laughed. "That's right. Okay, that's it. No more questions. It's time for bed. Let's go boys. Back to your room. I'll be there to tuck you in in a few minutes."

As the boys left, Luisa tucked in each of the girls and then turned off the light.

"Good night, *chiquitas*. See you tomorrow."

"Goodnight Luisa," they chimed back. "See you tomorrow."

CHAPTER 9

Claudia got a ninety percent on her biochemistry test, and Luisa suggested they go to the Botero Museum to celebrate. She said yes right away and asked if they could invite Sophia. Luisa wanted to say no but said yes.

Luisa had learned about Fernando Botero in her high school art class. He was a Colombian painter from Medellín, who drew people and objects larger and chubbier than they were in real life. They walked through the exhibit rooms slowly, standing in front of each piece and taking time to look at each of the paintings carefully. Luisa watched Claudia and Sophia take in Botero's chubby pears, chubby horses, chubby guitars, chubby people dancing, and chubby nuns. Claudia was intrigued. Sophia was not.

"The chubbiness of everything really throws off your perspective. I like that," said Claudia.

Luisa did too. And she really liked the way each of the paintings of everyday life in Colombia reminded her that she'd made it back home. Home to the love and care of the nuns at El Orfanato. Home to a place of salsa music and dancing. But then they came upon the portraits of Colombian politicians, guerilla fighters, and drug lords. Botero often painted them in the centre of scenes of murder and torture. Luisa couldn't look at any of them for very long. The scenes were very violent and forced her to see the brutality and pain Colombia's civil war had brought on its people.

When they came to Botero's drawing of a chubby Jesus Christ being crucified, Sophia was repulsed.

"I think it's provocative to see Christ on the cross with flesh on his face and his body," Luisa said. "It makes him look like an ordinary person. Someone you could meet on the street."

"But he isn't an ordinary person," replied Sophia. "He's the son of God and it's wrong to paint him like he isn't."

"Let's go see the sculptures now," said Claudia deftly changing the subject. Luisa caught her eye and gave her a grateful smile. Sophia caught the smile and narrowed her eyes. She wasn't enjoying herself.

They walked into the room with Botero's sculptures, and Luisa was immediately drawn to a bronze sculpture of a mother and child. It was called *Maternita.* Maternity. The child—it was hard to tell if it was a boy or a girl—had its hand on the mother's breast, but instead of looking down at the child as you might expect, the mother was looking away, her face anxious.

Claudia came to stand beside Luisa. "Look at her face," Luisa said. "She's worried. She's looking at something she didn't see coming. I wonder what it is."

"It could be many things," said Claudia taking her hand.

Luisa felt a tingling go up her arm. She could feel Sophia's icy stare behind her back.

"Being a mother, protecting your children is a big responsibility," Claudia continued, "What do you think Sophia?" trying to interest her in the sculpture in front of them.

"Yes, it could be many things," Sophia said. Detached. Disengaged.

Claudia and Luisa took their time to study each and every sculpture. Eventually Sophia got bored and said she'd meet them outside the museum. When they found her a half hour later, Luisa suggested they have coffee and cake at the café next door. Her treat. They each ordered a café con leche and shared a piece of *torta negra Colombiana,* Colombian chocolate cake.

"Have you tasted *torta negra* before?" Claudia asked.

"No! It's my first time having it. It's really good."

"Sometimes Sister Francesca makes it for a special occasion," said Sophia. She took another big piece on her fork. "So how do you like your life in Toronto?"

Luisa took a moment to answer. "It's complicated. I'm very lucky to have an adopted family that loves and supports me. But I'm sorry I didn't grow up in Bogotá."

"Is it difficult living with your mother's girlfriend?"

Luisa knew what she meant but pretended she didn't. "No. Marty's very easy going."

"No. I mean do people speak badly about your family?"

"Not very often. Some people have a bad reaction when they first find out about Harriet and Marty. Like Anita, who's the head of Global Family. When she first found out she refused to invite Marty to Seder. So Harriet, Ana, and Clare and I didn't go to Seder either. Harriet wouldn't go without Marty."

"What's Seder?"

"It's a meal Jewish people have on a holiday called Passover. It happens around the same time as Easter. Christ's last supper was a Passover Seder."

"Your family is Jewish?" said Sophia, eyes wide open with surprise. Luisa braced herself for a difficult conversation.

"Yes."

"Did you and Ana have to become Jewish too?"

Luisa wanted to say yes just to see what Sophia's reaction would be. But she didn't want to behave badly in front of Claudia.

"No."

"So do you go to church?"

"Yeah."

"Every Sunday?"

"At Christmas."

"That's all?"

"Uh, huh."

"Well, I'm glad I wasn't adopted into your family." It was blunt and mean.

Luisa looked over at Claudia who was shaking her head ever so slightly in disapproval.

"You know," Luisa replied, getting angry, "My family's been very good to me and Ana, even though they don't take us to church every week. Ana and Marty are very close. I like them too. A lot."

"That's good," said Claudia. She took Luisa's hand again. "We all have to make peace with the families we've been given." Then she took Sophia's hand. "And the families we've lost."

She waited for Sophia to say something. Sophia didn't say a word.

"Isn't that right, Sophia?" squeezing her hand.

"Yes," Sophia finally said to please Claudia.

And that was the last thing Sophia said that afternoon. On the taxi ride back to the orphanage, Luisa and Claudia talked about their favourite paintings and sculptures, but Sophia didn't join in. She spent the ride looking out at the rain through the window. Claudia let her be and Luisa followed Claudia's lead although she couldn't stop wondering what Sophia was thinking. And if somehow she was going to pay for Claudia's friendship.

That night Luisa had two scary bedtime stories to tell.

"Which one do you want to hear?" she asked. "The scary story that happened here in Bogotá or the scary story that happened in Toronto?"

"Both!" said Santiago, excited.

"Okay, which one first?"

"The one from here."

"Okay. The Story of When Ana Got Locked in the Bathroom."

Santiago moved closer to Luisa so he could hear every word.

"On the first night Ana and Luisa slept at the orphanage, they were in the bathroom getting ready for bed. Ana went into one of the stalls, locked the door and then couldn't open it. Luisa and Ana were the only ones in the bathroom. Everyone else was already in bed. Ana started banging on the door and shouting out Luisa's name. Luisa told her to jiggle the lock. It didn't move. Luisa tried to slide under the door to get in, but there wasn't enough room for her to slide underneath. She told Ana she was going to find Sister Francesca, but then Ana started to cry, begging her not to leave her so Luisa stayed."

"How old was Ana?" asked Paola.

"Four. Luisa told Ana they had to wait until Sister Francesca came to find them. Ana cried even harder. To make her feel better Luisa began to sing. A song their *mamá* sang to them before they went to sleep. It worked. Ana stopped crying. About a half an hour later Sister Francesca found Luisa sitting on the floor outside the bathroom stall singing. She went to find a screwdriver and unscrewed the hinges of the bathroom door so Ana could get out. Ana ran into Luisa's arms sobbing. Luisa started crying too. Sister Francesca gave them both a big hug and took them down to the kitchen and made them some hot milk. Then she gave each of them a cookie."

"Which ones?" asked Carolina.

"The ones with powdered sugar."

"*Polvorosas*!" shouted Paola.

"But we only have *polvorosas* on our birthdays and Christmas!" said Carolina.

"Really? Sister Francesca must have felt very sorry for us."

"What happened next?" asked Santiago.

"Sister Francesca took Luisa and Ana back to their room and tucked them in. She told Luisa she was smart not to leave Ana alone in the bathroom, and she was smart to start singing to calm her down. Sister Francesca said Ana was very lucky to have Luisa as her sister. That's when Luisa knew Sister Francesca really liked her. And that she really liked Sister Francesca. And that living at El Orfanato was going to be okay."

Everyone clapped.

"Okay, now tell the scary story from Toronto," said Santiago.

"Are you sure you want to hear it?" Luisa teased. "It might be too scary for you."

"It won't be," he said with certainty.

"Okay, then," Luisa replied looking directly into eyes. "The Day Luisa Got Lost at the Market. Once, not long after Luisa and Ana left El Orfanato to live in Toronto, Harriet took them and their sister Clare to the market."

"Was it big?" asked Santiago.

"Huge." He nodded in anticipation.

"Luisa stopped to look at a table of dolls from around the world. Three of the dolls were from Colombia, a father, a mother, and a little baby. The sign beside them said 'Colombia Campesina and Campesino Family in national costume.'"

"What did they look like?" asked Carolina.

"Well, both the father and the mother had straw hats. The mother was wearing a white shirt and black skirt with coloured ribbons at the bottom, and she was holding a baby."

"What was baby wearing?" asked Paola.

"A white lace dress."

"And the father?"

"Black pants, white shirt, and a wool scarf over one shoulder."

"What colour was the scarf?"

"I'm not sure. All kinds of colours. Orange. Green. Blue."

"Beautiful," breathed Paola.

"But how did you get lost?" Santiago wasn't interested in the dolls.

"Well, when I stopped to look at the dolls, I thought Harriet, Ana, and Clare were looking at them too. But they weren't. They had walked away. I panicked. I started running up and down the aisles of the market looking for them. I tripped over a box of vegetables that was sitting in the middle of the aisle and skinned my knee. It began to bleed."

"Just like you did here!" said Carolina.

"Because you didn't stay with the group!" added Paola. "Right?"

"Right," Luisa said, embarrassed. She hadn't realized the story of her skinning her knee at the market had become a cautionary tale for the younger kids.

"Was there a lot of blood?" asked Santiago.

"Tons of blood. It ran all the way down my leg, and the white socks I was wearing turned red!"

He was impressed. "That's a lot of blood."

"A woman who was selling vegetables nearby came running over to help me. Miraculously she spoke Spanish. She had a different accent than me, but she understood I was lost and needed to find Harriet.

"'Don't worry, we'll find her,' she said. 'But first let's fix your knee.' The woman tried to wipe away the blood with her handkerchief, but it wouldn't stop bleeding. So, she tied the handkerchief tight around my knee to stop the bleeding."

"Did it hurt?" asked Santiago.

"Yes, the handkerchief was really, really tight."

"Then what happened?"

"The woman took me by the hand, and we went to find the security guard at the main entrance. Harriet was there. So were Ana and Clare. They were crying. Harriet thanked the woman who'd found me over and over again. The security guard had a first aid kit and gave Harriet antiseptic to clean off my knee and a bandage."

"Did that hurt too?"

"Yes. It hurt a lot."

"Did you cry?"

"No. I wanted to be brave."

Santiago nodded in approval. "Then what?"

"Then we all went over to the woman's stall to buy our vegetables. On our way out, I showed Harriet the dolls from Colombia. For my next birthday, Harriet bought the dolls for me."

"All three of them?" asked Carolina. "Not just one?" reminding Luisa how easy it was for Harriet to buy three dolls for her birthday and how hard it was for mothers in Ciudad Bolívar to do the same.

Luisa nodded. "I named them after my *mamá* and my father. Inés and Juan Andres."

"What did you name the baby?"

"Guess."

"Luisa."

She smiled. "Good guess. How did you know?"

"It was easy. You wanted the *mamá* and *papá* dolls to watch over baby Luisa. Like they did before you came here."

Luisa nodded, moved at how clearly Carolina understood why the dolls had always been so important to her. "That's exactly right."

Later that night, after changing into her pajamas and brushing her teeth, Luisa slipped into Claudia's room quietly. She was studying. Luisa took out her guidebook and re-read every word about the Botero Museum, stopping every few sentences to look at Claudia taking notes from one of her textbooks. After a while Claudia turned off the light and said good night. In the dark, Luisa went over every moment of their visit to the museum. The best part was when they were looking at Botero's sculpture of the mother and her child and Claudia had taken her hand. She got goosebumps thinking about it. That was when Luisa first realized she was falling for Claudia. Just like Harriet had fallen for Marty. It surprised her. She'd never been attracted to girls before, and the only person she'd ever kissed in her entire life was Carlos.

Carlos was born in Toronto and didn't speak much Spanish. His parents were afraid he was going to lose it completely, so they enrolled him in Luisa's Saturday Spanish class. He didn't want to go, but his parents promised to buy him a car for university if he went every Saturday for his last year of high school. He took the deal.

Carlos and Luisa liked each other from the first day they met. He reminded Luisa of one of the older boys she had had a crush on when she lived at the orphanage. He had tight curly black hair and a wide and friendly smile. He also liked salsa almost as much as she did. When Carlos asked Luisa to his graduation dance, she was thrilled. They had a fantastic time, shared a few passionate kisses on the dance floor, and started hanging out over the summer. Carlos was Luisa's first real friend in Toronto. During the day, Luisa was busy with her summer calculus course, but at night they took long walks on the boardwalk along the lake and talked about all the things they wanted to do in life. Luisa asked Carlos if he wanted to go to Colombia to see where his family came from. He said there were other places he wanted to see first: Europe, Asia, Australia. Colombia could wait. It was the exact opposite for her. The world could wait. Colombia couldn't.

Most nights they'd end up in Carlos's parent's basement where they'd make out. Although Carlos was Luisa's first boyfriend, she wasn't his first girlfriend, and he knew how to kiss and stroke in just the right places to get her body humming.

Near the end of the summer, Carlos's parents went away for a week. They had the house to themselves. The first night they cuddled up on the sofa in the living room and watched a Colombian movie. Carlos's parents had an amazing collection of Colombian movies. When it was over, Carlos took Luisa's hand and led her upstairs to his bedroom. Luisa was excited, but a little nervous too. It was going to be her first time.

Luisa had thought long and hard about having sex with Carlos before going over to his house while his parents were away. She knew at the end of the summer he was leaving to go to university. Once he left, they probably wouldn't see each other again until Christmas. Maybe they'd pick up where they left off, maybe they wouldn't. Luisa wondered how it would feel to say goodbye in September and if it'd be easier if they didn't have sex. But then she thought about how good it felt when they were together and how much she liked him. She also knew that Carlos would never push her to do anything she didn't want to do. If they started having sex and she changed her mind, he wouldn't give her a hard time about it.

They started kissing. Knowing no one was home gave Luisa an incredible sense of freedom. She didn't change her mind. When it was over, Carlos wrapped Luisa in the blanket folded up at the edge of his bed, and walked into the bathroom, smiling. The blanket smelled of lemon laundry soap. Luisa smiled too.

Two hours later they got back into their clothes and went out to get some ice cream. Luisa was tingling all over. She felt amazing.

Carlos and Luisa spent as much time together as they could while his parents were away. But two weeks later, on Labour Day, he left for school in Montreal. In his new car. He didn't come back to Toronto for Thanksgiving, but they saw each other a few times at Christmas. The chemistry was still there, but they didn't get to spend any time to be alone together. Carlos was busy with his family and friends.

Because sex with Carlos had been easy and fun, Luisa thought she was straight. But the electricity she felt when Claudia had taken her hand convinced her she was as attracted to her as much as she had been to Carlos. For some people, finding out they might be bisexual or pansexual is a big deal. But crushing on Claudia didn't worry Luisa at all. The only thing that worried her was that Claudia might not feel the same way about her that she did about Claudia. And even if Claudia was interested, Luisa didn't how they would ever find a way to start a romance living in El Orfanato under the watchful eyes of Sister Lorena and Sister Francesca.

CHAPTER 10

The next day in Luisa's English class, Mariana asked about Harriet and Marty. In front of everyone.

"Is it true your mother's divorced and has a girlfriend?"

Luisa looked at Sophia. Go ahead, her eyes said. If you're so proud of your family, why don't you tell everyone about them?

Defiance made Luisa brave.

"Yes, it's true. Would you like to see a picture of them?"

Luisa took out her phone and looked for a picture of Harriet and Marty. It was risky. It was one more thing that made her different, but she did it anyway.

"Harriet's the shorter one. Her partner's name is Marty."

"When did your mother and father get divorced?" Mariana asked.

"When I was in grade six. Harriet started seeing Marty a year later."

"What's it like living with your mother's girlfriend?"

"The same as it was when we lived with her and my adoptive father."

Actually it wasn't. Jonathan and Luisa had become friends on the long drives across the city to her Spanish class. Although she wasn't lying when she told Sophia that she liked Marty, Marty was much closer to Ana and Clare than they were to Luisa. Marty and Luisa were still trying to find ways to connect.

"It can't be the same," said Mariana.

"Why not?"

She looked at Sophia. "Because it's not normal for two women to live together in that way."

Sophia nodded, a smug smile on her face.

"Who says it's not normal?" Luisa asked.

"Everyone," said Sophia with a certainty that got everyone else in the room nodding in agreement.

Luisa was used to answering all kinds of questions about Harriet and Marty, but it was different talking about them in Spanish. More personal.

"That's not true," she said. "In Canada, it's legal for two women to get married. In Colombia too. And it's legal for two women to adopt children here."

"Really?" asked Mariana.

"Yes."

"Are your mother and her girlfriend married?" asked Adriana.

"No."

"Why not?"

"I don't know. I never asked them."

"Is your sister gay too?" Mariana wanted to know.

"My sister? You mean Ana?"

"No, not Ana. Your other sister. Harriet's daughter."

"Clare? I don't know. She's only eleven. Why do you think Clare's gay? Because Harriet's bisexual?"

"Yeah."

"It doesn't work that way. Harriet's parents weren't bisexual. But Harriet is."

"But if Harriet's bisexual, why did she marry your father?" asked Sophia, crossing her arms and shaking her head.

Everyone else nodded, looking confused.

"I know it may be a little difficult to understand. Some people are attracted to both men and women but decide to get married to one or the another."

Luisa was about to tell them that not everyone identified as a boy or a girl. That some people identified as non-binary like Marty. But Alejandra wanted to know something else.

"Who are you attracted to?" she asked Luisa.

Luisa couldn't say Claudia.

"I had a boyfriend last summer," she replied.

"Was he Canadian?"

"Yes, but his parents were Colombian."

"Is that why you liked him? Because his parents were Colombian?"

"That was part of it."

The dinner bell rang but no one got up.

"We need to go," Luisa said. "Who has my phone?"

"Me," said Adriana. She got up and handed it to Luisa. Everyone else got up too and went to wash up, talking in low, excited voices on their way out. Sophia was the last to leave.

"I should be mad at you, but I'm not," Luisa said to Sophia. "I'm relieved. Now that everyone knows about Marty, I can finally talk about my family without worrying what to say and what not to say."

Sophia looked like she wanted to slap Luisa's face.

"Just because you live in Canada and have liberal ideas and can speak English and have money to spend on taxis and coffee and cake, don't think you're better than anyone else here. You're not any more special than the rest of us."

Sophia pushed by Luisa and left.

Luisa was stunned. She hadn't realized how much Sophia resented her.

Three seconds later Sophia came back. "And if you're not worried about what people think about your family, why haven't you told Sister Lorena about Harriet and Marty? Or Sister Francesca? You talk to Sister Francesca about everything."

She stormed off again, leaving Luisa with something else to worry about. If she didn't tell Sister Lorena and Sister Francesca about Marty, maybe Sophia would.

At dinner Luisa sat as far away from Sophia as she could and said as little as possible to the rest of the girls. Fortunately, Claudia had had an exciting day and spent most of dinner talking about what she'd learned from the midwife who'd visited her class. Everyone was listening and seemed to have completely forgotten about Harriet and Marty.

The next morning Sister Lorena called Luisa into her office. Luisa braced herself for bad news. Sophia had told Sister Lorena about Marty, and Sister Lorena was going to send her back to Toronto. There was no place at El Orfanato for a girl with queer parents. Even if they weren't really her parents. But when Luisa knocked on the door and sat down, Sister Lorena didn't want to talk about Harriet and Marty.

"I have some good news and bad news. Father Álvarez called. He was able to find your aunt and contact her. Unfortunately, she doesn't want to meet with you."

"Oh," said Luisa. Underneath that "Oh" was a whole mess of different feelings. Huge relief. Sister Lorena didn't know about Harriet and Marty. Then huge disappointment. Beatriz didn't want to meet her.

"Why?" she asked.

"I don't know. Father Álvarez didn't say. I'm sorry."

Luisa tried to think of a way to change Beatriz's mind. Maybe she just needed another push.

"Sister Lorena, would it be all right for me to write a letter to her? I have so few memories of my *mamá* and none of my father. I want to know more than I know now. It would help me feel . . ." She used Claudia's words, "more settled. If I wrote a letter to her, would you ask Father Álvarez to forward it?"

It took Sister Lorena a moment to answer. Luisa thought she was going to say no. But then Sister Lorena surprised her.

"If you keep the letter short, no longer than a page, I'll send it."

"Thank you."

"But you understand, there are no guarantees. Father Álvarez may decide not to send it to her. And even if he does, she may not write back."

"I understand."

"Good."

"Thank you, Sister. I'll write the letter tonight."

As Luisa left her office, she noticed two large black filing cabinets standing side by side inside the closet. She hadn't noticed them before. The closet door must've been closed the last time she was in the office. Luisa wondered what was in the filing cabinets. Maybe Sister Lorena kept the children's files there. Maybe her file would have some new information about Beatriz that could help her.

When Luisa got back to Claudia's room, she looked for the notepaper and envelopes she'd packed in her suitcase just in case she needed to write a letter. She pulled out a sheet and wrote Beatriz a letter.

Dear Beatriz Rodríguez:

Hello. This is your niece, Luisa. Inés's eldest daughter. I know you told Father Álvarez you don't want to meet me. I'm writing to try change your mind. I was only ten when I left Bogotá and don't know very much about our family. I want to find out as much as I can. I want to know who my grandparents were, where they lived, and what Ana and I were like as young children. I need to build some memories, and you're the only one who can help me. Here's a photo of Ana and me that we took in the photo booth at the Eaton Centre. It's a silly picture. We were both trying to make each other laugh by sticking out our tongues at each other, but it will give you an idea of what we look like. Father Álvarez says I look a lot like you. Do you see the resemblance too?

My return address at the orphanage is on the front of the envelope. If you're willing to meet me, please write back. If I don't hear from you, I won't bother you again.

Sincerely yours,
Luisa Gómez Rodríguez

Luisa re-read the letter three times, found the photo in her wallet, placed the letter and the photo into the envelope, and headed back to Sister Lorena's office. Maybe seeing a picture of them would change Beatriz's mind.

The following Sunday, Claudia and Luisa went to the Gold Museum. Claudia had invited Sophia, but to Luisa's great relief, Sophia said she had to study for an exam and couldn't go. Luisa didn't have to worry about Sophia's disapproving glances and remarks. And she could have the afternoon alone with Claudia. It was raining so Luisa asked the taxi driver to stop as close to the Gold Museum as he could. The closest he could get was a block away, and Claudia and Luisa opened their umbrellas and ran the entire block trying not to get soaked. They arrived at the museum laughing and a little out of breath.

The Gold Museum was probably the most famous museum in Bogotá. The guidebook said it owned more than 55,000 gold art pieces created by the Indigenous people who lived in Colombia before the Spanish colonizers came.

The museum was packed so they went straight up to the second floor where there were fewer people. The exhibits were organized by region, and the descriptions underneath each piece were written in English as well as Spanish. Luisa had to read most of them in English. They spent a lot of time looking at the animal figures—water birds, alligators, fish, a whole bunch of cats, and deer. Some of the animals were a mixture of two animals—a jaguar and frog, a man and eagle. But Luisa's favourite pieces were the gold women statues.

"See that one in the corner?" she said to Claudia. "She looks like you."

"No, she doesn't."

"Yes, she does. Her hair is down to her waist, and she has your cheekbones and your lips. She's beautiful. Just like you."

Claudia blushed and looked away. "Where do you want to go next?" she asked.

Luisa had embarrassed her. She needed to come up with a place to go that would make Claudia forget what she'd just said.

"What about The Art Shop? I could show you the painting of Sister Francesca I'm working on. Is that okay?"

"Sure."

The rain had let up, and they took their time wandering up and down the streets. When they came across a vendor selling *obleas,* Claudia asked if Luisa had ever had one. An *oblea* is made of two thin round waffles with something sweet in the middle. Luisa said she wasn't sure. Claudia ordered two *obleas* with *arequipe,* which looked like caramel candy. When Luisa took out some money, Claudia insisted on paying. She handed Luisa her *oblea*, and Luisa took a small bite. It reminded her of eating pancakes with maple syrup. The kind Ana made for everyone on Sunday mornings. Thin and crispy. Luisa took another bite. A hazy memory pushed its way through her thoughts. She closed her eyes to capture as much of it as she could. Luisa, Ana, and their *mamá* were standing in front of an *obleas* stand with a red umbrella. Their *mamá* was holding an *oblea* and gave Luisa the first bite. She took a tiny bite and then passed it to Ana. Ana passed it back to their *mamá*. They took turns taking tiny little bites until it was gone. Luisa opened her eyes, barely breathing. Another memory to add to her collection.

"How do you like it?" asked Claudia.

"It's really sweet!"

She laughed. "I haven't had an *oblea* for such a long time. My parents used to buy it for my sister and me. It was a big treat."

They started walking slowly to The Art Shop, eating their *obleas* along the way.

"What happened to your parents?" Luisa asked.

"They died. In a car accident. I was in the car with them. So was Luciana."

"Your sister?"

She nodded. "Our car was hit by a drunk driver." Her voice was flat. Like she was telling someone else's story.

"That's terrible."

"Everyone died. Except me. Father Álvarez came to see me every day. He told me when I left the hospital, I could live at El Orfanato."

"How old were you?"

"Twelve."

"Horrible."

"Christiane got me through. She was the nurse in emergency when they brought me in. She held my hand and talked to me the entire time I was there. She was there when I woke up from surgery. She was there when they told me my parents and Luciana died."

"How old was Luciana?"

"Nine."

Luisa took Claudia's hand. It was ice cold.

"Christiane helped me through the most awful moment of my life. I want to do that for other people. But emergency nursing is really difficult. Anything can happen at any time. People die. Children die."

"Yeah." There was more Luisa wanted to say, but Claudia took away her hand and changed the subject.

"Tell me about Harriet and Marty."

Luisa wasn't sure why she was asking about them.

"Well, they're great together. Marty's a lot of fun. Ana's crazy about them. They coach Ana's hockey team. They're really close."

"How did Harriet and Marty get together?"

"They were friends for a long time. But when Harriet and Jonathan got divorced, their friendship changed."

"Do you think Marty always loved Harriet? Always wanted to be with her?"

"I don't know. Maybe."

"I don't understand how a woman who was married to a man can suddenly change and love a woman."

Luisa took a silent deep breath.

"Harriet told us when she married Jonathan she was fully committed to the relationship. She thought she'd spend the rest of her life with him. But when he moved to Vancouver and they got divorced, she had an opportunity to explore her attraction to Marty. And it was strong enough for them to become more than friends."

"I can't imagine it."

The *oblea* Luisa had just finished started coming up her throat. She swallowed hard.

"No?"

"Can you?"

Luisa tried to play it cool. "Sure. A few of the girls at my high school had girlfriends."

"I don't know anyone who is bisexual like Harriet."

Yes, you do, Luisa thought. "No one in nursing school?"

"No."

"Well, I'm sure there are lots of bi people in Bogotá. There was a Pride parade here last summer."

"Really?"

"Yeah."

"Is there a Pride parade in Toronto?"

"Every year."

"Have you ever gone?"

"Lots of times."

"Even though you're not gay?"

Luisa wanted to ask her how she could be so sure she wasn't gay but settled for "Everyone goes to Pride."

When they got to The Art Shop, Laura gave Luisa a big hello and kissed her on both cheeks. Luisa introduced her to Claudia and asked if she could show Claudia the portrait of Sister Francesca she was working on. Laura went into the back of the shop to find it. Although Luisa still had to paint Sister Francesca's hands and face, the portrait was beginning to come alive. Claudia loved the way Luisa had exaggerated Sister Francesca's breasts and hands and feet. That made Luisa happy.

By the time they left The Art Shop, it was already after five. In the taxi on the way back, Claudia gave Luisa a big hug and told her she'd had a lovely afternoon. Luisa hugged her back and said, "Me too." But for Luisa, the afternoon together had been complicated. For the first time since arriving in Bogotá, Luisa had been able to talk about Harriet and Marty without being afraid. But the girl who she'd shared her story with couldn't imagine falling for Luisa the way Luisa had fallen for her. That left a rip in Luisa's heart.

CHAPTER 11

When Luisa arrived at The Art Shop the following Saturday, there were five easels set up, not four. Somebody new had signed up. Luisa had just finished unpacking her brushes and paints when Laura walked in followed by a boy with long black hair, tied in a ponytail like Diego's. He scanned the room and saw the empty easel beside Luisa.

"Hi, can I set up here?"

"Sure."

"Thanks." He smiled. He had a stunning smile. Open and confident. Just like Carlos.

As he placed a fresh new canvas on the easel, Laura began the class.

"Hello, everyone. Please welcome Daniel García to our class. Daniel, would you like to introduce yourself?"

"Sure. I'm Daniel García. But you already know that."

He was nervous. Luisa nodded her head and smiled to encourage him.

He nodded and smiled back. "I'm studying photography at the University of the Andes here in La Candelaria. I'm in my second year. I've passed by The Art Shop a couple of times. Last week I finally came in to look around. Laura was here. I told her I wanted to start painting again, and she said I should come to her Saturday class. So here I am."

"Great," said Laura. "Could you tell us about an artist who has influenced your work?"

"Sure. Last fall I saw the work of Kent Monkman in Toronto. He's a Canadian Indigenous artist. His people are First Nations Cree. The installation I saw was about the extinction of the American bison. The White settlers killed the bison for their fur and left the meat to rot on the bone. Then they collected the bones to use as fertilizer and for bone china. The museum showing the installation has a lot of pieces of bone china from that time period, so it was a way to give visitors a different history, a history of how the museum's beautiful collection of bone china came to be created. I love the idea of using art to challenge the history we learn in school, the history we learn in museums. I want to try experimenting with that idea in my own work. But I have to take a few history courses first. Monkman really knows his history."

Luisa stared at Daniel in disbelief. She loved Kent Monkman's work and had seen the bison installation twice.

"Thanks, Daniel," said Laura. "Okay, let's start painting."

As Daniel opened his sketchbook and placed it on the easel next to a fresh canvas, Luisa moved her easel a little closer to him so she could catch the best light in the room.

"You forgot to mention the infamous Miss Chief," she said with a smile that was just a little flirty.

She pronounced *Miss Chief* the way she would in English. Miss Chief was Kent Monkman's queer alter ego. She often popped up in his work. In the bison installation, she was standing on top of the cliff next to the stuffed bison, dressed in a sparkly red-sequined pantsuit and matching scarf. She was a First Nations warrior with long flowing black hair dressed up like a drag queen. Miss Chief was there to create mischief, to show people a different history than the one they'd learned in school. People usually laughed when they saw Miss Chief in Monkman's work. And that was the point. If they were laughing, they'd be more open to seeing things differently.

"You've seen Kent Monkman's work?" Daniel asked, surprised.

Luisa deepened her smile. "Many times. I live in Toronto."

"So, you understand what I want to do!"

"You want to play with history."

"Exactly. What's your name?"

"Luisa Gómez Rodríguez."

"Nice to meet you, Luisa Gómez Rodríguez."

"Nice to meet you too Daniel García."

"You're lucky to live in Toronto."

"And I think you're lucky to live here. There are so many museums and art galleries in Bogotá!"

"But if you live in Toronto, you can go down to New York for the weekend!"

That was true. Luisa had gone there with Harriet and Clare when Marty took Ana's hockey team to a tournament in Ottawa.

"So, what are you going to paint?" Luisa asked.

"This." He handed her his sketchbook. Taped to the first page was a photograph of the mountains surrounding Bogotá. The mountains were in the background, cradling the pink office towers and apartment buildings beneath them. In the foreground was a set of treetops, suggesting another set of mountains on the other side of the city.

"It's a terrific photo. Did you take it?"

"Yes. Now I want to try to paint it."

"You're going to have fun mixing all the different pinks for the buildings. And the different greens for the mountains. The ones in the very back almost look blue."

"What are you working on?"

"A portrait."

"Can I see?"

"Sure." Luisa stepped to the side so he could see her canvas. "This is Sister Francesca."

He looked at the painting. "Her breasts are huge!"

Luisa grinned. "I know. She has a lot of love to share."

Daniel grinned back and looked at the painting again.

"Which is why the little girl sitting on her lap is so lucky."

"Exactly."

"I really like Sister Francesca's eyes. Loving and determined."

Laura came over to see how they were doing.

"So, what are you working on today?" she asked Luisa.

"Her hands and face. But I'm having trouble mixing the right colour."

"What colour are you trying to find?"

"Caramel brown. I started by mixing yellow and red and adding some blue. But the brown was too dark. So I added a bit more orange. Then it was too light, so I added more blue. But it still isn't right."

"Try adding a tiny bit of gold to warm up the brown. I have some in the back. I'll bring it over."

When Luisa finally got the shade she wanted, she asked Laura to take a look.

"What do you think?"

"I like it. It's a warm, deep caramel."

"Yeah, I like it too."

By the time Luisa had finished painting Sister Francesca's hands and face, everyone else had started cleaning their brushes at the sink and she had a moment alone with Laura.

"Could I ask you about something?"

"Sure."

"It's about living in the Borderlands. It's . . ." She searched for the right word. "Unsettling."

"Why?"

"Because it's so much easier when you belong in one place. It's easier to fit in. Because I was born in Bogotá, at school I was never Canadian enough. And now that I'm back I speak Spanish with an accent so I'm not Colombian enough."

"I know what you mean."

"Do people ever ask you where you're from?"

She laughed. "'Where are you from?' could be the title of my autobiography!"

"So, what do you say?"

"I say, 'I was born in Mexico, immigrated to Canada when I was fourteen, live in Toronto for half the year and in Bogotá for the other half.'"

"And what do you call yourself? Mexican? Canadian?"

"Right now, Mexican-Canadian. What about you?"

"Colombian. Even though I became Canadian after I was adopted."

"How old were you when you were adopted?"

"Ten. My sister Ana was seven."

"And you've lived in Toronto for . . . ?"

"Seven years. Almost eight."

"So soon you'll have lived in Toronto as long as you did in Bogotá."

"If I stay there. I promised Harriet I'd go back for one more year. To try university. If I like it, I can stay. If I don't, maybe I'll come back here."

"Harriet's . . . ?"

"My adoptive mother." Saying adoptive mother felt okay. A lot better than saying mother.

"Is she from Colombia too?"

"No. She was born in Canada."

"And she's White?" Laura asked.

"Yeah."

"So, the schools you went to were mostly White?"

"Yeah. And affluent."

"It must've been hard to fit in."

"Brutal. When I first got there, there were a few really mean girls in my class who made my life miserable. What was your school like?"

"Most of the kids were Brown like me, and most spoke Spanish."

"That would've been much better for me. So, what's it like living half in Toronto and half here?"

It was a personal question, but Luisa really wanted to know.

"Fine. At least for now. I came last year to meet Diego's family, help him set up the shop, and see how I like living here. Then I went back to Toronto. Now I'm here again. I'm not sure what's next."

"Do you ever think about going back and living in Mexico?"

"I've been back to visit a few times, but I don't think I want to live there. My friends and family are in Toronto and Bogotá. But I still feel Mexican in my soul, so I call myself Mexican-Canadian."

"I feel Colombian in my soul. Even though people here think I'm a *gringa*."

Laura laughed. "Do you ever feel Canadian in your soul?"

"Hardly ever."

"But once in a while?"

"Maybe once in a while. Like when I tell the kids stories about my life in Toronto."

Luisa went over to the sink to clean her brushes. It took a while to wash out the gold. As she was drying them off with a rag, Laura came over.

"Listen, I have an idea. My neighbour Jessica was also adopted by a Canadian family. Just like you. She was born in Bogotá, adopted when she was two, and has come back here to live for a while. She says being adopted is an identity all its own. She's just started a group for adoptees called Patria. It means homeland. They get together once a month to talk. On Thursday nights."

"It sounds amazing but going out at night is a problem."

"Diego has a car. What if I pick you up at the orphanage and bring you back?"

"You'd do that for me?"

"Sure."

"That's really nice of you. I'll ask Sister Francesca."

Luisa packed up her supplies, said goodbye, and left. Right outside The Art Shop a crowd had gathered around one of the street artists. He was sketching a portrait of a tourist in charcoal using vine charcoal, which is soft and powdery. Beside him sat a little girl who looked just like him. It was hard to know how old she was, but Luisa guessed six or seven. Her father had given her a small piece of the charcoal and a piece of paper from his sketchpad. She was watching his every move and copying each one of his strokes carefully. Luisa moved closer so she could watch her work.

Like her father, she began by lightly sketching out the overall form of the tourist's face, keeping her arm moving.

Luisa moved to the side of the crowd, took out her sketchbook and a black pencil from her knapsack and started drawing the little girl. Twenty minutes later she was finished. But the face of the little girl didn't look like her at all. Instead, she had drawn herself sitting on the street sketching. It was bizarre.

As Luisa walked away from the crowd, wondering why she'd put her own face on the little girl who looked nothing liked her, she bumped into Daniel. He'd been watching the street artist as well and had seen her walking away.

"Hey," he said, running to catch up to her. "Luisa Gómez Rodríguez! Would you like to go out for coffee?"

"I'd love to," she said lightly touching his arm, "but I can't. I'll be late for dinner. What about tomorrow? I can meet you in front of The Art Shop after Mass. Around two?"

"You go to Mass?" She'd surprised him again.

"Every Sunday. With Sister Francesca."

"Sister Francesca from your painting?"

"Yes."

"Where are you living? In a convent?"

Luisa laughed. "No, an orphanage."

"Why are you living in an orphanage?"

"I'm volunteering there."

"For how long?"

"Six months. I have four and a half months left."

"Just four and a half?"

"Yeah."

He smiled. A sexy smile. "Too bad."

Luisa smiled back. "That's exactly how I feel. So I'll see you tomorrow?"

"See you tomorrow." He gave her a kiss on the right cheek. Colombian style.

CHAPTER 12

When they met at The Art Shop the next day, Daniel suggested they go on a tour of the street murals that could be found throughout La Candelaria. They began in a children's playground not far from The Art Shop.

On an old brick wall was a huge mural painted by an artist named Bastardilla, which means *italics* in English. The mural featured two giant faces. One was painted bright blue and looked like a robot. The other was painted pink and orange. It had a tongue made of swords, the kind you see in medieval movies. The pink and orange Indigenous warrior was holding the head of the blue robot in his hands.

"So what do you think it's about?" Daniel asked Luisa.

"It could be about lots of things," she said wanting to impress him. "The clash between the traditional lives Indigenous people used to live and the contemporary technological lives we have now. The Indigenous warrior's tongue of swords reminds me of the ways Indigenous people have had to swallow and carry the violence of settler colonialism."

Luisa wondered if she'd said too much and if Daniel thought she was showing off. She'd learned about how the White settlers from Europe invaded the land of the Indigenous people in grade twelve history (in elementary school the White settlers were called "explorers" who "discovered" and "founded" Canada), but maybe, she thought, she should've just left it at the clash between tradition and technology.

"So, you think the warrior's a man?" Daniel asked Luisa.

"Definitely."

"I think she's a woman."

"Why?"

"Look at her lips, then look at her hand."

Luisa looked at the mural again. It was possible she was a woman. Or non-binary. "Yeah, I can see why you think she's a woman."

"At first I thought she'd beheaded the blue robot and was carrying its head in her hands. But then I thought she was embracing the robot. Look at the tear in the robot's left eye. The warrior could be comforting her."

"So, the robot's a woman too?"

"Yeah."

Luisa wondered how he could be so sure. "Who's Bastardilla?" she asked.

"She's a street artist known for her paintings about violence against women."

That's how, thought Luisa. He knew the artist who had painted the mural. If anyone was showing off, it was him!

"So, the robot could be a woman who's been dehumanized by violence?" she asked.

Daniel grinned. "Exactly."

"And the swords are the violence women suffer at the hands of men?"

"Yes. Would you like to see some more of her work?"

"Sure."

But just as they were leaving the playground it began to rain. Within seconds it was pouring, so they ducked into a café.

Luisa ordered a café con leche, Daniel ordered a *café tinto*, and they shared a piece of *torta negra*.

"So, you're volunteering in an orphanage."

"El Orfanato Para Niños y Niñas."

"Where is it?"

"In Ciudad Bolívar. I used to live there."

"So, the little girl in Sister Francesca's arms is . . ."

"Me. Okay, your turn. Where do you live?"

"In an apartment near the university."

"By yourself?"

"No, I have two roommates. One's a photographer, one's a painter."

"Where did you grow up?"

"In the northern part of the city."

"In one of the rich neighbourhoods?"

"Yeah, I guess."

"Did you go to a private school?"

"Yeah."

"And they let you wear your hair in a ponytail?"

He laughed. "No, I only started growing it in university. I wasn't allowed to wear it long in high school."

"What did you look like before?"

"I'll show you."

He pulled out his phone and found a photo of a sweet young man with short hair wearing a uniform.

"You're adorable."

He grinned. "Thank you."

"Were you always interested in photography?"

"Always. My parents gave me my first camera when I was seven."

"So, you want to be a photographer?"

"Yeah. And a painter. But my father wants me to be an architect. He's an architect. He has his own firm."

"What does your mother do?"

"She's an interior designer."

"She works with your father?"

"It's a family business."

"What does she want?"

"The same thing he wants."

"So, you're going to have to fight to be an artist."

He sighed. "Yeah. And I think I'm about to lose."

"Why?"

"One of my father's colleagues is an architecture prof at Uniandes. He's coming to talk to me about starting the program next week."

"Next week! Don't you have to apply first?"

"I applied last summer to get my father off my back. I wasn't serious about going. I was hoping they wouldn't accept me. It's a very competitive program. But they did. I told my father I don't want to go. I want to finish my degree in photography. But he said photography is a hobby, not a profession. So is history. If I don't accept the offer to architecture, he'll stop paying my tuition."

"He'd really do that?"

"Yup." His attempt to seem casual couldn't hide how upset he was.

"Your turn. What—"

Luisa wasn't ready to let it go.

"You need to negotiate. Say you'll try it for a year to see how you like it, but only if you can keep studying photography as well. Say you'll try it if you can do a double major in architecture and photography."

Daniel looked at Luisa, excited.

"That's a not a bad idea. But what about history?"

"You might have to let history go for now. But at least you could still take photography."

"Yeah. Photography's more important. I can read history on my own."

"Do you think your father will go for it?"

"Maybe. It's worth a try. Thanks." He put his hand on her arm and gave it a light squeeze.

Luisa smiled. "Of course."

"Now, it's your turn again. What happened to your parents?"

Luisa took a deep breath and just came out with it.

"My *mamá* died of pneumonia because she couldn't afford antibiotics and my father disappeared in Medellín."

"Disappeared?"

"Yeah. He went to visit his mother and never came back. No one knows what happened."

Daniel's face grew dark.

"What?" asked Luisa.

"How old were you when he left?"

"I don't know. But it was before my *mamá* was sick, so four or five. Maybe six."

"When did you turn four?"

Luisa did the math. "2005."

"So, between 2005 and 2007. That was when Álvaro Uribe was president."

"President of Colombia?"

"Yeah. When he was elected, he promised to kill all the guerillas. He gave the army incentives to kill as many of them as they could. Some of the soldiers killed innocent men they said were guerillas so they could get the money. Lots of the civilian men they murdered were from Medellín."

Luisa was stunned. She leaned forward across the table.

"You think my father was murdered by the army?" she asked in a low voice.

"Maybe."

Luisa didn't believe it. Things like that happened in the movies, not in real life.

"Why didn't anyone stop them?"

"No one knew they were doing it. Not for a long time. When people finally realized what had happened, it was a big scandal. The United Nations came to investigate. They called the murdered men the *falsos positivos*."

The false positives. "How do you know all this?"

"We learned about it in history class."

"You think my father was one of the *falsos positivos*?"

"It's possible."

"How can I find out?"

"I don't know. But when the United Nations came to investigate, they wrote a report."

"Will you read it with me?"

He hesitated. "I don't know. The whole thing was very violent. Very disturbing."

"It's already very disturbing not knowing what happened to him."

Daniel didn't want to read the report.

"Please?" asked Luisa holding her breath.

"Yeah, okay," said Daniel, reluctant.

Luisa let out a quiet breath of relief. If she had to read the report all by herself, she wasn't sure she could've done it.

"Do you think it's available online?" Luisa asked.

"Let me check." Daniel took out his phone and started looking. "Found it."

Luisa handed him her phone. "See if there's an English translation. Tragically, my English is better than my Spanish. You read it in Spanish, I'll read it in English and then we'll compare notes."

"Okay."

"But first tell me everything you already know."

"How's your Colombian history?"

"Pretty basic," she answered, embarrassed.

"Well, you know there's been armed conflict in Colombia between the FARC guerillas and the National Army for the last fifty years, right?"

"Yeah, I saw Botero's paintings of the guerillas. But I don't know what FARC stands for."

"Fuerzas Armadas Revolucionarias de Colombia. They're the largest group of leftist guerillas in the country."

"Okay."

"Okay, so the story of the *falsos positivos* began to come out in 2008 when the bodies of sixteen men showed up in a mass grave in Ocaña. They'd been reported missing from Soacha. The army said the men were guerilla fighters and they'd been killed in combat. But they weren't. They were civilians. Ordinary people."

"How far is Ocaña from Soacha."

"Driving? About twelve hours."

"Okay, thanks."

Daniel found the English report for Luisa, and she started reading, her heart thumping louder and louder with every line she read. Almost all the people who were killed were young men who had been disguised to look like guerrilla fighters. Some were farmers. A few were homeless. Some were drug addicts or disabled. A recruiter working with the army targeted each man and tricked him with the promise of a job offer. Then the man was driven a long distance away to avoid being identified. That's how the sixteen young men from Soacha ended up in a grave so far from home. After the men were killed, the army dressed them in military clothes, placed a weapon and ammunition in each man's hands and took photographs. Then they buried them. Anonymously.

Luisa imagined her father lying in an anonymous grave somewhere, and her hands started shaking. She clasped them together tightly and told herself to take slow, deep breaths. In for three seconds, out for three seconds. In for three, out for three.

Daniel could see Luisa was struggling. "I think we should stop," he said.

Luisa shook her head. "Not yet," she said between breaths. "I need to know how the men in Medellín were recruited."

Daniel scrolled through the Spanish version of the report.

"It says 922 men were killed in the district of Antioquia. That's where Medellín is."

"How?"

"The same way they were killed in Soacha. Soldiers offered them work on a farm in Puerto Berrío. When they accepted, they got on the bus they thought was going to the farm. But the bus stopped at a place called Puerto Nare, and the soldiers told them to get off."

"Then what?"

"The men were picked up by other soldiers on motorcycles and were shot."

Luisa stood up, her legs shaking like her hands. "Let's go."

They walked out of the café into the rain.

Luisa fished her umbrella out of her knapsack and opened it. Daniel took her other hand. They started walking.

"How am I going to live with this?" Luisa asked Daniel.

"We don't know for sure your father was one of the *falsos positivos*."

"But even if my father didn't die that way, even if he died some other way, or even if he didn't die at all, the point is he could've died that way. And if my father didn't die that way, 922 other men died that way. What kind of country kills its own people?"

"That's what happens in civil wars."

Luisa started to cry. A bus stopped right in front of them. A long line of students waited for the doors to open.

"Let's get on. It's going to the university. I'll take you to my apartment and make some tea."

"No! Not the bus," said Luisa suddenly panicked. "Let's take a taxi."

"But the bus is right here."

"The last time I was on a bus, it was awful."

"Awful how?"

"Never mind. Trust me, it was awful."

"I'll stand right beside you. Nothing will happen."

Luisa reluctantly followed Daniel onto the bus. It was packed. They stood the entire way, jammed in beside everyone else who lived near the university. Luisa held her knapsack tightly under her arm. It was only a ten-minute ride to Daniel's apartment. Daniel put his arm around her shoulders, shielding her from the crowd. When they got off the bus, the rain had nearly stopped. Daniel took her hand again.

Daniel's apartment was on the top floor of a four-story walk up. The staircase was very dark and he pushed the button on the wall at the bottom of the stairs. A light came on for a few seconds, just long enough for them to climb the first flight. Then it went off again. At the bottom of each flight of stairs, Daniel turned on the light. It stayed on just long enough for them to reach the next flight. It was a little stressful. Luisa began running up the stairs to reach the top before the light went out.

The apartment had a kitchen, living room, and a small bedroom. Daniel and his roommates had managed to get two bunk beds into the bedroom and had installed floor-to-ceiling shelves along one of the walls. Each shelf had a set of baskets to store their clothes. The room was incredibly well organized and tidy. Ana wasn't the only one who was a neat freak.

Daniel told Luisa to make herself comfortable while he made her a cup of tea. She sat on the couch in the tiny living room and looked at the photographs on the walls.

"Are all of these yours?"

"Most of them, some are Miguel's."

"Your roommate?"

"Yeah." He handed Luisa a mug of tea and sat down beside her.

"Thanks."

Luisa took a few sips. It was nice and hot. She wanted to talk about anything but what they had just read.

"Tell me about your photographs."

Luisa half listened while Daniel talked about each of the pictures on the wall. Where he'd been standing. What the light had been like. What he'd been trying to capture. Luisa drank her tea while he talked. Listening to Daniel talk was calming. His world was safe.

"So, what are you going to do when you go back to Toronto?" Daniel asked, sensing Luisa was drifting off. "Go to art school?"

"No. I decided to take Spanish and Latin American studies."

"But you're going to keep painting, right?"

"Of course."

Daniel took her hand. "Good. You have to keep painting. Your portrait of Sister Francesca is spectacular."

"Because of her enormous breasts?" she teased.

"Yes! Those enormous breasts have something to say to the world."

Luisa laughed. "About what?"

"Loss and adoption," he said seriously. "And the power of love."

He leaned over and kissed her. A soft, sweet, lingering kiss. At first, Luisa kissed him back. But then the kiss got more passionate, more insistent, and she pulled away. It was still too soon. Too soon after everything they'd just read and talked about. Too soon after realizing she had feelings for Claudia. Although she was attracted to Daniel, she wasn't ready to make a choice between him and Claudia.

"No?" Daniel asked.

"No," answered Luisa. "I'm still trying to take everything in. That report we just read? It was brutal."

"It was."

"The government should protect its people. Not kill them."

"I know."

"Has anyone been arrested?"

"I think some of the lower-ranking officers have. But not any of the generals."

"Do people talk about it?"

Daniel sighed. "People talk about it. But the government says the problem of the *falsos positivos* was the actions of rogue soldiers and officers."

"Was it?"

"Not if you believe the human rights people."

He leaned back into the couch and put his arm around Luisa. She put her head on his shoulder.

"I know I told you I wanted to know, but maybe it would've been better not to know." Suddenly she felt incredibly vulnerable.

"It's never better not to know," said Daniel.

"Why not?"

"You can't change what needs to be changed unless you understand how it happened."

"Even when you understand what happened, it's hard to change things."

"But you can't stop trying. Look at Bastardilla and Monkman. They keep trying. If you can influence the way people see things, the way they understand things, then you've changed a little piece of the world."

"Do you think my father was one of the *falsos positivos*?"

"I don't know."

"What do you think I should do next?"

"I don't think there's anything you can do. Except mourn his death."

"How can I mourn his death when I don't remember anything about him?"

"You're an artist. You invent him."

CHAPTER 13

Dear Luisa:

To get to England from Germany we travelled through Holland and were put on a ferry. It was the first time many of us had ever been on a boat, and a lot of the younger children were sick. Susanne and I went around helping the little ones clean up with the towels my mother had squeezed into my suitcase. But when the stench made us both too nauseous to continue helping, we found a breezy spot at the back of the boat and encouraged each other to look out at the horizon. That helped. Soon some of the other older children joined us and we began to share our stories of Kristallnacht. A girl from Bavaria named Ingrid said the Jews in her neighbourhood were all forced to leave their homes in the middle of the night and march to a theatre in the centre of town.

"On the way," she said, in a voice barely above a whisper, "we passed the synagogue. The Nazis had taken the Torahs out of the synagogue and a stormtrooper was stomping on them, destroying them. Another one was beating up the rabbi. He was lying on the street, bleeding badly."

I imagined having to watch our beloved rabbi being beaten up and not being able to help him. The nausea I'd been holding back overwhelmed me, and I threw up over the rail of the ferry. Susanne handed me the last clean towel to wipe my face.

"When we arrived at the theatre," Ingrid continued, "we were told to sit down. When everyone was seated, the Nazis set up a row of tables and chairs on the stage. Then they grabbed all the men in the audience, forced them up onto the stage and told them to jump over each chair and table. If they couldn't

do it, they were whipped. *My father was one of the men who couldn't jump over the chairs. When one of the Nazis raised his arm to strike him, my mother covered my eyes with her hand. I could feel her body trembling beside me. After all the men had been publicly humiliated, the Nazis divided them into two groups. Men over sixty and men under sixty. The men under sixty were sent to Dachau, the nearest concentration camp."*

"Your father?" I asked, my stomach heaving again. I tried breathing deeply to stop the heaving.

"He was over sixty. But my best friend's father was fifty-five. He was taken away that night and never came back."

I leaned over the railing again, but there was nothing left to throw up. Just bile. When the heaving subsided, I went to stand between Ingrid and Susanne and reached for their hands. Then one by one everyone else reached out for a hand and we stood in silence until it got too cold to stay outside.

The next morning the ferry had arrived in England. We lined up to get off the boat and onto a double-decker bus. Everyone wanted to sit upstairs. There were so many of us, Ingrid was afraid the bus might tip. None of us had ever seen or been on a double-decker bus before.

It wasn't a long ride to Dovercourt, the summer holiday camp that had been turned into a temporary holding centre for us. Each of us were assigned a bed in one of the huts and given some bedding. Susanne and I were separated so that we could keep an eye on the younger children assigned to our huts. It was very cold in the camp. None of the huts, which had been built for people to stay in during the summer, had heating. We slept in every piece of clothing we had brought with us and ate our meals with our gloves on.

Even though there was room for a thousand children at the camp, there was a lot of pressure to find homes for us as quickly as possible. Every week brought hundreds of new children to Dovercourt, and they needed our beds. Every Saturday and Sunday we were told to put on our best clothes and wait for potential foster parents to come and meet us. We called it the cattle market. People walked around the dining hall and stared at us, trying to figure out if *they wanted to take us home or not. If someone picked you out the crowd, you were taken away from your table and interviewed.*

Many of the visitors to Dovercourt were surprised to find us so well dressed. They expected us to look bedraggled, wearing old and torn clothes. But when our parents helped us pack our suitcases, they didn't pack our ordinary, everyday clothes. One little suitcase didn't hold a lot. We came with our best clothes.

Most families wanted little blue-eyed, blond girls between the ages of three to seven. Little boys were popular too. Susanne and I knew we might not be placed with a foster family, but we had no idea what would happen to us if we weren't chosen. We also knew there weren't enough Jewish people coming forward to take us in, and there was a chance we'd be asked to live in a non-Jewish home. Having grown up Orthodox, I prayed it wouldn't happen to me.

After lunch on our second Saturday at Dovercourt, Susanne and I were on display at the cattle market, trying to distract ourselves from how awful it was by writing letters home. I was so involved in writing my letter that I jumped when one of the camp workers put her hand on my shoulder to introduce Mrs. Ross to Susanne and me. Mrs. Ross was from a seaside town called Brighton, and she was looking to foster an older girl. She was wearing a cross.

With the camp worker translating, Mrs. Ross asked us about our homes in Germany. Where we had lived, what our parents did for a living, how many brothers and sisters we had. Susanne went first. When I told Mrs. Ross my parents had run a shoe repair shop and I was an only child, she nodded seriously and asked me if we could have a private conversation. Susanne immediately got up, squeezed my hand, and went off to sit at another table. The camp worker stayed to translate. As she passed me, Susanne whispered in Yiddish, "Zol zayn mit glick." Good luck.

"My husband and I are chemists," Mrs. Ross said. "We have two shops on Elm Grove, and we work six days a week from eight in the morning until seven at night. Mother Ross, my mother-in-law, is losing her short-term memory. She'll put the kettle on, pour herself a cup of tea, but forget to turn off the stove. She'll draw a bath, get undressed while the tub is filling, but forget to turn the

water off and come back to an overflowing tub. My husband's decided it's time for her to come and live with us, and we're looking for an older girl to be her companion and look out for her during the day while we're at work. Someone who likes to walk. Do you like to walk?"

I nodded. "Will it be possible for me to go to school?"

She shook her head. "No, we'll need you at home all day. That's why we're looking for an older girl."

I tried not to show my disappointment. "Is there a synagogue in Brighton?"

"Yes. Downtown. That's how we found out about the Kindertransport. The rabbi came to speak at our church about needing foster homes in Brighton."

For a brief moment I felt a little better. "My family is religious. Will I be able to attend services on Saturday?"

"We'll need you at home on Saturday. You can have Sunday morning and afternoon to yourself when we take Mother Ross to church."

A bigger disappointment. "Will it be possible to buy Shabbos candles and light them on Friday night?"

"We'll give you a small allowance every week so you can buy things you need. If you want to spend it on candles, that's up to you."

"You know Jews don't eat pork. I won't be able to eat pork."

She didn't know but did her best to cover it up. "That's not a problem. You can make yourself something else the nights we have pork."

The camp worker turned to me. "So, you'll go with Mrs. Ross?"

I wanted to say no. But I could see Mrs. Ross was well dressed. A chemist with two shops might have friends or neighbours or customers who could hire my parents and get them a domestic worker's visa. Besides, how could I tell anyone who was willing to take me in that I'd rather be in a Jewish home when there wasn't a Jewish home for me to go to?

I nodded. Turning to Mrs. Ross, I offered the English words I'd been practicing since my arrival. "I am very grateful for your kindness."

She was pleased. "I'm afraid we don't have much time before our train leaves back to Brighton. We need to leave in twenty minutes to catch the bus to the station."

I asked the camp worker if Mrs. Ross could write her address down for me on the back of the letter I was writing. When she was done, the three of us stood up. I looked for Susanne in the dining hall but couldn't find her.

"You need to get your things right now," said the camp worker, so I walked back to my hut, picked up my suitcase, which we had been told to pack that morning in case we were offered a home. I took out a piece of writing paper and quickly wrote out a note to Susanne with my new address on it.

"Please write and let me know where to write you back. I'll be waiting to hear from you."

Then I walked out of the hut and out of the camp, leaving my note to Susanne with the camp worker. I wondered if I'd ever hear from her again.

Not being able to speak each other's language, neither Mrs. Ross nor I said much to each other on the train ride from Dovercourt to London. I finished the letter to my parents and gave them my new address. I'd have to find a place to buy stamps in Brighton. In London, we had to rush to catch the train to Brighton, so there was no time to stop for food. By the time we arrived at the house it was almost nine, and we were both famished. The Rosses had a housekeeper who cooked and cleaned for them. She'd left a cold plate of food for us in the fridge. Ham. Mrs. Ross found me some cheese and bread and made us both a cup of tea. Neither Mr. Ross nor Mother Ross came into the kitchen to say hello. I assumed they'd gone to bed. After a quick bite, Mrs. Ross and I also went to bed. The day ended on a better note when Mrs. Ross showed me my room. I wasn't expected to sleep with Mother Ross.

The next morning was Sunday, and everyone got up early to go to church. I joined them in the dining room for breakfast, a quiet meal with very little talk. Mrs. Ross busied herself making tea and toast. Mr. Ross read the newspaper. Mother Ross ate her toast, refusing to look at me. After everyone had left for church, I unpacked my suitcase, put my clothes away in the tiny closet and the one drawer that had been emptied for me. Then I took a look around the house. It had three bedrooms, none of them very large, a medium-sized living room and dining room, and a bright kitchen. There were very few books in the house, but there was a piano in the living room. I didn't play piano myself, but Susanne did, and seeing the piano made me think of her and wonder once again if I'd ever hear from her. As you can imagine, it would have been easy to sink into deep sadness at that moment, but on the long train ride from Dovercourt to London and then from London to Brighton, I decided I would try to remain as optimistic as possible, learn English as quickly as possible, and do everything I could to find work for my parents in England so they could leave Germany. Feeling sad wasn't going to get my parents out.

I decided to go for a walk and get to know the neighbourhood. It was still very, very cold, but I put on every piece of clothing I had, just like I had at Dovercourt and ventured out. I found the Rosses' chemist shops on Elm Grove and searched for houses that looked big enough—as big as the Rosses' house—to need a housekeeper and maybe a gardener. There weren't any. By the time I got home, the Rosses were back, and Mrs. Ross was getting ready to serve lunch. I helped the best I could, following her gestures of how to set the table and following her lead when it was time to bring in the food. Lunch was just as quiet as breakfast. Mother Ross still refused to look at me, even though I tried to catch her eye several times.

After lunch, I helped Mrs. Ross clear the table and do the dishes, and just as we were finishing up, there was a knock on the front door and several people came in. After taking off their winter coats and boots, they settled into the living room, someone began playing the piano and everyone started singing. I didn't know if I should join them or sit in the kitchen. No one invited me into the living room, so I sat in the kitchen, listening to the music and watching the Rosses through the open kitchen door. I didn't recognize any of the songs, and I didn't understand any of the words, but I could tell the Rosses were having a wonderful time. Even Mother Ross was singing.

About a half hour into the singing, there was another knock at the door. When Mr. Ross went to see who it was, a youngish looking man wearing a long black overcoat and a black hat was standing in the doorway. He had a beard and reminded me of the younger men from our synagogue. The music stopped. Mr. Ross recognized the man, invited him in, and introduced him to everyone. Everyone nodded respectfully. Even Mother Ross. Then Mr. Ross came into the kitchen and gestured for me to follow him into the living room.

"Hello!" the man greeted me in English. Then, in Yiddish, he said, "I'm Rabbi Goldberg and I've come to welcome you to Brighton!"

It was shocking to hear him speak Yiddish to me in the Rosses' living room, and I began to cry.

"I'm sorry," I said. "No one's spoken to me in Yiddish since I left home."

"I understand," he said, his voice soft and kind. "Mr. Ross wants to introduce you to his friends. He didn't think you wanted to join them because they are singing hymns. Christian hymns."

I nodded at Mr. Ross, who introduced me.

I put on my most polite smile and acknowledged each of their hellos. When it was time to say hello to Mother Ross, I looked her straight in the eye and said in English, "I am very grateful for your kindness."

Like Mrs. Ross, she was pleased.

"I'm sorry I don't speak English," I added.

Rabbi Goldberg translated.

"Never mind," she said. "I'll teach you."

It was totally unexpected, and I gave her a real smile. "Thank you."

Rabbi Goldberg asked if I'd like to come to his home and meet his family. It was a twenty minute walk.

"I'd love to. If it's alright with Mr. and Mrs. Ross."

"Mr. Ross said it's fine. Sunday is your day to do whatever you want."

It was still very cold, and we walked quickly. At the end of the first block, I asked the rabbi about finding work for my parents.

"This is East Brighton. It's a working-class neighbourhood. You won't be able to find your parents work here. You can come talk to the congregation, but I don't think the families there will be able to employ your parents either."

"I need to do whatever I can to get them out!"

"Of course. I'll talk to the rabbi at Middle Street Synagogue. He might know of a family who can help."

We walked in silence for a while. I looked for landmarks so I could find my way back downtown the following Sunday. We passed by a big park that Rabbi Goldberg said was Queen's Park.

As we turned onto Edward Street, the rabbi stopped and said, "I have another idea. Before coming to Brighton, I was the rabbi in a synagogue in London. Some of the families there may have enough money to give your parents work. We can go there, you can talk to the congregation, give them a report of what's happening in Germany and tell them that you're looking for a family to employ your parents on a domestic visa. What do you think?"

"I think it's a wonderful idea. Thank you. But the only day the family doesn't need me is Sunday."

"We'll go next Sunday."

When we got to Lansdowne Road, the rabbi stopped in front of his shul. It was an ordinary-looking building and without the Star of David over the front doors. I wouldn't have guessed it was a synagogue.

"Welcome to Brighton and Hove Liberal Synagogue."

"It's not Orthodox?"

"No. Your family is Orthodox?"

I nodded. "I told Mrs. Ross I can't eat pork and I want to light Shabbos candles on Friday night. Do you know where I can buy Shabbos candles?"

"We have a lot of them at home. I'll give you some." We walked a little further until the rabbi stopped in front of a small house. Smaller than the Rosses' house.

"Here we are."

The first thing I saw when we stepped inside was a row of open trunks full of books and clothes and dishes.

"Are you going somewhere?" I asked.

"We're moving to the United States."

"You're going to America? When?"

"In three weeks."

I must have looked stricken because he quickly added, "But don't worry, we'll go to London next Sunday. Before I leave."

"But who's going to take your place at the shul?"

"The new rabbi started yesterday," said Mrs. Goldberg, coming into the living room from the kitchen. "Welcome to Brighton! How's your foster home?"

"They're not Jewish!" I knew I sounded childish and ungrateful, but I couldn't help myself. "And they don't speak Yiddish."

"Never mind," she said. "You'll learn to speak English in no time. Come into the kitchen and we'll have some tea."

Mrs. Goldberg had made some honey cake to go with the tea and for a moment I felt as if I was sitting in my own kitchen back home.

Rabbi Goldberg asked how bad the situation was for the Jews in Germany, and I shared the stories the kids on the ferry had told me.

"My father says it will blow over. But I don't think it will."

"Neither do I," said Rabbi Goldberg. "But you're safe in Brighton now, and we'll do what we can to get your parents out."

When it was time to go, Mrs. Goldberg packed me a bag of warm winter clothes and Shabbos candles.

"Don't you need these?"

"I have enough to share. Is there anything else you need?"

"Stamps? I don't know when I'll get the allowance Mrs. Ross talked about, and I want to send my parents my new address as soon as I can."

"Of course. We have stamps. Anything else?"

"A dictionary? A German-English dictionary? To help me learn English?"

"That I don't have, but I'll ask around."

On the way home, Rabbi Goldberg told me to lead the way to make sure I could get back to the Rosses by myself. When we arrived, he told me he'd pick me up at nine the following Sunday so we could walk back to town and take the morning train to London. In the meantime, he advised me, just as my mother had, to live the best life I could in Brighton. My safety and home with the Rosses were a gift from God and shouldn't be wasted.

"You have to learn English as quickly as you can and tell people what is happening in Germany," he said. "People here need to understand what

happened and how it happened. We can't change what needs to be changed unless we understand how it happened."

And this, my darling precious Luisa, is what I'm hoping will happen for you while you are in Bogotá. That once you understand the circumstances that sent you and Ana to El Orfanato, you'll be able to somehow work for change so that other children don't lose their mamás the way you and Ana did.

Lots of love,
Nana Lottie

CHAPTER 14

The taxi Luisa took from Daniel's apartment pulled up two minutes before the dinner bell rang. Luisa made it to the dining room on time but couldn't eat anything. After clearing, washing, and drying the dishes, she went back to Claudia's room to try to organize her thoughts. She had the room to herself. Claudia was working late at the hospital. Luisa found Nana Lottie's second letter, the one where she went to live with the Rosses and met Rabbi Goldberg. She re-read it four times. Rabbi Goldberg's advice to Nana Lottie was the same as Daniel's advice to her: "We can't change what needs to be changed unless we understand how it happened." But it was hard to think about changing things when what needed changing hurt so much.

Exhausted from everything she had learned, Luisa fell asleep until the sound of Claudia opening the door to the room woke her up. When Claudia turned on the light, she was surprised to see Luisa. Luisa was supposed to be in the younger girls' room telling the kids a bedtime story. Claudia sat on the edge of Luisa's bed.

"What's wrong?"

Luisa told her what she'd found out and began to cry.

Claudia began to rub her back and stroke her hair. Without thinking Luisa looked up at her and kissed her. Pleasure raced through her body.

Claudia pulled back in shock and got off the bed.

"What are you doing?"

Luisa was as shocked as Claudia was. She hadn't planned on kissing her. It just happened.

"I don't know. I, I'm, I'm sorry."

"Don't ever do that again."

"No, of course. I won't. I'm sorry."

But Claudia didn't hear her apology. She'd already left the room, grabbing one of her textbooks on the way out. Claudia didn't come back for three hours and when she returned, she wouldn't talk to Luisa. She gathered up her night gown and toothbrush to get ready for bed. And when she came back from the girls' bathroom upstairs, she turned off the light and went straight to bed without even saying goodnight.

Luisa was sure Claudia was going to talk to Sister Lorena about what had happened. She spent a sleepless night rehearsing what she was going to say when Sister Lorena summoned her to her office to tell her she was sending her back to Toronto.

The summons came right after breakfast. As Luisa sat down in front of Sister Lorena's desk, she scrutinized her face.

"Daniel García phoned early this morning. Why are you interested in the *falsos positivos*?" she asked.

Luisa allowed herself to feel a moment of relief. Sister Lorena hadn't called her into her office to explain why she'd kissed Claudia. She had called her in because Daniel had told her that they thought her father might be one of the *falsos positivos*.

"Father Álvarez said my father disappeared in Medellín," Luisa said. "Lots of the *falsos positivos* came from Medellín."

Sister Lorena shook her head. "The men who were killed there were young men with no family who might ask questions about what happened to them. Your father had family in Medellín. It's unlikely he was one of the *falsos positivos*."

"Then what happened to him?"

"I don't know. And we may never know. Not knowing is something you're going to have to live with. It's a heavy burden to carry, but you'll find a way."

"I'm not so sure." Luisa's voice trembled. "I already have a lot to carry."

"I know. But you're strong. Stronger than you think."

Nothing had changed but knowing that Sister Lorena thought she was strong made Luisa feel a little better.

"I told Daniel you'd text him to let him know you're okay." She looked at her watch. "Make it fast, it's almost time for your class."

Luisa texted Daniel then went next door to the meeting room to teach the pre-school kids. When she got there, she started to laugh. Claudia hadn't told Sister Lorena about the kiss. She was safe. The kids had no idea why Luisa was laughing but they started to laugh too. They spent the first five minutes of the class laughing.

But Luisa's relief was short-lived. When she got back to Claudia's room after her last class with the older kids, there was a note on the floor by the door. It was folded in half and had her name on it. She opened it and looked at the signature. It was from Sophia, who hadn't shown up for class.

"I saw you kiss Claudia," the note said. "Claudia's door was open, and I saw everything. It was disgusting. You're disgusting, and I'm going to tell Sister Lorena. You can start packing now."

Luisa was reading the note again when Claudia walked into the room.

"What's that?" she asked.

Luisa handed her the note. She covered her mouth with her hand in panic.

"You have to go talk to Sister Lorena right now! You have to tell her it was you who kissed me, not me who kissed you. If she thinks it was me, I could lose my scholarship. You have to tell her I had nothing to do with it. If she tells you to leave, you'll have to leave."

"What?! I can't leave now. Not before I meet Beatriz! She's the only connection I have to my *mamá* and father. I can't leave Bogotá without talking to her."

"If I lose my scholarship, I'll have nothing. Do you understand? Nothing!" She looked at her watch. "It's almost six. Sister Lorena leaves at six. Go! Go now! I'll look for Sophia."

Claudia gave Luisa a little push, and she ran down the hall to Sister Lorena's office. The door was partially open, and she heard Sophia's voice.

"Claudia and Luisa were sitting on the bed together. Then Luisa kissed her! On the lips. She shouldn't be allowed to stay here."

Breathing heavily, Luisa knocked loudly on the door and walked in without waiting for permission.

"Sister, I want to explain what happened."

Sophia stood up to protest, but Luisa had Sister Lorena's full attention.

"I was very, very upset after finding out about the *falsos positivos*. Claudia was trying to comfort me. The kiss . . . it just happened. I take full responsibility for it. She didn't encourage it and told me never to kiss her again. I won't. I promise."

"Being upset is not an excuse," said Sophia, righteous.

Luisa ignored her, keeping her eyes on Sister Lorena.

"Sister, please don't ask me to leave. I can't leave. Not yet. Not before I meet my aunt. If Claudia would rather not share a room with me, I can move into the older girls' room."

"What!" Sophia shook her head.

"Or if Sophia doesn't want me in her room, I could move into the younger girls' room."

Luisa was proud of herself. She'd said what needed to be said without bursting into tears. She'd taken responsibility for the kiss so Claudia wouldn't be implicated. If Sister Lorena decided to kick her out, at least she'd done her best for Claudia.

The dinner bell rang.

"Sophia, it's time for dinner. You may go. Close the door behind you."

Sophia got up slowly, gave Luisa a look of disgust, and left the office slamming the door behind her. Slamming the door was against the rules. It was one of the things that had gotten Luisa sent down to the kitchen to peel potatoes for Sister Francesca when she was seven. Sister Lorena frowned, then turned her attention back to Luisa.

"You know, you're not the first girl to tell me she kissed another girl."

Luisa was surprised. "Really?"

"Of course, not. The girls and boys who live here aren't any different than anywhere else. I know what the Church teaches about homosexuality. But I went to a progressive Catholic college in the United States. My own view is everyone is a child of God no matter who they love."

Luisa realized she'd been holding her breath ever since Sophia left the room. She allowed herself to breath.

"However, the kiss was unwanted, and you need to apologize to Claudia."

"Of course, Sister. I already have, but I'll apologize again, and assure Claudia it won't happen again."

Sister Lorena nodded in approval. "I'll speak to Claudia. If she no longer wants to share her room with you, we'll make other arrangements."

"Thank you, Sister."

"You're part of the El Orfanato Para Niños y Niñas family. You and Ana lived here for three years, and now you've come back to care for the children who live here just like others cared for you. There'll always be a place for you here."

Luisa's eyes teared up. It was the last thing she expected to hear. Sister Lorena had just promised Luisa that there would always be place for her at El Orfanato! She'd let her stay no matter what. Just like Luisa's *mamá* would if she was still alive.

"Thank you, Sister," she said lowering her head in gratitude.

"You should go to dinner now."

"Yes, Sister."

Luisa got up, left the office and ran back to Claudia's room to tell her the good news. When she got there the door was closed. Inside Claudia was talking to Sophia. Luisa could hear every word they said.

"Why did you write such a mean note?"

"Because she kissed you! It's not normal."

Shame heated Luisa's face. She touched her cheeks. They were on fire. Luisa stood at the door and listened.

"Sister Lorena might tell her to leave."

"Good, I want her to leave."

"Why?"

"She doesn't belong here. Her mother's divorced and lives with a woman. That's not normal either. And she doesn't even care! She needs to go back to Toronto where no one else cares either."

Luisa's shame turned into anger, and she burst into the room.

"You've no right to say Harriet and Marty aren't normal! You've never even met them."

Claudia stood up and grabbed Luisa's arm.

"What happened with Sister Lorena?"

"I told her it was my fault. She believed me."

"Thank God!" The relief in Claudia's voice made Luisa's heart hurt. Claudia had so much at stake. There was no room for any mistakes.

"It's going to be okay. It's going to be fine," Luisa said.

Claudia sat back down on the bed and put her face into her hands. Her shoulders started shake. She was crying. Luisa wanted to comfort her but was afraid to touch her. Sophia put her hand on Claudia's shoulder, but Claudia shook it off. Sophia got up to give Claudia some space and stood beside the door, as far away from Luisa as she could. It took a while, but eventually Claudia stopped crying and wiped away her tears.

"Do you have to leave?" Claudia asked Luisa.

"No."

"She's letting you stay?!" Sophia was shocked.

Luisa ignored Sophia and kept her eyes on Claudia.

"But Sister Lorena is going to ask you if you want me to move out of your room. Can we talk about this in private? Can you ask Sophia to leave?"

Claudia turned to Sophia and gestured her head to the door. Sophia left, giving Luisa a nasty look on her way out. Luisa knew she was standing just outside the door listening but let it go.

"So do you want me to move out?" she asked Claudia.

"Yes? No? Maybe? I don't know. Things are complicated now."

"Look, I was upset. You were kind. It just kind of happened. Of course, I should have asked first. It won't happen again. I promise."

It was the right thing to say, but the pain inside Luisa's chest was fierce. Claudia's rejection hurt.

"Don't believe her," said Sophia from outside the door.

"When I make a promise, I always keep it," Luisa said placing her fist on her heart.

Claudia nodded. "I believe you."

"Thank you."

"Sophia," Claudia called out. "Come back in and apologize. Tell Luisa you're sorry."

Sophia came back in but refused to look at Luisa. She looked directly behind her at the closet door. "I'm sorry. Please accept my apology and forgive me." It was the most insincere apology Luisa had ever heard.

Luisa exploded. "No! I won't accept your apology. Because you're not really sorry. You're not sorry at all."

Sophia also exploded. "You're right, I'm not."

Sophia stormed out of the room. So did Luisa. But in the opposite direction.

There was nowhere for Luisa to go but outside. It was cold and she didn't have a jacket. She started walking to keep warm and made it around the block twice until she was too cold to keep walking. Luckily, Luisa thought, Sister Francesca didn't see her leave.

Luisa was still too angry to go back to Claudia's room, so she went to the reception room to calm down. She walked around looking at the children's art the sisters had put up. She was drawn to a painting of a young woman holding the hands of two little girls. It was hanging at the back of the room, and she hadn't noticed it before. The girls were standing in front of a brown building. A small building. Two stories. The young woman was wearing a white t-shirt and jeans. The girls were wearing red t-shirts and shorts. One of the girls had long curly black hair. Her shirt was bright red, the other had long straight brown hair. Her shirt was the same bright red. Luisa looked for the name of the artist and gasped. Luisa Gómez Rodríguez, age 7. She looked carefully at the brown apartment building and tried to remember something about it. Was it on a busy street? Were there other buildings beside it? What floor did they live on?

Luisa closed her eyes and tried to visualize the apartment building. She saw her *mamá* go in the front door and start climbing the stairs. Her *mamá* was holding several plastic bags of groceries in one hand and Ana's hand in the other. She was climbing the stairs behind them. Their *mamá* was singing. Luisa didn't recognize the song, but she recognized the voice. It sounded just like Ana's. Luisa opened her eyes and studied the painting. No one was smiling. They all looked worried. There was no sign of her father. He was already gone.

Luisa knew if she wanted to stay at El Orfanato and try to find out what happened to him, she had to accept Sophia's apology.

She walked back to Claudia's room. The door was open. Sophia was back. Luisa looked over at her. She was sitting on Claudia's bed, arms crossed. Still not looking sorry.

"I accept your apology."

"Thank you." Sophia said it so quietly Luisa could hardly hear it.

"Good." Claudia turned to Sophia. "Now you have to promise you won't mention what happened to anyone else. I don't want to hear any gossip. If I do, I'll be very disappointed."

"I promise."

"All right." Claudia looked at her watch. "We've missed dinner. Maybe Sister Francesca saved us something. Let's go."

The next afternoon, Sophia was absent from class again. She told Sister Lorena she didn't want to go to Luisa's class anymore. Sister Lorena wasn't happy. If Sophia dropped out, the others might drop out too. She told Sophia she could take the rest of week off but had to be back in class the following week. Then she told Luisa she needed to tell Sophia she'd be welcomed back.

Luisa was sure Claudia would skip out of their weekly study session for her biochem test. But when Luisa returned from telling the kids their bedtime story, Claudia had her pile of cards ready to go. As if nothing had happened. It was like she'd erased the entire thing from her memory. But Luisa knew she hadn't. Because instead of moving her desk chair beside Luisa's bed, she sat at her desk. When Luisa finished asking her all the questions, Claudia thanked her politely, then opened her biochem book to read through the chapter one more time. No little chat about Luisa's day, no little chat about the next day, no little chat about anything at all. Luisa knew she was going to pay for that kiss for a very long time.

CHAPTER 15

Dear Luisa:

The day after my visit to Rabbi Goldberg's house I began my job as a companion to Mother Ross. The housekeeper, Mrs. Bell, arrived at seven and made breakfast for Mr. and Mrs. Ross who left the house at seven forty-five to open the shops at eight. Mother Ross came downstairs to the kitchen after they had left, and we had breakfast together. She began teaching me the words for bread, toast, jam, and tea. She'd point to an item, say its word in English and then point to me. I'd repeat the word and do my best to memorize it so I could say it back to her when she quizzed me five minutes later. By eight thirty Mother Ross was restless and left the table. I followed her to the hall closet and watched her take out her winter coat and boots. It was time for our first walk. I ran upstairs, threw on the heavy wool sweater and hat Mrs. Goldberg had given me and then rushed to put on my boots, my mother's winter coat, the cashmere scarf she gave me, and my gloves. Mother Ross had already left the house and was walking down the block. I ran to catch up to her. She was headed towards downtown Brighton, walking down the same street Rabbi Goldberg had taken me. Suddenly she took a different turn and walked us down to the promenade beside the beach. It was a very windy day. Watching the ocean toss and turn reminded me of my ferry ride to Dovercourt. I felt nauseous all over again. We walked down the promenade to Middle Street towards Middle Street Synagogue. The one Rabbi Goldberg had talked about. It was magnificent, at least three times the size of Rabbi Goldberg's synagogue.

The shul was built in what my beloved Harry, may he rest in peace, would have called a Classical style, a style that imitates Greek and Roman architecture. It was made of yellow brick and had two large granite columns on either side of two beautiful wooden doors. A Hebrew inscription carved in stone above the doors included the date the synagogue was opened, 559, or 1875 in the Christian calendar. I couldn't believe there'd been a Jewish community in Brighton for at least sixty-three years. Maybe even more. Mother Ross could see how happy I was to see the synagogue and smiled. She tried to open the front door, but it was locked. I wasn't surprised. Unless there was a funeral or special event planned, the synagogue probably wouldn't be opened again until Friday night. We turned around and walked back home the same way we came. On the way we stopped at a news agency and Mother Ross bought two newspapers, The Daily Express *from London and* The Argus, *a Brighton paper. By the time we got home it was ten, and Mrs. Bell made us a cup of tea. Mother Ross opened* The Argus *and continued my English lessons. She chose a short news story with a picture from the first page and read it aloud, pointing out each word as she read. Then she read it again. And again. And again. The story must have been funny because she laughed every time. I began to understand what Mrs. Ross meant when she said Mother Ross had lost her short-term memory. The fifth time she read the article, Mother Ross had me repeat each word of the first sentence. When we came to the end of the sentence, she repeated the whole sentence and asked me to read it. I had no idea what I was reading, but I managed to repeat the sentence correctly.*

By the time we worked our way through the story sentence by sentence, it was time for lunch, which I later found out was called dinner in England. After dinner we went for another walk, this time around Queen's Park. We came home, had another cup of tea and a biscuit to fortify us, and started out for a third walk around the neighbourhood. By the time we got home at five it was dark, and my legs and feet were aching. Mother Ross was finally tired enough to sit down and rest before Mrs. Bell served us tea (dinner) at six. After tea we listened to the radio, waiting for Mr. and Mrs. Ross to come home from work. Mrs. Bell left at seven, and the Rosses came home at eight fifteen to the meal Mrs. Bell had left for them.

In the evenings, after Mother Ross went to bed, I wrote letters to my parents and Susanne who'd been offered a room in London if she worked as the family's maid. Susanne hadn't realized she was expected to work as a maid and was shocked when her foster mother showed her the uniform she wanted her to wear to scrub the front steps. Susanne refused to wear the uniform but reluctantly agreed to clean the house. Susanne had a strong sense of what was right and what was wrong. She also had a lot of spirit. You remind me a lot of her.

Every day at the Rosses unfolded in the same way except for Sundays when I had the day to myself. Every day was predictable and a little dull, but every day I learned more and more English and soon I was able to read both The Argus *and* The Daily Express *out loud and understand what I was reading. I worked hard to live the best life I could, just as my mother and Rabbi Goldberg had told me to. At night, while I tried to fall asleep, I'd imagine walking along the promenade next to the beach with my parents, showing off Middle Street Synagogue, and then taking them to services at Rabbi Goldberg's shul.*

At first I spoke English with a German accent, and wherever Mother Ross and I went, people would ask her why she was out with a German girl. Mother Ross would say the same thing every time. "She's a Jewish refugee from Germany, and our family is keeping her safe from the Nazis." I worked hard to lose my German accent, and by the time I left London to come to Toronto I sounded English. Then when I came to Toronto, I had to work hard to lose my English accent because it sounded snobby to Grandpa Harry's family and friends. By the time your mother was born, I sounded Canadian. I had what people used to call "a good ear."

On the Sunday after our first visit, Rabbi Goldberg came to pick me up at nine just as he said he would, and we took the train to London to talk to the Orthodox congregation of Finchley Synagogue in Kinloss Gardens. The shul was in the northwest part of London in the middle of a vibrant Jewish neighbourhood filled with kosher restaurants and bakeries. As I passed by store windows full of apple strudel, rugalech, and chocolate and cinnamon babka, I immediately felt at home and knew if my parents and I ever moved to London, this is where we would want to live.

Finchley Synagogue was made of red brick, and while it wasn't as grand as Middle Street Synagogue in Brighton, it was attractive in its own way. I hadn't been to shul since Kristallnacht, and as I climbed the stairs to go inside, I savoured how normal the moment felt. Life hadn't felt normal for a very long time. I had no idea how many people would come to hear a Jewish refugee girl speak about her life in Germany, so I was surprised to see a big crowd sitting in the main sanctuary. I followed Rabbi Goldberg's advice and shared my own story about Kristallnacht and the other stories I'd heard on the ferry. People were shocked, some cried. But when I talked about the urgency of getting my parents out of Germany with domestic worker visas, people looked away and refused to catch my eye. After my talk, several people came up to thank me for coming to speak to them, but no one offered to give my parents work. I wasn't sure if Rabbi Goldberg had been mistaken and that people couldn't afford to hire my parents or if I had said something wrong. Maybe my stories were too shocking. Maybe I'd scared people. Maybe people didn't want to bring the suffering we'd endured into their homes.

I was bitterly disappointed, and when the rabbi at Finchley promised he'd keep looking for a family to hire my parents, I had to work hard to graciously thank him and show my gratitude. Rabbi Goldberg also thanked him and gave him the Rosses' address and phone number. Then we left to catch the train back to Brighton. When we arrived, Rabbi Goldberg walked me back to the Rosses and said that he'd write to see how I was doing.

It was a tough goodbye. Although we had just met, I knew I'd miss him. He was my only link to the Jewish home I'd left behind.

"I wish you all the best in America," I said shaking his hand, a little melancholy.

"And I wish you all the best here," he replied hearing my sadness. "Don't give up. Your parents are still alive, and it's still possible to get them out of Germany. It's not over yet."

As I watched him walk away, I repeated his words over and over. "It's not over yet. It's not over yet." Maybe saying them again and again could make them true.

So, my darling Luisa, with his advice not to give up, his reminder it wasn't over yet, Rabbi Goldberg helped me find a way to live in my lowest moment since Kristallnacht. I hope and pray there will be someone in Bogotá who will be there for you when you need them.

Lots of love,
Nana Lottie

CHAPTER 16

O n the Thursday after the infamous kiss, Laura texted to say she'd pick Luisa up at seven to go to the Patria meeting. Luisa had forgotten all about it. She waited for Laura on the edge of the blue bench, ecstatic to get out of the orphanage for a few hours. Sophia's hostility and Claudia's careful politeness were wearing her down.

Laura pulled up in a little white Volkswagen bug. Luisa waved and hurried over to the car. Jessica, Laura, and Diego's apartment building was close to Uniandes, Daniel's university. Jessica was taking Spanish classes there. That's where she met a few other adoptees and decided to start Patria.

Traffic was bad, and Laura hadn't driven in Ciudad Bolívar before, so at first they didn't talk much. But once she hit the streets she knew well, Laura relaxed.

"How's your week been?" she asked Luisa.

Luisa thought about how to describe the last few crazy days.

"Intense. Very intense."

"What happened?"

"I think I'm bisexual," Luisa blurted out in English.

Laura looked at her for a quick second, then back at the road. She switched to English too. "That's exciting."

"You think so? I think I think so too, but . . ."

"But?" Laura asked, eyes still on the road.

Luisa kept her eyes on the road too. It made it easier to talk. "But it's also a little confusing. I was sure I was straight until I met Claudia."

"The girl who came into the shop with you?"

"Yeah. I kissed her."

"Did she kiss you back?"

"No. She pulled away and told me to never kiss her again."

"Oh. That's hard." Laura reached over and quickly touched Luisa's arm before returning it back to the wheel.

"That's not all. Claudia's friend Sophia saw me kiss her and told me I was disgusting." Luisa's voice cracked. "Now, I feel ashamed. Even though I don't think I have anything to be ashamed of. I kissed a girl I have a crush on. No big deal, right? Except for not asking Claudia if it was all right to kiss her. I should've asked first."

"Yes, you should've asked first, but I agree. Kissing someone you have feelings for is nothing to be ashamed of. The person who should feel ashamed is Sophia for being so judgmental and mean."

"Do you think kissing Claudia means I'm bisexual?"

"I think it means you're attracted to Claudia. It'll probably take you a while to figure out who you want to love and how you want to love."

Luisa nodded, taking this in, happy to have a chance to talk about what kissing Claudia might mean.

"You need to give yourself some time," Laura added. "Go out with a lot of different people and see how it feels to be close to them. There's no rush to define yourself."

"Did it take you some time?"

"Yes. A long time."

"Have you ever been attracted to a woman?"

"Yes. More than one." Laura smiled.

"Does Diego know?"

"Of course."

"And he's okay with it?"

"It's part of who I am," Laura said, confident in a way Luisa hoped she might be one day.

"But what does it mean for your relationship?"

"Diego and I are in a committed relationship. When I'm here and when I'm not here. The part I'm figuring out is whether or not I want to be here all the time. It's hard being so far away from my family in Toronto."

"Have you ever had a serious relationship with a woman?"

"Yes."

"What was it like?"

"Wonderful. Until it ended. Then it hurt."

Luisa nodded in sympathy.

"Harriet's in a relationship with a non-binary partner. But I don't feel comfortable talking about Marty here. Sister Francesca still doesn't know Harriet's divorced and that Marty's living with us now. I've talked to Sister Francesca about so many things, but not about Marty."

"Sister Francesca loves you very much. She won't reject you because Harriet and Marty love each other. And . . ."

She hesitated.

"What?"

"And I don't think she'd reject you if, one day, you told her you were in love with a woman or a non-binary partner."

"How do you know?"

"From the expression you painted in her eyes. Her eyes tell me how much she loves you."

"You know, it was hard for Harriet to come out after she and Jonathan split up. Everyone thought they were a great couple. They were shocked when Jonathan moved to Vancouver and Harriet stayed behind with us. And they were even more shocked when she started seeing Marty. Everyone in her life thought Harriet was straight. When Harriet told Anita she wanted to bring Marty to the Global Family Seder, our first Passover without Jonathan, Anita told her she couldn't. The other Globals would feel uncomfortable or disapprove. So, Harriet didn't go and neither did

Ana, Clare, or I. And that not only hurt us, it hurt the kids who were looking forward to seeing us. And when a few of the Globals stopped bringing their kids to Colombia Night at our house, those kids lost the chance to connect with the friends they'd made at our house."

Laura nodded and took another quick glance at Luisa before turning her eyes back on the road. "Coming out later in life can be hard."

"You know, Harriet never acted as if it was. But now I'm beginning to think it must have been hard. Really hard."

"How did it go when Harriet came out to you and your sisters?"

"When Harriet told us about Marty, she told us not to worry. She was the same person she always was. Life was going to go on the same way it always had. And eventually it did. The parents and kids who missed us at Seder put pressure on Anita to invite us the following year, but I'm sure Harriet was devastated when Anita dumped her that first year she was out. I'm sure Claudia would like to dump me if she could. But because we share a room she can't."

"When did this all happen?"

"A few days ago."

"Claudia may come around."

"I don't think so."

"You never know. She may surprise you."

Luisa doubted it but really appreciated Laura's support.

"I hope so. Thanks for listening."

"Of course."

Luisa felt a little better. Now she knew Laura was there for her. Just like Rabbi Goldberg had been there for Nana Lottie.

They arrived at Laura's apartment building, and she found a place to park about a block away. The building looked a lot like Daniel's. It had the same dark staircase and the same light switch at the bottom of each flight of stairs. Jessica's apartment was on the third floor. When Laura knocked on the door, Jessica called out in English, "It's open," and they walked in. Everyone was already there, sitting in a circle. Suddenly Luisa felt a little shy. Laura put her arm around her shoulders, introduced Luisa to everyone, told her to text her when the meeting was over, and slipped out the door. Luisa was on her own.

"Come and sit down next to me," said Jessica. "We've just started. We've been taking turns sharing our adoption stories. It's Bianca's turn this week."

"Thanks," Luisa replied. After mostly speaking Spanish for six weeks, it was a little weird for Luisa to be speaking in English again. Bianca started.

"So, I found out I was adopted when I was eighteen. And that's when I found out I was born in Colombia. I've always been a lot darker than my parents, but they told me it was because I looked like my father's family who are a lot darker than my mother's family. But whenever I went out of the house people thought I was Latina and tried speaking Spanish to me. Even though I didn't know a word of Spanish! After my parents finally told me I was born in Bogotá, I got a job and started saving so I could come here for a year and learn Spanish. So here I am. Doing the best I can to learn the language and the culture. But it's hard. Really hard. Some adoptive families look for ways to keep their children connected to their birth culture. Mine didn't. I was raised to be the White daughter of a Jewish family that's been living in the United States for three generations. My entire life's been whitewashed."

Bianca started tearing up. The girl beside her took her hand. Luisa could barely breathe.

Jessica responded. "It's incredibly hard finding out you're adopted after years of not knowing. And it's incredibly hard trying to fit into a White family when you don't look White! So many White parents don't know how to talk about race. Or refuse to talk about race. My mother thinks there's only one race: the human race. She thinks being colour blind means she's not racist. But what she doesn't get is how much my race is part of my life. When she refuses to see my race, she refuses to see a big part of me. And I can't talk to her about the racism in my life."

Bianca nodded. "I can't talk to anyone in my family about racism either. When I started telling people I'd been adopted from Colombia, I got some very nasty questions. Like how much my parents had to pay for me."

Luisa gasped.

Bianca looked at her. "You too?"

"I thought I was the only one."

"You're not. But for me, that isn't even the hardest thing about being adopted. The hardest thing is people expecting me to feel grateful. To appreciate the good life I've been given. They don't understand it's more complicated than that."

Lots of people in the circle nodded.

"But I am grateful," said the girl sitting beside Luisa. "I appreciate everything my adoptive family has done for me."

"Maybe what we need," said Jessica, "is to give ourselves permission. Permission to say being adopted is difficult. Permission to feel the loss and grief of what happened as well as the gratitude."

And there it was. Permission for Luisa to feel everything she'd been feeling for the last seven years. From the moment Jonathan stood up from the blue bench in front of the orphanage, took her hand, and led her to the taxi waiting to take them to the airport. Permission to feel the pain nobody wanted to talk about.

"Let's all take a moment," said Jessica. "A moment to remember and grieve."

"And be grateful," said the girl beside Luisa while the girl on the other side of her rolled her eyes.

Luisa closed her eyes and remembered. Taking Jonathan's hand. Walking to the taxi. And turning around to wave to Sister Francesca one last time. The memory was excruciating. The sob that came from deep inside joined the other sobs in the room. Jessica reached for Luisa's hand and squeezed it tightly. She understood, Luisa thought. In a way no one else in her life ever had.

CHAPTER 17

On Saturday Luisa arrived at The Art Shop early to help Laura set up.

"I want to start something new today," she said opening her sketchbook.

"Can I take a look?" Laura asked, intrigued.

"Sure."

Laura began looking through the pages, taking time to notice the differences between each of the sketches. "They're all different drawings of the same man. Who is he?"

"My father. Ever since the meeting on Thursday I've had a strong desire to draw him. But I don't remember what he looks like. I've sketched him tall, short, slim, fat, with a beard, without a beard. But I still don't recognize him." Luisa could hear the sadness in her voice.

Laura nodded, moved. "Just keep drawing until you do."

When Daniel arrived a few minutes later, Luisa was deep into sketching another version of her father and barely heard him come in. This time, her father was taller than Luisa but not as tall as Jonathan who was six foot two. And he was slimmer than Jonathan but had a fuller face.

"Hi, how's it going?" asked Daniel, interrupting Luisa's concentration. She looked up from her sketch.

"Hi."

"I've been worried about you. You didn't answer any of my texts." He looked more concerned than angry.

"I'm really sorry," said Luisa. "I was having some big feelings after reading the UN report, and I wasn't ready to share them yet," giving him the most honest answer she could.

"Yeah, I get it," he said touching her shoulder lightly. "What are you working on?"

"How to paint my father. But as you can see, I have no idea what he really looked like."

Luisa handed Daniel her sketchbook and watched him flip through the sketches.

"I have an idea," he said looking up, excited. "Tear out all the drawings and lay them on floor. Then just choose one. That's the one you'll paint."

Luisa tried it. Going on nothing but instinct she chose the drawing she thought might resemble her father the most. Then she blocked out the painting. Like Sister Francesca, her father would have a big chest, big hands, and big feet. Like Sister Francesca, he'd be sitting down. But instead of holding one little girl, he'd be holding two.

When Laura came by, she took a long look at the emerging figure on Luisa's canvas and nodded to herself. "Is that the same blue bench Sister Francesca is sitting on?" she asked.

"I don't know," answered Luisa. "Maybe." She stepped back a bit and looked at it again. "Actually yes. You're right. It's the blue bench outside the front of the orphanage. The way it used to look when Ana and I were living there."

"What happens on that bench?"

"It's where the parents wait while their adopted children say goodbye to their friends and the sisters. When the kids come out, the parents take them to their new home."

Laura smiled. "So, it's a place where children make family."

Luisa nodded but didn't smile back. "Yes, but it's also a place where children say goodbye to family."

And suddenly she understood. Painting her father on the bench was a way to touch the grief of saying goodbye.

At the end of the class, as they were packing up to go, Daniel told Luisa he had some news to share. She searched his face to see if it was good news or bad news.

"What is it?"

His eyes lit up.

"The negotiation was successful. I pitched the double major idea during our visit with Professor Suarez. Suarez liked it a lot. He said what I'm learning in photography will help me in architecture. So, my father's agreed to the double major. You're brilliant."

He leaned over to kiss her. Luisa caught it on her right cheek.

"I'm really happy for you!" she said.

"I'm really happy for me too! Let's go out tomorrow to celebrate."

"Sure," she replied, picking up her knapsack and putting it on her back. "In fact, I was going to ask you if you were up for a drive tomorrow."

"A drive?" he asked. "Where do you want to go?"

"I'll tell you tomorrow. Meet me here at two."

"After Mass?"

Luisa smiled. "Right."

But Luisa had no intention of going to Mass. When the breakfast bell rang, she went into the kitchen in her pajamas and told Sister Francesca she hadn't slept all night. She needed to go back to bed. Sister Francesca believed her and made her a cup of coca tea. After Sister Francesca left for church, Luisa went into her bedroom and searched for the keys to Sister Lorena's office. She knew what she was doing was wrong, especially after both Sister Francesca and Sister Lorena had been so kind and trusting. She also knew it was dangerous. If she was caught, she'd probably be asked to leave El Orfanato despite what Sister Lorena had said about there always being a place for her there. But she did it anyway.

The deep sadness Luisa was feeling ever since the Patria meeting had sharpened her need to find out what happened to her father. It had been two and a half weeks since she sent her letter to Beatriz, and she hadn't heard a word. Luisa was sure Father Álvarez hadn't sent it. She needed to find Beatriz herself.

Sister Francesca was the guardian of the keys on the weekend. She'd probably taken them with her to Mass, thought Luisa, but it was worth a look anyway. Luisa found them in the top drawer of her desk. She couldn't believe her luck.

Sister Lorena had labelled all the keys so that in an emergency Sister Francesca wouldn't have any trouble finding the key she needed. The labels were colour coded. The office keys were labelled in blue. It took no time to open the door and to open the closet. There were only four filing cabinet keys and they were labelled one, two, three, and four. Luisa opened the first drawer and looked at the name on the first file folder: Alonso, Adriana. Sister Lorena did keep the children's files in the cabinet! They were filed alphabetically. Rodríguez would be at the end of the third drawer or at the beginning of the fourth, thought Luisa. The last file folder in the third drawer belonged to Pérez, Mariana. Her file would be in the last drawer. Luisa crouched down to reach the last drawer and was about to open it when Sister Francesca walked in.

Luisa was busted.

"What are you doing?" Sister Francesca looked at Luisa in disbelief, alarmed.

Luisa stood up. "Looking for my file."

"How did you get in?"

Luisa thought about telling her the door had been open but knew Sister Francesca wouldn't believe her.

"I found the keys in your desk drawer."

"Give them back to me." Sister Francesca held out her hand.

Luisa stepped back. "I have a right to see my file. I'm eighteen."

Luisa was surprised at how defiant she sounded. But Sister Francesca remained calm. She'd spent a lot of time talking to defiant children.

"You haven't been given permission to see it."

"I know. But I'm sure it's there, in the last drawer. All I need is ten minutes to look at it, and I'll never ask to see it again."

Luisa knew she sounded desperate. But desperation didn't work any better than defiance.

Sister Francesca's face had the same steely determination Luisa had painted in her eyes. No amount of pleading was going to change her mind.

"Give me back the keys."

Luisa walked over to Sister Francesca and gently put the keys in her hand, remorseful. Sister Francesca walked over to the cabinet and tested each of the drawers to make sure they were locked. For Luisa, it was humiliating.

"Okay, let's go," she said nodding towards the door, waiting for Luisa to leave the office first so she could follow her out and lock the door.

"I can't tell you how very disappointed I am, *pequeña.* You have more integrity than that."

Luisa wanted to disappear.

"Get dressed. We're going to Mass."

It wasn't an invitation. It was a command. Luisa quickly put on her church clothes, and they walked to Mass together. In silence. Until they got to the bottom of the hill.

"Are you going to tell Sister Lorena?"

"No. But you're going to have to learn to control your impatience. It's a flaw, *pequeña,* and you are going to have to work hard to fix it. Your impatience hurts people. People who love you. You hurt Harriet and now you've hurt me." She was angry.

"I'm sorry," said Luisa. It came out as a whisper.

Mass felt even longer than usual to Luisa. If she believed in Sister Francesca's God, Luisa would've asked for forgiveness. But she didn't so she just sat beside Sister Francesca reliving the moment Sister Francesca had told her how disappointed she was in her. When Mass was over, Luisa returned to the orphanage with everyone else, helped Sister Francesca serve lunch, and asked for permission to go meet Daniel. She was sure she was going to say no. But she didn't. Luisa thought Sister Francesca probably wanted her out of her sight for a while.

When she arrived at The Art Shop, Daniel was already there. He waved and gave Luisa his stunning smile. At least someone in Bogotá is happy to see me, thought Luisa. She smiled and waved back feeling happy to see him too.

"Hi!" she called out.

"Hi!" he answered, putting his hand on her arm and leaning over to kiss her. He waited to see if Luisa was going to offer him her lips or cheek. When she offered him her cheek, Luisa saw a flash of disappointment in his eyes. But just a flash. He wasn't going to make a big deal about it. She was relieved.

"So where are we going?" he asked.

"Back to Ciudad Bolívar."

"What?! Why?"

"Look at this," Luisa said, excited.

She passed him her phone. She'd taken some pictures of her painting.

"It's a kid's painting." He swiped through all the pictures.

"Yeah. Guess who drew it."

"You?"

"Me. I was seven."

"Wow. So that's you and Ana and your *mamá*?"

"Yeah. But I don't remember anything about living in that building. I want to take a taxi to Father Álvarez's church, drive around the neighbourhood and look for buildings just like that one. Maybe I'll see something that sparks a memory. Are you up for it?"

"Sure."

They called a taxi, and Daniel explained to the driver where they wanted to go and what they wanted to do. He agreed, and they took off in the direction Luisa had just come from.

They passed the church, and Luisa stared out the window as they bumped along the dirt roads. Most of the apartment buildings were two stories tall and made of brown brick. The odd one had been painted green or blue. Her family could've lived in any one of them. Most of the buildings looked shabby and, unlike El Orfanato, uncared for. When Luisa had marched by the same buildings in Father Álvarez's parade they hadn't looked as scruffy. Maybe the festive atmosphere—the horns, the drums, the kids' excitement—made the worn-out neighbourhood look more vibrant than it was. Luisa looked for landmarks. They passed a corner drugstore, a pizza shop, a convenience store selling time on the internet. Nothing looked familiar. Wild dogs ran up and down the streets, dodging traffic. They looked mean. After they'd driven around for a while, Luisa asked the driver to take them back to La Candelaria. He dropped them off at the Plaza de Bolívar, and they found a place to have coffee.

"I'm sorry nothing looked familiar," Daniel said as they sat at a small table across from each other waiting for their café con leche.

"Me too," Luisa nodded, disappointed and sad. "But I'm glad we tried. It gave me an idea of how we might have lived before my *mamá* died. Pretty bleak, no?"

"Yes and no. When we passed the school, the kids were having a blast playing soccer."

"Still, would you want to grow up in one of those apartment buildings and worry about getting bitten by one of those dogs?"

"No."

"Me neither."

They were quiet for a moment and then Luisa began a conversation she knew Daniel wouldn't be happy about.

"So about last Sunday."

"Which part?"

"The part when we read the report. It was very intense."

"Very."

"And the part when you kissed me? I stopped because I was overwhelmed. From everything we'd read. And . . ."

"And . . . ?"

"I didn't want to make a mistake."

Daniel tensed up, sitting up very straight on his chair. "What kind of mistake?"

"I didn't want my feelings about what may have happened to my father to be the reason I kissed you back."

"Was it?"

"I don't know. That's why I stopped."

"So, what are you saying?"

Luisa put her hand on his arm. "For now, can we be just friends?"

Daniel covered her hand with his own. "I really like you. I don't want to be just friends."

"I know," she said, gently removing his hand. "I really like you too. But for now, that's all I can handle. Is that okay?"

Daniel didn't answer right away. It wasn't okay.

Luisa took a deep breath. "I could really use a friend right now. I'm totally on my own out here."

Daniel took the high road.

"I know. Sure. We can be friends."

Luisa took his hand and squeezed it. Just like Claudia. "Thanks."

They finished their coffee and Luisa called a taxi. Daniel waited outside with her until it arrived. It had begun to rain, and Luisa opened her umbrella to cover them both.

"See you next Saturday," she said handing him the umbrella as the taxi pulled up beside them. "You can give me back the umbrella then."

"Okay, thanks. See you next Saturday." He gave her a kiss on her cheek. The kind he'd give to his mother, his sister, or a good friend. It was exactly the kind of kiss Luisa wanted.

When she got back to the orphanage, Luisa went up to the older girls' room to find Sophia. She was there alone doing her homework.

"Hi."

Sophia didn't answer back but acknowledged Luisa with a nod of her head.

"Everyone missed you in class last week. They're happy you're coming back tomorrow."

"The only reason I'm coming back is because Sister Lorena says I have to."

"I know."

"If it were up to me, I would never talk to you again." Her eyes were mean. Luisa cringed.

"Look, you don't have to like me. And you don't have to approve of my family. All you have to do is show up to class and learn a little English. Who knows? Maybe it will help when you start university. Claudia says students who speak English are placed in the best hospitals in the city during their practicum."

"Watching *The Amazing Race* won't teach me enough English to work in the best hospitals in the city."

"No, but if you take an English course at the university this summer, build on what you learn here, that might be enough. You're very smart. You're picking it up faster than anyone else in the class. Some people have a gift for languages. I don't. I had a really hard time learning English. But Ana has the gift. You have it too. If you want, I can ask Harriet to send me an English grammar book. The two of us can start working through it. That will be more challenging. And it will prepare you for taking English in university."

"Why would you do that for me?"

Luisa tried to ignore how bitter Sophia sounded. "Because you deserve it," she replied in a softer voice. "You deserve every opportunity that comes your way."

"I don't know if I have time to work through a grammar book."

"I understand, think about it."

Luisa left the room feeling that she'd done what she could to make peace.

Another week began. Sophia agreed to working together, Harriet sent Luisa a grammar book, and they began working together every night after Luisa had tucked the younger kids into bed.

On Thursday Laura picked Luisa up to go to the Patria meeting. Jessica asked Luisa if she wanted to tell her adoption story. Luisa told her she wasn't ready. Two days later, on Saturday, Carolina and Paola's adoptive parents arrived to take them to Toronto. They were leaving the next day. That night Luisa told the younger kids the story she hadn't wanted to share at the Patria meeting.

"When Luisa was ten years old, Ana was seven. They'd lived in the orphanage for three years. Luisa took very good care of Ana and was like a mother to her. She taught her how to tie her shoes and braided her hair for school. She tucked her into bed every night. Luisa knew she and Ana were very lucky to have each other. None of the other children in the orphanage had any brothers and sisters. But Luisa was worried. She was worried one day someone would come and adopt Ana, but not her. Sister Francesca told her not to worry, she wouldn't let anyone adopt Ana without adopting Luisa as well. Luisa couldn't stop worrying. Who would want to adopt two girls? But someone did."

"Just like us!" said Carolina joyfully.

"Just like you. One day Sister Francesca brought Luisa into the kitchen. She told her a man and a woman from Canada wanted to adopt her. Before she could say they wanted to adopt Ana too, Luisa started screaming she wouldn't go without Ana. Sister Francesca took her in her arms, held her very tightly, and kept telling her, 'Ana, too! Ana, too!' until Luisa finally understood. The man and the woman were arriving in a few days to meet them and take them to place called Toronto in a country called Canada. Luisa was scared. She asked Sister Francesca if Toronto was very far away. She said it was and that after dinner she would show Ana and Luisa a map of the world so we could see where Canada was. Then Luisa asked if people in Toronto knew how to speak Spanish. Sister Francesca said some people did, but her new parents didn't. They would have to learn English."

Luisa caught Carolina's eye.

"She said it might be hard in the beginning, but she knew they could do it. Sister Francesca was right. At the beginning, it was hard. It was harder for Luisa than it was for Ana. But soon both Luisa and Ana were speaking English as well as they could speak Spanish."

"How long did it take?" Carolina asked in a thin voice.

"Two years."

"Two years!"

"But it won't take you two years. You already know a lot of words in English. I didn't know any."

"That's true." Carolina sounded relieved, and Luisa was pleased.

"What was it like meeting Harriet?" asked Paola.

"We met in the reception room. Sister Francesca brought us in. She went in first and then Ana and I followed. Ana was holding my hand so tight it hurt. But I didn't shake it off. Harriet and Jonathan brought small gifts for us. Things we could do together."

"Like what?" she asked.

"A puzzle. Ana and Jonathan did a puzzle together."

"So, you played with Harriet?" asked Carolina.

"I did."

"Did you love her right from the very beginning?"

"Well, you know, love takes time." Truthful, Luisa thought, but not mean.

"Like learning English," said Carolina.

"Exactly."

"I don't want to leave," said Paola, grabbing Carolina's arm.

Everyone looked surprised. Paola had never said anything about not waiting to leave El Orfanato.

"Don't be silly," said Carolina pulling Paola's hand off her arm.

"I'm not silly. I want to stay here. I don't want to leave Sister Francesca and all my friends."

"But you're going to have a new *mamá* and a new *papá*. And live in a house."

"I don't want a new *mamá* and a new *papá*."

"Everybody wants a *mamá* and a *papá*."

"Not me." Paola began to cry.

Luisa got up from the bed she was sitting on, moved over to Paola's bed and took her hand. She needed to say something comforting. Quickly.

"I have an idea."

"What?" asked Paola.

"In English class on Monday, all of us are going to write you a letter. And then I will mail all of them to you, so soon you will be receiving a lot of letters from your friends at El Orfanato. Then you can write one letter back to all of us and we will write more letters to you, and I'll send them. And we'll keep writing letters to you and you'll keep writing letters to us."

"But who will help me write my letters in English?" Paola asked, about to cry again.

"You can write them in Spanish. And you can ask your parents to help you say a few things in English. Carolina can help you too. What do you think? Is that a good idea?"

Paola nodded.

"Good. So that's what we'll do." Luisa looked at her watch. "Okay, it's getting late. Boys, get ready for bed, I'll be there in a minute."

The boys left, and Luisa tucked the girls into their beds. Then she walked over to Carolina and Paola for a final goodbye. Paola had climbed into bed with Carolina.

"See you in Toronto," she whispered.

"See you in Toronto," they whispered back.

"Paola, don't forget to watch out for our letters!"

"I will. I love you, Luisa."

"I love you too. Both of you." Luisa wanted to cry. She walked to the door, steadied her voice and turned off the light.

"Good night, *chiquitas*."

"Good night, Luisa!"

After tucking the boys in, Luisa was restless. She picked up her jacket from Claudia's closet and went to sit on the old blue bench in front of the orphanage. It creaked and moved beneath her weight.

Luisa's story about the day Sister Francesca told her they were going to be adopted had triggered all kinds of big feelings. So did Paola's reluctance to leave El Orfanato. She'd told the kids she'd been scared but, in fact, she'd been terrified. She had tried to hide it so Ana wouldn't know.

And then, in a way that Luisa hadn't expected, telling Carolina and Paola she'd see them in Toronto made her a little homesick. She missed walking along the beach, being able to see Lake Ontario and the horizon beyond it. The Andes Mountains surrounding Bogotá were magnificent, and she never got tired of looking at them, but once in a while they felt claustrophobic. Especially on rainy days.

Luisa was lonely. After sharing a bedroom with Ana for seven years she missed her. Even though they argued a lot during the day, at night they shared their secrets. Ana was the only one in the world who knew how awful the girls in Luisa's first grade five class were. Luisa also missed Clare. There weren't many people in the world who loved her the way Clare loved her. And then there was Harriet. While Luisa had been furious with her when she cancelled the family trip back to Bogotá, Luisa knew Harriet loved her and usually had her back. She was also a lot more flexible than Sister Francesca. Harriet never called her impatience a flaw.

The only person Luisa had become close to at the orphanage besides Sister Francesca was Claudia. But any intimacy they'd built up disappeared after Luisa kissed her. One impulsive move had destroyed their friendship.

Thunder clapped in the distance. It was going to start pouring any minute. Luisa went inside and locked the front door. She could smell the lemon cleaner the girls used to clean the floor. Everyone at El Orfanato worked so hard to keep life clean, neat, and organized. It was the only way to keep the chaos of life outside under control.

The next day, Luisa told Sister Francesca she felt closer to God when she was painting than she did in church and asked for permission to stay behind and paint instead of going to Mass. Sister Francesca appreciated her honesty and said she could stay behind. Then she shook her purse to let Luisa know the keys to Sister Lorena's office were inside.

Luisa nodded, embarrassed.

Luisa usually stored her work at The Art Shop between classes, but the day before she'd taken her father's portrait and her easel back to the orphanage. She set up in the reception room because it had the best light. It was against the rules to use the room without permission, but no one would know. Luisa had two hours to paint and clean up before everyone came back.

When Luisa started painting that day, she wanted to show the love her father had had for his two little daughters and the love they'd had for him. But as she finished painting their eyes, it wasn't love she captured. It was terror. The faces of her father, Ana, and herself all carried the terror of what was to come. The terror of their father's disappearance and the terror of their *mamá*'s death. Luisa's fear was on display for everyone to see. She knew she needed to paint over everyone's faces and start again. But it was too late. The sisters and the children would be back in ten minutes. She cleaned up quickly and slipped out before everyone returned. She'd have to wait to erase the terror.

CHAPTER 18

Dear Luisa:

While I waited to hear from the rabbis I received a letter from my parents. They had moved to Kippenheim, a village on the edge of the Black Forest. My father had a cousin there who wanted to set up a small shoe repair shop in his home. My parents were invited to come and run the business with him and his wife. "Everyone needs to get their shoes repaired," my mother said in her first letter from Kippenheim. In the letters that followed, my parents seemed to be managing well enough, but I knew they'd never be safe until they left Germany. So every Sunday, after writing my parents and Susanne, I wrote to all three rabbis—the one at Brighton Liberal, the one at Middle Street, and the one in London—and asked if they'd found anyone to give my parents a job. Week after week, month after month, the answer was no, sorry, not yet. It became impossible to get to sleep at night even after four hours of walking with Mother Ross. I'd lie awake trying to think about new ways to find my parents work. Finally, I worked up enough courage to write to the rabbi at the Finchley shul to ask if I could speak to the congregation again.

I was waiting to hear back from him when Prime Minister Neville Chamberlain declared Britain was going to war with Germany. I was in the living room sitting with the Rosses when he came on the radio. I was shattered. My entire life in Brighton had been built around the hope of being reunited with my parents. Everything my parents and I had said to each other in our letters, "We'll see each other soon, we'll find a way," was suddenly impossible.

How was I going to live here without them? How were they going to survive? Every night, in the privacy of my bedroom, I cried. Not for days. Not for weeks. For months. I cried until I got a letter from Susanne telling me she was going to join the Women's Auxiliary Air Force when she turned eighteen and I should too. Like me, Susanne hadn't been able to find work for her parents, and like my parents, her parents were trapped in Germany with her younger sister. "We need a new purpose," she wrote. So on my eighteenth birthday, about a year after I'd come to Brighton, I said goodbye to the Rosses and got on a train to London to join the WAAF.

The goodbyes weren't difficult. The Rosses and I had established a connection, but it was a shallow connection built on my gratitude for a place to live and their gratitude for the companionship I gave Mother Ross. The connection I'd developed with Mother Ross wasn't much deeper. Our conversations lived in the moment. Although she sometimes asked about my life in Germany or how my parents were managing, Mother Ross couldn't remember anything I told her, so we couldn't build on any of our conversations. While I didn't think she'd actually miss me, I did want to find her another companion, so I wrote to the people working with the Refugee Children's Movement and asked them if they needed a home for an older girl who liked to walk. The Kindertransport had stopped bringing children to England after Britain declared war on Germany, but there were still children who had recently arrived and hadn't been placed in foster homes. The RCM found someone to take my place so when I left Brighton, I left knowing Mother Ross would continue living the best life she could.

Joining the WAAF took a few weeks. It began with an interview at the recruiting office. When I began answering the first question, what was still left of my German accent—which really wasn't very strong at that point— made the recruiting officer nervous so I quickly explained that I was a Jewish German refugee who had come on the Kindertransport and had been living in Brighton. The recruiting officer had never heard of the Kindertransport, and I had to explain that as well. It wasn't until I told her the reason I wanted to join the WAAF—to fight Hitler—that she began to relax and ask me about my work experience. I knew taking walks with Mother Ross wouldn't impress her, so I talked about working in my father's shoe repair shop and helping him with the accounting. That pleased her, and she said they'd be happy to take me. I'd be hearing from them soon. Did I have a London address? Knowing I'd need a place to stay in London because there was no room for me at the home where Susanne was living, I'd written to the rabbi at Finchley Synagogue. He offered me a room in his home until I was sent for basic training. I gave the officer the rabbi's address and waited to hear from them. It didn't take long for a brown envelope to arrive at the rabbi's house, giving me the day and time to show up for a medical exam. If I passed, I'd be sent for basic training, but if I failed, I'd be sent back home. The WAAF didn't know I didn't have a home to go back to, and my whole future depended on me passing the exam. It had been a long time since I'd seen a doctor, and I had no idea what kind of health problem might come up. I was often nauseous, but I assumed it was because I was so worried about my parents. But maybe I had some kind of stomach issue that would keep me out of the WAAF.

When I arrived for the exam, there were lines and lines of women waiting to see different doctors. They were tall, they were short, they were thin, they were stocky. And they all looked as nervous as I felt. Would we be strong enough to pass all the tests ahead of us? The doctors checked our hearts and lungs, stretched our arms and legs, tested our reflexes, examined our eyes, ears, feet, looking for reasons why we might not be suitable recruits for the WAAF. At the end of a very long day, I was passed as fit and healthy. After three weeks of basic training, I was assigned a trade. The least popular assignments were cook and orderly because they came with very long working hours. I was lucky. I was assigned to pay accounts, maybe because I had kept track of the shoe repair orders in my parents' shop. All the women assigned to pay accounts were sent to Wales for accountancy training. When I arrived in Penarth, a Welsh town by the sea like Brighton, I was assigned to equipment accounts instead of pay accounts. Sixty of us began equipment account training all at the same time. The course was extremely difficult, and a large number of girls who'd attempted the course just before us flunked. We were given an extra week of training to improve the pass rate. We were all very anxious about the final exam. If we failed, we could end up working in the kitchen or cleaning out latrines after all.

It didn't take me long to understand why the course was considered so difficult. It required an extremely good memory. There was a different form for every possible situation that involved the issue of items in the Air Force, and we were expected to learn the official number of each of them. Form 647 was used to request a new item, but if the item in question was replacing an old item or an item that had worn out, then form 673 was required instead. The list of numbers was endless, and we had to memorize all of them. We also had to remember how many copies of each form were required and where each copy had to be sent. On top of that, every nut, bolt, and screw, every piece of clothing, every item of food that went through the Air Force stores had its own number, and we had to memorize them as well. Every night I'd go over the long list of forms and parts again and again. Finally, the dreaded day arrived, and I took the exam along with the other sixty girls in the course. By the time I finished the exam, I had only answered a little more than half of the questions. I had no idea if that was enough to pass. The following day, we were all lined up on the seafront in alphabetical order. One by one, our last names were called out and our results were read off in front of everyone. The pass mark was very low, forty percent, but even so many of the girls whose names were called out before mine had failed. It didn't take long for the sergeant to make it down to the letter E. "Englehard," she barked. "Fifty-five percent. Pass." I'd made it.

The girls who passed the exam were marched off for a series of shots. The girl in front of me, exhausted from the stress of the exam, fainted as soon as she saw the needle. When it was my turn to be jabbed, I looked away so I couldn't see how big the needle was. The next day, we were issued railway warrants to take us to our new postings. I was posted as a supply equipment clerk at RAF Titchfield, a balloon squadron, in Hampshire. The base was a two-hour train ride to London. Close enough to visit Kinloss Gardens on my days off.

Susanne trained as a mechanical transport driver and was posted to an RAF base in Yorkshire, about a four-hour train ride to London. It was too far to visit, so we kept in touch by letters. Susanne loved her job and was thrilled to be sharing a room with a corporal at her base. When the corporal was transferred, Susanne applied for a promotion so she could fill her position. Susanne's commander agreed to send her for training and told her that as long as she passed the "discip" course, the job was hers. The hardest part, Susanne told me, was learning how to lead the parade. She had to time her commands very carefully. An order had to be issued just as the left foot was passing the right so that everyone moved together on the next step. Once, when Susanne was commanding her cohort, the instructor told her to give the order "About turn!" But when Susanne stared at all the feet marching in unison to find the right moment to give the command, she became transfixed. Before she knew it, her troops had marched off the parade ground and were walking through a giant aircraft hanger where a group of engineers were repairing a damaged plane. The instructor was forced to go running after them, frantically shouting out the order to prevent Susanne's troop from marching into a wall. Despite that one horrible moment, Susanne did well through the rest of the course and was promoted to corporal. In her letters, she wrote about leading her flight of girls to breakfast each morning and patrolling the camp at night looking out for girls who were out with their boyfriends when they were supposed to be in bed.

After the war broke out, it was difficult for my parents and I to write to each other. Their letters from Germany couldn't be sent to me in England. They had to be sent to someone living in another country who would then send them on to me. Luckily the family my parents were working with in Kippenheim had a relative in Holland who agreed to send their letters to the Rosses, who then sent them to Finchley Synagogue. In their letters, my parents never told me very much about what was happening to their lives. Everything was always fine. There was no need for me to worry. But of course, I worried anyway. I knew they wouldn't be safe until I could get them out of Germany.

Several months after I'd been assigned to my post as equipment supply clerk, keeping track of what equipment came in and out the base, I went back to London to attend a Shabbat service at Finchley Synagogue. It was in November 1940. The rabbi I'd stayed with when I joined the WAAF had left to take up a position in Australia, but one of the members of the Finchley Sisterhood offered me a place to stay.

Rose Caplan lived alone in a small house in Kinloss Gardens. She had been widowed at fifty and had a son who was married. She had such a kind way about her that when she invited me to stay in her guest room anytime when I was on leave from the base, I accepted. Rose and I got along extremely well. She was also an avid reader and always sent me back to the base with books she thought I'd like. We could talk about books for hours. She always looked for the bright side of things, which wasn't easy during wartime with its rations and blackouts and air raids. I felt very lucky to have met her.

One Saturday at the kiddush after the Shabbat service, Rose introduced me to someone who'd recently emigrated from Kippenheim to London. She thought he might have some news about what was happening there. He did have news, but it was the news I'd been dreading. All the Jews from Kippenheim had been deported to France.

At first, I didn't believe it. "But not my parents. They weren't deported."

"Yes," he said. "I'm sorry, your parents too. They were all deported."

"No," I said, "Not my parents." I was heavy, heavy into denial.

But after that, when I didn't hear from my parents for a very long time, I began to wonder if it was true. But I refused to give up hope. As Rose said, it was wartime and there were all kinds of reasons why their letters weren't reaching me. They couldn't buy stamps. The mail was unreliable.

Several months later, in the spring, I finally received a letter from my parents. It was dated November 30, 1940. At the top of the letter my father had written their address. The letter had come from Camp de Gurs, in Vichy France. They had been deported.

"At least now you know they're still alive," said Rose when I told her the news. "Where there is life, there is hope."

These are words to live by my darling Luisa. "Where there is life, there is hope."

Lots of love,
Nana Lottie

CHAPTER 19

The day after Luisa skipped Mass to work on her father's portrait, Sister Lorena walked into her class holding a letter.

"It's from your Aunt Beatriz."

Luisa was stunned. It was the last thing she expected to happen that day.

"Open it!" Adriana called out.

Luisa tried to open the envelope, but her hands were shaking. She gave it back to Sister Lorena.

"Could you open it for me?"

Sister Lorena opened the envelope and handed Luisa the letter. It was folded in two. Inside was a photo of a young woman and man in their twenties. The woman looked just like Ana.

"Show us the picture!" Adriana demanded.

Luisa held it out, and Adriana got out of her seat and took it. "Who is it?"

"My parents."

"Oh," she breathed. "Read us the letter!"

Luisa looked at Sister Lorena.

"Go ahead."

"Dear Luisa, thank you for your letter. You asked if you look like me. You do. You look a lot like me. I know Inés would've wanted me to meet you and answer as many of your questions as I could. So I've changed my mind. Let's meet at one in front of Father Álvarez's church on Sunday.

There's a park close by where we can talk. Here's a photo of your parents on the day they got married. It's the only picture I have of them. I've made a copy for myself. You can keep the original. Sincerely yours, Beatriz Rodríguez."

The kids began to clap.

Sister Lorena smiled. "I'm very happy for you."

"Thank you, Sister." Luisa could hardly breathe. "I'm very happy too."

After the picture had been passed around and Adriana gave it back to Luisa, she looked at it again. Her father had his arm around her mother's waist. They looked happy. Excited. No hint of the terror yet to come.

After dinner Luisa went back to Claudia's room and took her painting out of the closet and put it against the door. She looked carefully at the photo Beatriz had sent and then at her painting. The man in the photo was younger and thinner than the man in her painting. His nose was a little longer, and so was his chin. But she had captured her father's hands. His slim fingers, his neatly trimmed nails. She had remembered his hands perfectly. But the terrified eyes in the painting looked nothing like her father's happy, smiling eyes in the photo. At least now she knew how she could change them.

On Thursday, Luisa brought the painting to the Patria meeting of adoptees. Laura asked if she could stay and listen to Luisa talk about it. Everyone said yes. Luisa placed the painting on a chair in front of the kitchen counter. Laura came forward to look at it and then took two steps back.

"His eyes!"

"I know."

"Ana's eyes! Your eyes!"

"I know. I'm going to re-paint them."

"No! Don't touch them! It's really difficult to paint terror."

"But I don't want to paint terror. I want to paint love. His love for us. Our love for him."

"Sometimes love is terrifying," Laura said. "When someone you love has been taken away from you, it's terrifying. You've captured the terror. It's amazing."

Luisa hadn't thought about it that way but wasn't convinced. It was excruciating to look at her portrait of terror. She'd never hang it up anywhere. She wanted to paint a portrait people could look at.

Jessica called everyone else over to take a look but asked them not to say anything until Luisa had finished talking about it herself. Luisa really appreciated her thoughtfulness but didn't know where to begin. Jessica suggested she begin with what she remembered about her father.

"I don't remember anything," Luisa said with a sadness that sat on her chest like a huge rock. "But I'll tell you what I know. He wasn't there when my *mamá* got sick with pneumonia. He wasn't there when she sent us to El Orfanato in Ciudad Bolívar. He wasn't there when she died. And he wasn't there when Harriet and Jonathan adopted my sister and me and took us to Canada. I don't know why he wasn't there. I only know that he wasn't there, and," Luisa nodded towards her painting, "his absence was terrifying. For all of us."

Luisa stopped there. Nobody said a word for the longest time. Then Jessica asked in a voice so quiet it was hard to hear her. "Who else had a parent who wasn't there? Who else had a parent whose absence led to them being adopted?"

Every single person around the circle except Laura raised their hand.

"How many people don't know why their parent wasn't there?"

Again, every single person in the circle except Laura raised their hand. Every single one of them. And then, without anyone saying anything, they all took each other's hands and sat in silence for a long time. Laura caught Luisa's eye and nodded her head towards the people who had tears in their eyes. Her painting had unleashed the pain that comes with losing your parents too soon. That's what art can do sometimes. Unleash pain. Unleash hurt.

Luisa carried the ache of her father's absence with her for the rest of the week. But on Sunday she woke up feeling more hopeful than she'd felt in a long time. She was finally going to meet Beatriz. Maybe Beatriz could tell her something about her father. Like Nana Lottie had written, "Where there's life, there's hope."

Luisa left the orphanage before lunch, so she'd get to Father Álvarez's church before Beatriz did. She was wearing her teaching outfit and had put her hair up in a bun. She also dug out the tube of red lipstick she'd packed away in a secret pocket in her suitcase. It had been a long time since she'd worn lipstick. None of the other girls at the orphanage did, so Luisa didn't either. Putting it on made the day feel special.

When Luisa stepped out of the taxi, there was a young woman in her mid-twenties standing in front of the church. She was wearing jeans and a pink t-shirt and had long curly black hair just like Luisa's. Her hair was tied in a ponytail, with a small pink ribbon that matched her t-shirt. She looked a little young to be Luisa's aunt, but who else, Luisa thought, would be waiting all by themselves in front of the church? Luisa took a deep breath and put a friendly smile on her face.

"Hello, I'm Luisa." She stuck out her hand for Beatriz to shake.

Beatriz took her hand. "I'm Beatriz."

Then they both started to laugh. The resemblance between them was remarkable. Just like Father Álvarez had said. They were the same shade of deep caramel brown and both had long curly black hair.

"The park is just two blocks away," Beatriz said. She looked up at the sky. "It might rain, but I brought an umbrella."

"Me too."

Although sharing a laugh had broken the ice, they both felt shy in each other's company. For the first few moments, they didn't know what to say to each other.

"Is this your first time back?" Beatriz finally asked. She had a very quiet voice.

"Yes."

"How do you like it?"

"I like it a lot. I love being able to speak Spanish all day. It wasn't easy to keep it up in Toronto. But I worked really hard at it. I always knew I'd be coming back."

Luisa could see she had made Beatriz uncomfortable.

"How's your family?" she asked changing the subject.

"Everyone's fine."

"Are they coming to visit too?"

"Not right now. Maybe next year. The one who wants to come the most is my adoptive sister Clare. I think Ana's afraid to come back."

"But you weren't afraid."

"No."

"That's because you're a spicy girl. Like your mother. She wasn't afraid either. I'm more cautious."

Luisa caught her breath.

"How was my mother spicy?" She tried to match Beatriz's quiet reserve and not sound too eager.

Beatriz took a few seconds to think about it. "Inés had a lot of opinions. About everything. And she wasn't afraid to tell you what she thought."

"How do you know I'm spicy like her?"

"From the letter you sent me. You don't take no for an answer. And the way you walk. With your head up high. Just like her."

"Did she have a temper?"

Beatriz smiled, just a tiny smile, and nodded. "Sometimes. Especially when she thought someone wasn't treating her fairly."

"That's just like me!"

They arrived at the park. The same park Luisa had marched in during the Día de los Reyes Magos parade. She looked for the empanada stall. It wasn't there.

Beatriz pointed to a wooden bench with a back that faced away from the street. "We can sit here."

They sat down on either end of bench, Beatriz keeping as much space as she could between them. Luisa started with an easy question.

"What else can you tell me about my *mamá*?"

Beatriz hesitated. "I'm not sure. She was a lot older than me."

"How much older?"

"Fifteen years. I was only seven when she married Juan Andres. We didn't live together in our parent's home for very long."

"Seven. That's how old I was when she died."

"I know."

Beatriz shifted on the bench, putting a little more distance between them.

"How old was she when she got married?"

"Twenty-two."

"And how old was she when I was born?"

"Twenty-two."

"If *mamá* was twenty-two when I was born, she was twenty-five when Ana was born and twenty-nine when she died."

"Yes. Twenty-nine."

"So you were . . ."

"Fourteen."

"Ana's age. Were you and my *mamá* close after she got married?"

Beatriz shook her head. "When Inés and Juan Andres got married, they moved away, and we didn't see them much. We only visited them twice. Once for your first birthday and once when Ana was born. We couldn't stay long. Just one night, each time. It was far. It took two hours to get there on the bus and two hours to get back. We had a business, we sold empanadas. We couldn't be away for long."

"So that's why I didn't remember you! You only visited twice. When I was really young. And that's probably why I didn't remember Father Álvarez. We didn't go to his church, we went to a different church."

"That's right."

"But why did they move away?"

"Juan Andres couldn't make enough money doing construction work in Ciudad Bolívar to support a family. One of his friends was living in La Candelaria. He was an artist. So was Juan Andres. They sketched portraits of tourists on the street and sold them. Between construction jobs."

"My father sketched portraits? I paint portraits!"

She nodded. "I'm not surprised. Inés said you loved to watch your father draw."

"Can I show you something?"

Luisa pulled her sketchbook out of her knapsack.

"A few weeks ago, I was watching a street artist draw a portrait of a tourist in La Candelaria. He had his daughter with him. She was copying his movements, learning to draw by watching him. I sketched her. But instead of drawing her face, I drew my own. Here it is. At the time I didn't understand why, but now I think maybe it's because watching the little girl draw reminded me that I used to watch my father draw. What do you think?"

Luisa opened the sketchbook to the page of the drawing of the street artist and his daughter, reached across the bench and handed it to Beatriz. She took a look at the little girl's face before handing it back.

"It's possible, I guess. The little girl does look like you when you were younger."

"I can't believe my father was an artist!"

Beatriz gave Luisa a little smile. "I'm glad you're happy."

"I'm very happy! Do you draw too?"

"No. I'm not artistic at all."

"So was I born in La Candelaria, not Ciudad Bolívar."

"That's right."

"And we lived in an apartment building? Maybe four floors?"

"That's right."

"And it was brown?"

"Maybe. I don't remember. Like I said, I was only there twice."

Luisa nodded. "Where did you sleep when you came to visit? Did you sleep with Ana and me?"

"Yes. Inés gave my parents the bed. The rest of us slept in the living room."

"What else?"

"When Ana was born, your *mamá* made dinner and my *mamá* made a cake. We sang 'Happy Birthday.' You were just turning three, but you knew all the words already."

"What was I like?"

"You were very happy to have a little sister. I remember when your *mamá* fed Ana you sat beside her leaning against her shoulder."

Luisa closed her eyes trying to remember leaning against her *mamá* while she breastfed Ana. She couldn't remember the moment.

"Did we ever come back to Father Álvarez's church to march in the Día de los Reyes Magos parade?"

"Every year. Inés brought you back to visit us and say hello to Father Álvarez."

"That's why I remembered the horns and drums. And that's why Father Álvarez remembered me and Ana," said Luisa. "Did you march with us?"

"No. I had to help my parents sell empanadas. We made good money that day. There were always lots of people in the park."

My heart raced. "Your stall was near the park?"

"Near the entrance."

"Did we ever go there?"

"Of course. After the parade, you came to see us and have some empanadas."

"We still love them. I make them in Toronto. For Colombia Night."

"Colombia Night?"

"It's a night when all the adopted children from Bogotá get together to celebrate our culture."

Beatriz nodded and edged even further away from Luisa, moving so close to the end of the bench Luisa thought she was going to fall off. This time Luisa changed the subject.

"There's something I want to ask you. I've been wondering about it for a long time."

"What is it?"

"Why didn't anyone come visit us at the orphanage?"

Luisa thought the question might surprise her, catch her off guard. But it seemed as though Beatriz had been expecting it.

"We all wanted to. But when I asked Father Álvarez to take us there, he said it was better we didn't go. It would upset you."

"Upset us!" Luisa raised her voice. "How could he say it would upset us? I can't believe Father Álvarez said you shouldn't visit. It would've meant so much to us to see you!"

Beatriz got up off the bench.

Luisa leaped to her feet, lowered her voice, and struggled to stay calm. "I'm sorry. I'm not angry at you. I'm angry at Father Álvarez. Please, let's sit down again."

Beatriz didn't move.

"Please. I promise I won't raise my voice again."

She nodded and sat down again at the edge of the bench.

"You have your *mamá*'s quick temper. She was angry too."

"At Father Álvarez?"

"No. At dying."

"People with pneumonia don't have to die."

"No, but she did."

They fell silent. A lot had been said. They were both trying to process what they'd discovered. After a long minute, Beatriz broke the silence.

"I did come to see you and Ana."

"At the orphanage?"

"Yes. But you'd already left."

"When was this?"

"About a year after you'd been adopted. The sister I talked to wouldn't tell me where you were."

"She wouldn't tell you?"

"'Out of the country.' That's all she said. 'Out of the country.' She said you and Ana were living with new parents now. They loved you and cared for you. You had lots of food, nice clothes, a nice house."

"Which sister was it?"

"The one who was the director."

"What was her name?" Luisa knew it couldn't have been Sister Lorena. She'd only been the director for a year.

"I don't know."

"You don't remember?"

"No. She said I should be happy for you because you had a father and a mother now."

"But they forced us to leave all the people we knew and trusted," Luisa protested, trying not to raise her voice again. "The place that had become our home. Sister Francesca was like a mother to me."

"I didn't know what to do. How to find you. Lawyers cost a lot of money." Luisa could hear the shame in Beatriz's voice.

"I know," she said, trying for a sympathetic tone.

"The sister thought she was doing the right thing," Beatriz continued.

Luisa exploded, raising her voice even louder than before.

"The right thing? You came to see us. The sister knew where we lived. You could've written us letters. We could've written back. Ana and I could've known you and you could've known us. They took that away from us. They had no right to take that away from us!"

Luisa hit the bench hard with her hand. It stung. Beatriz was on her feet again.

"Let's go for a walk," she said.

They walked for a good five minutes before Beatriz picked up the conversation. Walking just ahead of them was a young woman with two young children heading for the children's playground in the middle of the park.

"*Mamá*, let's go to the swings first," said the older one. "I want you to push me. High."

"Me too," said the younger one. "I want you to push me high too."

Two children excited to be going to the park with their mother. Two children who hadn't lost their mother. Or their aunt.

Beatriz must have been thinking the same thing.

"It wasn't the sisters' fault," she said very quietly so the woman in front of them wouldn't hear. "It wasn't their decision."

"Whose decision was it?" Luisa asked trying to match her tone and keep calm.

"Father Álvarez's. He was the one who told the sisters not to tell me where you were. He said it was better that way."

Luisa stopped walking. "But it wasn't! It wasn't better that way. Not for me." She was shouting again. The woman in front of them turned around to look at them and then led her children in another direction.

"I think I should go now," Beatriz said.

"No! Please! Not yet." Luisa lowered her voice. "Before you go, I want to ask you about my father."

Beatriz took a moment, deciding if she wanted to keep talking to Luisa.

"What do you want to know?" she asked tentatively, sounding like she wanted to end their conversation as soon as she could.

"Father Álvarez said he went to visit his mother in Medellín and never came back. When did that happen? How old was I?"

She turned to face Luisa. "Five, maybe six."

"What do you think happened?"

"I don't know. All I know was that he went to see his mother, and he didn't come back."

"Do you think he left us for someone else?"

"No," she said shaking her head with certainty. "He loved Inés, and he loved you and Ana." Her certainty was reassuring to Luisa.

"Father Álvarez says he thinks he's dead. What do you think?"

She looked away again to the street. "He's probably right."

"There's one thing I don't understand."

"What's that?"

"Why didn't my *mamá* have a plan?"

"A plan for what?" Beatriz turned to face Luisa again.

"A plan for what would happen to us if she died. She only agreed to send us to the orphanage until she got better. There must've been a moment when she knew she wasn't going to get better. Why didn't she have a plan?"

Beatriz started walking again. Quickly. Luisa hurried to catch up, her boots clacking on the concrete path.

"She did have a plan," Beatriz said still walking, her voice was so low Luisa almost didn't hear her.

"What was it?"

"She wanted you and Ana to come to live with our parents and me. She wanted me to leave school and start working full-time to help support the family."

Luisa grabbed Beatriz's arm. "What happened?"

She stopped walking and shook off Luisa's arm. Luisa stepped back to give her some space.

"Father Álvarez met with the entire family. First with my parents and me. He told us he'd spoken to my teachers. They said I was an excellent student. I shouldn't quit school. He said if I finished high school, he would find money to send me to nursing school so I could learn a profession. He said it'd be better for all of us if you and Ana stayed at the orphanage he worked with. The sisters could take care of you. I could finish high school. Once I was working as a nurse, I could help you and Ana go to university. Then he went to talk to Inés and told her the same thing."

"So *mamá* changed her mind?"

"She wanted the best for all of us."

"She decided to leave us at El Orfanato?"

"She wanted a future for all of us. She respected Father Álvarez's opinion. We all did."

"So, he chose you over us."

The moment the words were out of her mouth Luisa regretted them. Shame and grief washed over Beatriz's face, and she walked away again.

Luisa wasn't sure if she wanted to let her go or follow her.

"I'm sorry," she called out, running to catch up to Beatriz. "Ana says sometimes I have a very big mouth. I don't think before I speak. It was a terrible situation. For everyone."

Beatriz stopped and turned to face her. "Yes, it was." Luisa took a deep breath of relief. She hadn't lost her yet.

"I think it's wonderful that you went to nursing school. What kind of nurse are you?"

"I work in emergency."

Luisa thought of the emergency nurse who had helped Claudia.

"It's not easy to work in emergency. You see a lot of death. A lot of trauma. Your parents would have been very proud."

Beatriz teared up.

"How did they die?"

"*Papá* had a heart attack. *Mamá* died from complications from diabetes."

Luisa took a risk and offered her her hand. Beatriz didn't take it, and Luisa stuck it in her jacket pocket.

"Do you have a family of your own?" Luisa asked.

"Not yet."

"So, you live by yourself?"

"No, I share an apartment near the hospital with three other nurses."

"That's good. That's better than living alone."

"I'd hate living alone."

"Me too."

They'd found common ground.

It began raining. Hard. They opened up their umbrellas and left the park walking quickly.

"I'll find you a taxi," Beatriz said as they reached the street, cars rushing past them.

"Okay, but before I go, there's something I don't understand. If the plan was for you to go to school to become a nurse and come get us once you had a job, then why weren't you allowed to visit us at the orphanage? And why were we adopted?"

"I don't know."

"We had a family that wanted us. The plan was for us to stay in the orphanage until we could come live with you. Father Álvarez didn't respect the plan."

Beatriz didn't respond. She flagged down a cab.

The cab stopped in front of them, and Luisa grabbed her hand. "Can we meet again?"

Beatriz pulled it away and shook her head.

"Why not?! Everyone's gone. Your parents are gone. My parents are gone. The only family we have left is each other."

"I know, but this is too hard."

Luisa took a good look at her face and saw she was trying hard not to cry. Luisa knew she needed to say something. Something that could keep the two of them connected in some small way. She couldn't let this be their one and only meeting.

"Would you give me your phone number so I can text you?" asked Luisa. "Or your e-mail? I promise I won't harass you. I'll only write once or twice a year. Just to let you know how Ana and I are doing. How you can reach us if you want to. Just so I have a way to let you know when I'll be back in Bogotá in case you change your mind and want to see me again."

Luisa waited while Beatriz struggled. She wanted to say no so she could forget the past and focus on the future. But she also felt some compassion for Luisa.

The taxi driver honked his horn. They ignored him. He honked again.

Finally, Beatriz reached into her purse for her wallet, pulled out a business card, and handed it to Luisa. It was from the hospital she worked at.

"My e-mail's on the card."

"Thank you."

Beatriz opened the door for Luisa.

"Take care of yourself," she said and gently shut the door.

The driver asked Luisa where she was going.

"El Orfanato Para Niños y Niñas."

Back to the orphanage. Knowing a little more than she knew before but not much.

CHAPTER 20

Sister Francesca was waiting for Luisa at the front door.

"What are you doing here?" she asked. "Why aren't you at your parents?"

The last Sunday afternoon of every month, Sister Francesca visited her family. Luisa was surprised to see her.

"I wanted to be here when you got back. How did it go?"

"She doesn't want to see me again."

"I'm sorry, *pequeña*." She took Luisa's hand.

"Beatriz said she came to find us a year after we were adopted. But the sister in charge wouldn't give her our address in Toronto. Did you know she came to visit?"

Sister Francesca looked directly into Luisa's eyes. "I knew."

Luisa pulled her hand away. "You had our address. Why didn't you give it to her?"

"You know why."

"Father Álvarez told you not to." The contempt in her voice was harsh.

Sister Francesca sighed. "Of all the vows I made when I became a nun, the hardest one to keep is obedience. But I work very hard at it. I've only broken it once."

"When?"

"When I answered your letters."

"Father Álvarez said you couldn't write to me?"

"He said you needed to forget us and start a new life in Toronto. But I knew you needed to hear from me, and I needed to hear from you. So,

I wrote to you anyway. I mailed the letters on Sundays when I visited my parents. If I'd given your aunt your address and Father Álvarez had found out, there would've been questions. How did I know your address? Was I in contact with you? It was too risky."

Luisa thought of Sister Francesca, secretly mailing her letters to Toronto when she'd been told not to. She felt deeply loved.

Luisa reached out for Sister Francesca's hand. She gave it to her, and Luisa held it tight.

"All those letters you wrote sustained me," she said.

"And yours sustained me."

Luisa reached over and hugged her. She hugged her back.

"Now that you're eighteen we can write to each other as much we want. But the letters I sent you all those years? They're a secret."

"Did you ever secretly write to any of the other girls?"

"No, *pequeña*. Just you. Come into the kitchen and I'll make you a cup of tea."

After two cups of coca tea, Luisa asked Sister Francesca to let her into Sister Lorena's office so she could text Harriet. She joked she didn't need to break into the filing cabinets anymore. She'd found Beatriz. Sister Francesca let her in and left her alone so she could have some privacy. Luisa had promised Daniel she'd check in after her visit with Beatriz, so she texted him first.

"Not the brilliant visit I was hoping for. But I'm okay. Don't worry. *Besos.*" Kisses.

Then Luisa texted Harriet.

"My father was an artist."

Harriet texted back immediately.

"Just like you! What else?"

"Beatriz doesn't want to meet again."

"What? Why?"

They got cut off. Luisa turned her phone off and then back on again. No service. She'd have to try again later.

That night Luisa dreamt she and Ana were swinging in the park near Father Álvarez's church. Their *mamá* was pushing them, and the swings were climbing higher and higher. Luisa's hair was in a ponytail tied with the red ribbon her *mamá* had bought her. It waved in the wind as she soared into the sky and flapped against her back when she came back to earth. Luisa was laughing like crazy, excited by how high she was swinging. Suddenly her *mamá* stopped pushing her, and the swing began to slow down. Luisa turned around to tell her not to stop, to keep going, but she wasn't there. Luisa jumped off the swing and went to find her. She ran all around the playground, calling out her name, but she didn't answer. Luisa went back to the swings to find Ana. She was sitting on her swing all by herself. Luisa looked around. They were all alone in the playground. Everyone else had left.

Luisa woke up in a sweat, breathing heavily, enraged. When Father Álvarez took them to the orphanage, she and Ana lost their family forever. Her *mamá* had had a plan. Father Álvarez didn't respect it. Luisa thought he owed her an apology. It wouldn't change anything but at the very least, Father Álvarez had to acknowledge that he was wrong to keep them away from Beatriz and their grandparents.

The next morning, right after breakfast, Luisa called a taxi to take her to Father Álvarez's church. It was raining again, but she'd forgotten to take an umbrella. Luisa paid the driver and opened the door. There was a huge puddle between the car and the sidewalk. It was impossible not to step into the water. The stairs were slippery, and she had to grab onto the railing so she wouldn't fall. By the time Luisa walked into Father Álvarez's office, her shoes were squeaking and her feet were swimming in water.

Camila, who heard her squeaky footsteps, greeted her. Cordial, but cool. She said she'd see if Father Álvarez was available. He was very busy that day. She slipped inside Father Álvarez's office and came out a few seconds later.

"He said he'll see you. Briefly. You can go inside."

Father Álvarez rose as Luisa came in. All six feet four inches of him. Imposing as always.

"Good morning."

"Good morning, Father." Civil, but cool like Camila.

"How have you been?" He matched Luisa's tone.

"Not very well."

It was clear they weren't going to have a nice, pleasant chat.

"I'm sorry to hear that." Father Álvarez gestured to the chair in front of his desk. "Sit down."

Luisa sat down on the hard, wooden chair and folded her hands in her lap. They were ice cold. The man who'd changed her destiny was sitting right in front of her, forehead creased, furrowed eyebrows, not pleased to see her again.

"How can I help?" he asked in a dispassionate, distant voice.

"I met with Beatriz yesterday," said Luisa. "She told me my mother had a plan. She wanted us to live with my grandparents. You changed her mind."

Luisa's anger was unmistakable. Father Álvarez remained calm, his hands folded on top of his desk.

"We all agreed," he said. "It was better for everyone if you and Ana stayed at the orphanage and Beatriz finished school. High school was Beatriz's way out of a life of selling empanadas and cleaning other people's houses."

"But there was a plan. Beatriz was supposed to bring us home once she graduated and started working. You didn't respect the plan. You told Beatriz she shouldn't visit. You gave strangers permission to adopt us and take us half way around the world even though you knew my grandparents were waiting for us to come home. If you hadn't interfered, we would've grown up in the same house my *mamá* grew up in. We would've heard stories about her and my father. Lots of stories. We'd have memories of them both and of our life together in Bogotá."

Father Álvarez leaned forward and went on the attack.

"You're romanticizing what it would've been like. By the time Beatriz graduated from nursing school, both your grandparents were sick. She spent her days working at the hospital and nursing her parents at night. There was no time to take care of two young girls. It would've been impossible for you to go live with them. You would've stayed at the orphanage and gone out to work like the others when you turned sixteen. Instead, you were adopted by two professional parents who lived in a house in a good neighbourhood with time and money to take you to art and Spanish classes."

Luisa wondered how he knew about the art and Spanish classes. Maybe Sister Francesca had told him.

"You were never hungry, and you never had to worry about seeing a doctor because you couldn't pay him. You learned to speak English, finished high school, and are going to university. The world is full of opportunities for you. You should be grateful."

The word sent Luisa flying off her chair, and for a moment, standing tall on her side of the desk, she towered over him. "All those opportunities, they came with a price. All those years in Toronto, they were incredibly painful. You have no idea how painful they were."

Father Álvarez stood up too and now towered over Luisa. "Life is full of pain." He sounded arrogant, and it infuriated Luisa.

"Who gave you the right to play God?"

Father Álvarez's eyes narrowed, surprised by Luisa's impertinence. "I did what was best for everyone. For Beatriz, for you and for Ana."

"No, you didn't. You know what would've been best? Respecting the plan. Driving our family to the orphanage to visit us. Moving us back into their home when Beatriz finished school. That's what would've been best. Why didn't you respect the plan? Maybe it was because of the money. How much did Global Family pay you so they could bring two little Colombian girls back to Toronto?"

Luisa knew she'd gone too far. Father Álvarez came around the desk and firmly grasped her elbow.

"It's time for you to go. Camila will show you out."

Luisa didn't budge. So he left the office instead, pushing past Luisa in a burst of anger.

Camila came in to get rid of her.

"Follow me," she said to Luisa.

Luisa knew Father Álvarez wasn't going to apologize. Not now. Not ever. She followed Camila out of the church through the back door and was left standing next to a garbage can that stank of rotten fruit. Camila walked away without saying goodbye.

Hands shaking with shock at being kicked out so forcefully, Luisa took out her phone and called a taxi. The line was busy. She looked out at the yard at the back of the church. There was a small cemetery just beyond the back door where she was standing. Luisa felt goose bumps again. This time she knew what they meant. She'd been in this cemetery before. Her *mamá* was buried in this cemetery.

Luisa ran from the back door of the church into the soaking wet grass of the cemetery and started reading the names on the gravestones. There weren't that many. About forty. Luisa forced herself to take her time and read each name out loud. Her *mamá* was buried in the last row. Beside a pine tree. Luisa kneeled down on the grass in front her gravestone. All the rage she was carrying came pouring out. She screamed at the gravestone. In English.

"Why did you let him change your mind? Why didn't you stand up to him? Why didn't you protect us?"

The wind picked up and the rain slashed her face. She was shivering.

"What kind of mother doesn't protect her children? A bad mother. Only bad mothers don't protect their children."

Luisa began to cry. She cried until her teeth started chattering. She knew she had to get out of the wind and rain. She walked around to the front of the church, called for a taxi, and waited in the pouring rain for it to arrive.

CHAPTER 21

That night Luisa began to cough. The next morning she was still coughing and couldn't take a deep breath. Claudia said she needed to see a doctor.

"Do you have enough money?"

"I can use my credit card. The government will pay me back."

"The government in Canada pays for people to see a doctor?"

"Yes."

Claudia shook her head in amazement. "I'll take you to the family health clinic at the hospital. I know people there. We need to take a taxi. You shouldn't be on a bus."

"But you have to work today."

Claudia had just started her new practicum.

"If we leave right now, I can take you to the clinic and go straight to work. It should be fine."

They took a taxi to the hospital, and Claudia set Luisa up in the waiting room of the clinic.

"Text me when it's your turn and I'll try to come up."

Luisa sat in the waiting room of the clinic for two hours because she didn't have an appointment. She felt too sick to read so she just sat and waited. Finally she was called into one of the treatment rooms. She texted Claudia.

A medical student came in to take Luisa's medical history. He was tall, had curly black hair, and wore glasses. Round wireframe glasses like Sister Francesca. His nametag said he was Alejandro Hernández.

Claudia walked into the treatment room just as Alejandro was about to ask Luisa his first question. He was surprised to see her, but she looked as if she'd known he'd be there. When he asked how she was, Claudia blushed and said fine. Then when she tried to explain who Luisa was and why she was there, she stumbled on her last name and blushed again. Luisa couldn't figure out what was going on, then clued in. Claudia had a crush on Alejandro. A little wave of hurt washed over her heart.

Alejandro began to ask Luisa questions about her medical history and her symptoms. After she'd answered all of them, he asked, "Where are you from?"

"Bogotá."

"But you speak Spanish with an accent."

Luisa asked herself what Laura would say. "I was born here but live in Canada."

"So, you're Canadian!"

"No, I'm Colombian."

The doctor came in and asked Alejandro to present Luisa's symptoms. Then he listened to her lungs with a stethoscope and told her she had a serious case of pneumonia.

"How do you get pneumonia?" Luisa asked.

"You get it when you inhale a virus or bacteria. If your immune system is not able to fight it off, an infection grows in the air sacks of your lungs. I'm giving you a prescription for an antibiotic. Fill it at the pharmacy downstairs and start taking it right away. Stay in bed, get plenty of rest until you're feeling better, and drink extra fluids."

"How long will it take to recover?"

"Usually it takes a week or two. But in your case, maybe three or four."

"Four weeks! I can't be sick for four weeks! I'd be an extra burden to Sister Francesca who would insist on taking care of me for a month."

He signed the prescription and started to leave.

"Before you go, I want to ask you something," said Luisa. "It's about my immune system. I had a bad case of altitude sickness when I first got here. Did it weaken my immune system? Is that why I caught pneumonia?"

"Maybe. It's not impossible. You know, people who experience altitude sickness once usually experience it again."

Luisa nodded. Not only did she have a wicked case of pneumonia that would take weeks to recover from, every time she came back to Bogotá she was probably going to be sick with altitude sickness for a week.

"Before travelling, try taking acetazolamide one or two days before you leave. That helps some people."

"Okay, thanks."

The doctor left, but Alejandro lingered to talk to Claudia.

"So how long's your practicum?"

"Four weeks. I'm working downstairs in emergency."

"That's intense."

"For sure." Claudia looked at Luisa. "But I'm up for it." Luisa nodded.

Alejandro smiled. "Well, I'm still here, as you can see. Come by and say hello."

Claudia blushed again. "Okay. If I have time."

He turned to Luisa. "Take care of yourself. You should feel better in a few days."

"Thanks. I hope so."

Alejandro left the examining room, and Claudia brought Luisa downstairs to the pharmacy, which wasn't far from the emergency room. There was a long line of people ahead of them. Claudia found Luisa a seat and told her to wait there. She'd drop off the prescription, go back to work, and then come get her when the prescription was filled.

"It's okay. I can get back to the orphanage by myself."

"Text me when it's filled, and we'll see."

Luisa's seat was close to the cash register. There was a woman with a baby at the front of the line dumping all the money she had onto the counter.

"It's all I have," she said looking down on the counter, ashamed.

The cashier counted up her bills and coins.

"It's not enough."

"I'll come back and give you the rest."

"I can't give you the prescription until you have enough money."

"But my baby's so sick."

Luisa stood up, but too quickly. The room started to spin. She sat down again.

"How much do you need?" she called out.

The woman told her. Luisa found her new wallet in her knapsack and gave her 5,000 pesos.

"God bless you," she said to Luisa as she came over to take the money.

"Good luck," she replied, aware of how easy it was for her to part with 5,000 pesos and how difficult it was for the woman to find it.

It took forever to fill Luisa's prescription. By the time her little white bag was ready, Luisa's cheeks were burning up, and she'd started to shiver again. She texted Claudia who came up immediately.

"Do you have any water?" she asked.

"Yeah."

"Okay, take two pills. Then we'll leave."

"Just put me into a taxi and go back to work."

"No, you have a fever. I'll go back to the orphanage with you."

"You don't have to."

"I want to."

It had begun to rain, and the traffic was bad. It took the taxi almost double the time to drive to the orphanage than it did to drive to the hospital. Luisa coughed for the entire ride. Claudia put on a mask.

They were halfway there when the car in front of them suddenly stopped and the driver had to slam on his breaks to avoid hitting it. They were thrown forward and then backward in their seats. It was a good thing their seatbelts were on, otherwise they might have flown right through the front window. Claudia grabbed Luisa's arm and held on tight. Her face went white.

"It's okay. It's fine. We're fine," said Luisa, trying to reassure her. "It was just a sudden stop. It's okay. We're okay."

"I hate driving. Especially on busy roads. Especially in the rain."

The taxi started moving again, slowly because of the heavy traffic. Claudia relaxed and let go of Luisa's arm. The colour returned to her face.

As they got closer to the orphanage, Luisa asked about Alejandro.

"I think he likes you."

Claudia didn't answer.

"He wants you to come by and say hello."

"So?"

"So, he wants to talk to you, get to know you."

"If I go say hello, he might ask me to go for a coffee. And if we go for a coffee he'll ask about my family. And if he asks about my family, I'll have to tell him I have no family. I live in an orphanage."

"There's no shame in living in an orphanage."

"Yes, there is," she turned away from Luisa and looked out the window.

Luisa really didn't want to help Alejandro get a date with Claudia, but she hated hearing Claudia was ashamed of where she lived.

"Why? It's not your fault. You were in a terrible accident, and there was no one left to take care of you. The sisters took care of you."

"It doesn't matter. Boys from good families don't go out with poor orphan girls without families," she said still looking out the window, resigned.

"You're not a poor orphan girl. You're a brilliant, hard-working nursing student who won a scholarship to go to university! Tell him that!"

Claudia didn't answer, but she smiled. Just a little bit.

When they got back to her room, Claudia took Luisa's temperature. It was thirty-nine degrees Celsius, 102 degrees Fahrenheit.

"It'll come down once the antibiotics start to work. Try to sleep now."

"I'm sorry you had to leave work."

"It's all right. I'm going back now. I'll stay late to make up for it."

Luisa closed her eyes. All she wanted to do was sleep.

"Before you go, could you give my tablet to Sophia? Tell her to finish *The Amazing Race* with the older kids. They all want to see who wins."

"Okay."

"Thanks for everything."

"Of course. You helped me and now I'm helping you. That's what we do here. Help each other."

Later that day just before dinner, Sister Francesca brought Luisa some coca tea and soup. She took a couple of sips of the tea but couldn't eat much soup. She'd completely lost her appetite.

The next day Harriet arrived. Luisa couldn't believe her eyes when Harriet walked into Claudia's room wearing a mask. She thought she was hallucinating.

"What are you doing here?"

"Sister Lorena called me."

"She told you to come?"

"No, I asked her if could come."

Luisa was glad to see Harriet. Relieved she'd come. Now there was someone to take care of her besides Sister Francesca.

"Where are you staying?"

"The guest house where all the parents stay."

"What about work?"

"I asked for a supply teacher to cover for me for the rest of the week. Marty's taking care of your sisters. I can stay until Sunday afternoon. Can I get you anything?"

Luisa shook her head.

"How about some water?"

"Okay."

Harriet handed Luisa a bottle of water, and she took a few sips. After Harriet settled herself at the end of her bed, Luisa tried to sit up, but the room started spinning. She lay back down.

"I found my *mamá*'s grave."

"Really?! Where?"

"In the cemetery behind Father Álvarez's church. But I was angry and said some terrible things to her. I need to go back and tell her I didn't mean it."

"Of course. As soon as your fever's gone and you get some of your strength back."

It took the antibiotics a few days to kick in but once they did, Luisa began to feel better. Her temperature went down, the chills stopped, and she coughed less. She was able to eat more of the soup Sister Francesca kept bringing her and could sit up for half an hour at a time. But she mostly slept. Harriet spent most of her visit reading in Claudia's desk chair, which she placed beside Luisa's bed. It rained every day Harriet was there. After three days of rain, Harriet asked Luisa if she found the constant rain hard to take. Luisa told her, yes, sometimes.

On Friday, Harriet asked Luisa to come back to Toronto with her.

"It's still cold, but the days are getting longer, and Marty says it's been sunny every day since I've left. You can recover in your own bed with the sun coming through the window. No more rain."

Luisa closed her eyes and imagined herself in her bedroom in Toronto with the sun on her face. It was tempting.

"I know you're feeling better, but you're still not eating very much. If you come home with me, I can keep an eye on you. Claudia checked with your doctor. He says now that you're on antibiotics it's okay for you to fly with pneumonia. What do you think?"

"I don't know. I need to think about it. I'm not ready to go yet. I still don't know what happened to my father. If I stay, maybe . . . I mean, I don't know how, but . . ."

"I know," Harriet nodded, "I understand. No pressure. Just think about it."

CHAPTER 22

Part of Luisa wanted to go, part of her wanted to stay. She'd become very attached to the younger kids, and she knew they'd miss her if she left. She talked it over with Claudia. After taking Luisa to the hospital, Claudia had begun to warm up again. Luisa didn't know why. Maybe it was because Luisa was sick and Claudia felt sorry for her. Maybe it was because Luisa encouraged her to have coffee with Alejandro. But in the end, thought Luisa, it didn't matter why. What mattered was Claudia was friendly again.

"What should I do?" Luisa asked her.

Claudia pulled over her desk chair beside the bed the way she used to. Before the kiss.

"Let's go back to the beginning," she said. "Why did you come to Bogotá?"

"To find out why my *mamá* died of pneumonia and why my father wasn't there to take care of us."

"Do you feel more settled knowing what you know now?"

"No! I feel angry. If my father had come back from Medellín, there would've been enough money for *mamá* to buy antibiotics right away. My *mamá* would've gotten better, and we wouldn't have been adopted far away from everyone we knew and loved."

Claudia nodded. "So, what are you going to do with your anger?"

"I've thinking about going back to Toronto and applying for medical school. And raise money to build a health centre in Ciudad Bolívar."

Claudia smiled. "Yes, of course. That's exactly what you should do. But first, I think you need time to heal. You've been through a lot. I think you should go back to Toronto and let Harriet and Marty and your sisters help you. But if you're not sure you should go talk to your *mamá*."

The next day Luisa made plans to go back to the cemetery. Harriet asked to go with her. To pay her respects to *mamá*. Before they left, they stopped by the reception room to look at Luisa's drawing.

"Look at our faces," Luisa said.

Harriet moved closer to the drawing to look at each of their faces.

"Devastated. Everyone looks devastated." She moved back to take in the entire picture.

"But did you notice both you and Ana are wearing red t-shirts? Your *mamá*'s shirt is white. But yours are red. For me red means strength. Courage. Survival. Your drawing says you and Ana will survive." She turned away from the picture and looked at Luisa.

"You drew a future for yourself and Ana." She started tearing up. "And I got to be a part of it. Lucky me."

Luisa teared up, too, but didn't say anything.

"Ever since you left, I've been wondering if we did the right thing. Taking you so far away from home. I had no idea it'd be so difficult for you. It was all so simple for me. There were children out there who needed a home. I had a home. There were children who needed a family. I wanted a family. The children were from Colombia. So what? It didn't matter. But it did matter. It was painful for you leave, painful to start a new life, painful to come back. If I'd known . . . It hasn't been as difficult for Ana. But for you . . . I'm sorry. I'm very sorry."

By this time, the tears were rolling down both their faces. Luisa could see Harriet wanted to move closer, maybe give her a hug. But she wasn't ready, so she kept her distance, and Harriet followed her lead.

"Maybe this is as bad as it gets," Luisa said.

"I hope so. I really hope so," answered Harriet.

Luisa wiped the tears off her face. "Let's go see my *mamá*."

Half an hour later under a gray, cloudy sky that threatened rain, they stood in front of Luisa's *mamá*'s grave. A simple white wooden cross. Luisa translated the epitaph for Harriet. Inés González Rodríguez. Daughter, sister, wife, and mother. Harriet spoke to her first. Luisa moved in close beside her so she could hear every word she said. In a voice that was a little formal, a voice she used for people she respected a great deal but didn't know very well, Harriet introduced herself and told Luisa's *mamá* living with Ana and Luisa was one of the great joys of her life.

"Luisa has become a very talented artist. But she also does exceedingly well in biology, chemistry, and physics. Luisa can study anything she wants in university. Become anything she wants to be. Ana is a talented musician with a stunning voice. She sings like an angel. I promise you I will do everything I can to make sure their lives are as safe and happy as possible." Then she stepped aside and went to stand three graves away so Luisa could speak to her *mamá* alone. Close enough for Luisa to see her, to know she was there, but far enough to give her some privacy.

"*Mamá*, I'm sorry I was so angry the last time I saw you. Coming back to Bogotá has been hard. Harder than I expected."

The rain began to spit, and Luisa could feel the sting of rain drops falling onto her head.

"*Mamá*, Harriet's asked me to go back Toronto with her. I hate leaving not knowing what happened to *papá* but maybe I can learn to live with not knowing. I'm not the only adopted kid in the world whose father has disappeared. But I want to know what you think. Do you think it's time for me to go back?"

The sky became darker, and it began to rain harder. So hard it was clear what Luisa's *mamá* thought. It was time to go back.

Harriet had started inching closer so she could cover Luisa with the umbrella she'd brought.

"I think we should go," Harriet called out.

"Okay, just one more a minute."

Luisa placed both hands on her mother's cross, brown hands on peeling white paint. Her fingertips traced her name.

"*Mamá*, I've been thinking about what to do with my anger. I need to do something that takes me forward, not backwards. I'm going to follow Nana Lottie's and Claudia's advice and become a doctor. So other mothers in Ciudad Bolívar don't die of pneumonia and their children don't have to grow up without them. Now that I know what happened, I can try to change things, make things better. My English is better than my Spanish so I'm going to have to study in Toronto. But I promise I'll come back to see you. As often as I can. *Te amo mamá. Te veo pronto.*"

Then Luisa reached into her pocket for the small stone that she'd picked up from the gem store in La Candelaria and placed it in front of her *mamá*'s grave, Jewish style. To show the world someone had come to visit, someone remembered her.

Luisa grabbed Harriet's hand and they ran to the back door of the church to get out of the rain. Luckily, the back door was unlocked, and they were able to walk through the hallway to get to the front. Father Álvarez's office door was closed, and Camila wasn't at her desk. Luisa was relieved. She had no desire to talk to either of them.

While Harriet called for a taxi, Luisa went into the sanctuary. White walls, wooden pews, and two simple stained-glass windows. She sat down in the last row of the pews and looked around. She was sitting in the very room her *mamá* had sat in as a child. Each window featured a large yellow cross mounted against a blue backdrop with a green vine circling up the cross. The earth, the sky, and faith. Luisa's *mamá* would have stared at the same windows every week. Luisa closed her eyes and imagined her *mamá* sitting next to her parents and Beatriz. Did they sit in the front or the back? What part of the window had she been drawn to most? The blue sky? The green vine? The yellow cross? Did going to church sustain her when her husband didn't come home?

"The taxi's on its way," Harriet said from the doorway.

Luisa opened her eyes and turned around to face her.

"Okay."

"You don't have to get up just yet. How are you feeling?"

"Okay. I'm glad we came."

"Me too."

Luisa moved over so Harriet could sit beside her.

"So, you want to be a doctor!" said Harriet.

"If we can afford it."

"Don't worry, we'll find a way."

"It means I'll be around for a while."

"Fine with me."

Harriet tried to sound casual, but Luisa could see she'd started to cry again.

Luisa put her arm around Harriet's shoulder and gave her a hug. Then the taxi driver drove up, honked his horn, and they walked out of the sanctuary into the Bogotá rain together.

When the taxi pulled up in front of the orphanage, Sister Francesca was waiting for them at the front door with a big smile on her face. She was excited.

"Come in out of the rain! Another letter just came for you from Beatriz!"

"Your aunt?" asked Harriet.

"Yes. I didn't expect to hear from her again."

"I was praying she'd write to you again," said Sister Francesca grasping Luisa's arm. "And now she has! Come into the reception room."

They followed Sister Francesca into the reception room and sat down on the couch. Sister Francesca handed Luisa a letter opener she'd found in Sister Lorena's office so Luisa could open the envelope without tearing it. Luisa's hands were shaking badly.

"Could you open it for me?" she asked Sister Francesca.

"Of course, *pequeña*."

"And could you read it aloud for me?"

As Sister Francesca read the letter aloud, Luisa translated for Harriet.

During one of Beatriz's shifts in the emergency unit, a man about Luisa's father's age brought in his elderly mother who was having trouble breathing. Beatriz began to collect the mother's medical history, and when she took down her name and address, she realized the family lived in her old neighbourhood in Ciudad Bolívar. The son, whose name was Ricardo, worked in construction and had been friends with Luisa's father before he and Inés moved to La Candelaria.

"I asked Ricardo if he knew why your father had never come back from Medellín," Beatriz wrote. "He was surprised and wanted to know why I was asking after all these years. So I went to my locker, found my wallet, and took out the photo you sent me."

"I can't believe it," Luisa said to Sister Francesca in Spanish and then to Harriet in English. "Beatriz kept the photo I sent her in her wallet!"

Sister Francesca wrapped her in a big hug. "I'm so happy for you, *pequeña*."

When she finally let go, Luisa asked, "What happened next?"

Sister Francesca continued reading. "When I showed the photo to Ricardo, he stared at it for a long time. Finally, he told me to meet him in front of the hospital after my shift." Luisa stopped translating while Sister Francesca read the rest of the letter.

In an empty corner of the hospital parking lot, Beatriz heard the story Luisa had come to Colombia to hear. While her father was visiting his sick mother in Medellín, he was offered work outside the city. His mother needed to see a specialist. Specialists cost money so he took the job. Even though his family was waiting for him to return to Bogotá. Luisa's father called her mother and said he'd be gone for a few weeks. When he didn't come back his mother, Luisa's paternal grandmother, didn't know what to do. She was afraid to go the police. So was Inés.

"So it's possible," Beatriz said at the end of letter, "your father was one of the *falsos positivos*, but no one knows for sure. He could have had an accident on his way to the job that was never reported. Or an accident on the job. I don't know what to say except I'm very sorry. And that I'm glad we met. Both your parents would be very proud of the young woman you've become. Keep making your *mamá* and *papá* proud."

Hearing Beatriz's story hurt. It opened a wound that was still deep and raw. Harriet saw the hurt on Luisa's face and wanted to know what the last part of the letter said. Luisa asked Sister Francesca to read the whole letter again line by line so she could translate it into English for Harriet. When they were done, they all started to cry.

"Even if we still don't know exactly how your father died," said Harriet, "We do know he died trying to take care of his family. Maybe we can take comfort in that."

Sister Francesca nodded. She could see Luisa's grief was Harriet's grief. They were family.

Harriet and Luisa walked back to Claudia's room so Luisa could lie down and rest. Harriet asked if Luisa wanted her to start packing for the trip back to Toronto. Luisa told her she'd find her suitcase under the bed.

When she opened the mostly empty suitcase, which was now sitting at the bottom of Luisa's bed, Harriet found the package of letters Nana Lottie had sent for her birthday. Harriet could see Luisa had already read the letters because the five envelopes had been hastily tied together. Nana would have tied them together neatly. Harriet asked Luisa what Nana had written. When she told her, Harriet couldn't believe it and dragged Claudia's desk chair over next to Luisa bed so they could talk about the letters.

"I've asked for her years to tell me about Germany and England," said Harriet, "but she never told me very much. She always said that part of her life was over, it happened a long time ago and she didn't want to bring up sad memories. Have you read all five of them?"

"Yes. Some, four or five times. Would you like to read them together?"

"Yes!" Harriet reached over to squeeze Luisa's hand. "I'd love that!"

After a short nap and another bowl of soup for lunch, Harriet and Luisa sat down on the couch in the reception room and began taking turns reading Nana Lottie's letters aloud. When they got to the end of the second letter and Luisa read the rabbi's words, "We can't change what needs to be changed unless we understand how it happened," she stopped reading.

"What?" asked Harriet.

"That's exactly what Daniel said when we were reading about the *falsos positivos*."

"Daniel?"

"From art class. He was the one who told me about how the soldiers killed innocent people who didn't have a lot of money or family to protect them. I felt so sick, I had to run to the bathroom to throw up. When I came back, I told Daniel I was sorry I'd found out. It would've been better for me not to know. That's when he said, 'It's never better not to know. You can't change what needs to be changed unless you understand how it happened.'"

Harriet nodded.

"Can you imagine how Nana felt when she went to school and saw the synagogue and her school burning? And how she felt when she ran to her parents' store and found Nazis closing it down? Not knowing if they were going to hurt her? Or maybe even shoot her? And how she felt leaving on a train to a place she'd never been all alone without even her little sister with her?"

Luisa stopped. Nana didn't have a little sister. She was the one with a little sister.

Harriet reached for Luisa's hand and held it tight.

"No, I can't imagine. But you can."

Luisa squeezed her hand back and let the tears she was holding back flow.

They sat there holding hands until Luisa was ready to keep reading.

"Okay, letter three. It's your turn to read," Luisa said, handing Harriet the letter.

"Okay, letter three." Harriet put her glasses on. "The day after my visit to Rabbi Goldberg's house I began my job as a companion to Mother Ross."

"Wait. Did you adopt Ana and me because someone took Nana Lottie in?"

The question was so direct it took Harriet by surprise. She took off her glasses and took a moment before answering.

"Did you ever hear of a book called *The Diary of Anne Frank?*" she asked.

Luisa shook her head.

"Nana gave me a copy when I was in grade six. Anne was my age and living in Amsterdam with her family when the Nazis invaded and occupied the Netherlands. Her family went into hiding for two years in a place she called the Secret Annex, which she wrote about in her diary. They were safe for two years until someone betrayed them to the Nazis and they were sent to concentration camps. There were eight people who lived in the Secret Annex and only one of them, Anne's father, survived. Anne and her older sister Margot died in Bergen-Belsen, not very long before the camps were liberated."

"How old was she when she died?" asked Luisa.

"Sixteen. The same age as Nana Lottie when she left Germany on the Kindertransport. I knew if Nana hadn't left Germany, she would've been sent to a concentration camp like Anne. She probably wouldn't have survived. I knew right then and there that I as soon as I was ready to have a family, I'd offer a home to a child who needed one. I'd take care of them and give them whatever I could to help them live the best lives they could.

"The moment I saw the picture of you and Ana in the Global Family newsletter I knew I wanted to offer you both a home. Jonathan wasn't sure it was the right thing to do. He thought you might be happier living with a family in Bogotá. But I argued hard. I told him that you and Ana had been at El Orfanato for three years and it was unlikely a local family would adopt two older girls. I told him the reason your pictures were in the newsletter was because it was difficult to find you a home. We could afford to adopt two sisters. We'd make sure you kept up your Spanish and stay connected to your Colombian culture. We'd offer you a university education. He finally agreed.

"When Nana Lottie talked about the cattle market at Dovercourt in her letter, I could understand why she thought she was lucky to have been taken in by the Rosses. But when she wrote how desperate she was to get her parents out of Germany, I also began to understand what she lost the day she got on the train to England. Nana never talked about what she had lost when she left Germany, so I never thought about what you and Ana might be losing when Jonathan and I brought you home with us. I only thought about what we could offer you."

Harriet searched Luisa's face. Luisa knew she wanted to know if she'd made the right choice adopting her and Ana.

"Like Nana," Luisa began carefully, "I lost a lot. All those Spanish classes didn't stop me from losing my Colombian accent. People here think I speak like a *gringa.* I never learned any Colombian history. If I had, maybe finding out about the *falsos positivos* wouldn't have been so shocking. But the biggest thing I lost was the chance to spend time with Beatriz and my grandparents before they died. Beatriz came to El Orfanato to take Ana and me home. But we'd already left."

Harriet was shocked. "No one told us," she said. "I didn't know. If I had known, of course we would have—"

"I know, I know. El Orfanato kept it from all of us." Luisa knew she sounded bitter.

Harriet folded her hands on her lap and lowered her head. "I don't know what to say."

Luisa struggled to break through the bitterness.

"There's nothing you can say that will change what happened," she finally said in a voice that was as soft and gentle as she could manage. "There's nothing you can do but sit beside me while I grieve what I've lost. What both Ana and I have lost. And help us live the best life we can. Just like Nana Lottie."

Harriet nodded, her head still lowered to hide the pain and shame.

Luisa stood up and started pacing around the room. "Do you think that's why Nana Lottie wrote me the letters? Because she knew I'd find out how much I lost?"

Harriet looked up, keeping her eyes on Luisa's face as she walked back and forth. "I think it's very likely. I know she's been very worried about what going back to Bogotá might bring up for you. Do you want to take a break?"

"No. Let's keep going," Luisa said. "Unless you need a break?"

"Actually, I need a moment. Can you pick up where I left off?"

"Okay."

Luisa sat down again and continued reading Nana's third letter. When she came to the end, she went back and re-read what Rabbi Goldberg had told Nana just before he left to the United States, "Don't give up, it's not over yet."

"You know," said Luisa to Harriet, "there were so many times in the last few weeks I repeated Rabbi Goldberg's words to myself over and over again. 'Don't give up.' Your *mamá*'s gone, but your *papá* may still be alive. Or someone else in your family may still be alive. 'Don't give up, it's not over yet.' And then I found Beatriz. And although she says she doesn't want to see me again, she put the photo of Ana and me in her wallet and took the time to write and tell me what she'd learned from Ricardo. Maybe the next time I come back to Bogotá, Beatriz will agree to meet again. 'It's not over yet.'"

"No," said Harriet. "You're right. It's not over yet. It's far from over yet. Do you want to read the next letter?"

"Sure."

Luisa read the fourth letter to Harriet, the one that talked about Nana's parents moving to Kippenheim to start a shoe business and how when war was declared Nana cried not for days, not for weeks, but for months until her friend Susanne encouraged her to join the Women's Auxiliary Air Force and fight the Nazis. When she finished reading, Harriet's head was bowed again and Luisa could see she'd been crying.

Luisa put her hand on Harriet's shoulder. "There's one more letter left. Do you want me to keep reading? Or should we stop for now."

"Let's stop for now. I think the sun is finally coming out. We can go get some ice cream."

"Sure."

They walked down the hill to the convenience store and bought two ice cream cones. Vanilla for Harriet. Chocolate for Luisa. Then they walked back up the hill—slowly—not saying very much to each other, each of them thinking their own thoughts about what Nana Lottie had shared in her letters. When they got to the old blue bench they sat down carefully to make sure it could hold them both and finished their ice cream. Then Luisa wiped her hands, took Nana's last letter out of her pocket and began reading it aloud.

CHAPTER 23

Dear Luisa:

It was Rose from the Finchley shul who found out I could send money to my parents in Camp de Gurs. There was a black market run by farmers who lived close to the camp. They sold things to the prisoners through the barbed wire fence. I saved as much as I could from my WAAF salary and sent my parents money every week. I'm not sure how much money actually got to them, but I hope they received at least some of it and that it helped them in some way.

I got the occasional letter from both my mother and father. The last letter I received from my father was dated August 9, 1941. He wrote, "Tomorrow I'm going to be deported again, but I don't know where. It may be a very long time before you hear from me again."

Then I received a letter from my mother, dated about a month after my father's letter, September 1, 1941. She told me what I already knew. My father had been deported, and she had no idea where he'd been sent. Then she wrote, "Tomorrow I'm also going to be deported from here. Shver iz dos lebn in goles. Life in exile is difficult. Continue to be the exceptional person you are, hardworking, courageous. Hold your head high, keep the faith, and never give up hope. I love you."

Living in exile in England during the war was not as difficult as living with the uncertainty of what was going to happen to my parents. The uncertainty wasn't just difficult. It was almost unbearable. Worse than living through the Blitz when Nazi planes dropped bombs every night for almost two months. The minute the air raid siren went off, we all had to run to shelter. If I was in Kinloss Gardens with Rose we'd run to the nearest subway station and join the crowds of people sitting inside on the platforms, anxiously waiting for the all-clear signal. Often, we had to spend the night there listening to people quietly crying in the darkness.

It was Rose who helped me through the absolutely dreadful time of uncertainty. After I'd found out that both my parents had been deported from France, she wrote to me at the base every day. Her letters were delivered to me during the long tedious days of keeping track of what equipment came in and out of the base, not knowing if anything I was sending out ever helped anyone to fight the Germans or stay alive. The notes were a lifeline. They reminded me I wasn't completely alone in the world and that someone cared about me and what I was doing.

At the end of every note Rose reminded me I could come and stay with her in Kinloss Gardens as often as I wanted. When I was able to get to London to visit, she kept me busy from the moment I got up until the moment I went to bed. I became a member of the Finchley Sisterhood and spent afternoons putting together Jewish care packages for the Jewish soldiers fighting in Europe. Kosher salami donated by the delis in the neighbourhood, mandel brot from the bakeries, socks, cigarettes, books. Working beside Rose, tying one brown paper package after another with string helped. So did going to shul. I tried to arrive in London on Friday evening so I could go to services Saturday morning. My mother wanted me to keep the faith, and praying helped me feel close to her. I prayed for my parents' safety, for their survival. I prayed for the strength to stay optimistic, hopeful. I asked God to help me become the exceptional person my mother believed I was, and I thanked God for bringing Rose into my life.

The last note I received from my mother was a postcard dated September 4, 1942. Her handwriting was very shaky. She said she was travelling to the east. I knew travelling east meant she was being sent to one of the concentration work camps in Poland. But I didn't want to believe it, so I told myself maybe she was travelling back east to somewhere else. There was still a chance I'd see her there after the war. I just had to wait for the war to be over. I stayed hopeful. I stayed optimistic. Until the newspapers began reporting that Hitler's concentration camps had become extermination camps and millions of people, mostly Jews, were being murdered. That's when I lost my optimism. What were the chances that my parents were alive when millions of Jews had been gassed in Hitler's extermination camps?

People think that optimism is something you're born with. They talk about people they know who have a sunny nature, people who always look on the bright side of life. But optimism can come and go, and it can disappear completely. Once you lose it, you have to fight hard to find it again.

Rose found a Jewish social worker who ran support groups for people whose loved ones had been sent to concentration camps. People who had to live with knowing and not knowing what had happened to them. Every time I came to London, Rose would find out when the group was getting together and came with me to the meeting so I could learn how to live with the grief. The grief of knowing and not knowing.

Then one Saturday morning Harry came to the Shabbat service at Finchley. I didn't even notice him until after the service when he came over to say hello at the kiddush. He was wearing a Royal Canadian Air Force uniform, and the first thing I noticed wasn't how handsome he was, although he was quite handsome, but how familiar-looking he was. Tall with curly black hair that had been cut short. He looked like the older brother of one of the boys I went to school with. A Jewish airman! From Canada! He asked me what kind of work I was doing for the WAAF, and when I told him I was an equipment supply clerk he said it was one of the most important jobs in the Air Force. Without the right equipment sent to the right base, the pilots couldn't get their planes off the ground.

I didn't believe him but was flattered anyway. I asked him what squadron he was attached to. He was part of the Bomber Command group who went out on nighttime raids bombing German factories and bridges.

"Are you a pilot?"

"No, a navigator."

The navigators were the airmen who kept the planes on course and made sure they reached their targets. Then they had to guide the crew safely back to home base. It was a very dangerous job.

"Do have plans for the rest of Shabbat?" asked Rose.

"No, not really."

"Come home with us. We'll have lunch, show you the neighbourhood and then Lottie and I will make dinner."

"I'd love to."

Harry thought Kinloss Gardens was wonderful. He said it reminded him of Kensington Market, the Jewish neighbourhood he lived in in Toronto. Rose asked him what it was like for the Jews in Toronto.

"It's not Nazi Germany, but there's antisemitism there just like there is almost everywhere. But Kensington Market is wonderful. A strong, tightly knit Jewish community."

After dinner, Rose and I walked Harry back to the train station to catch the last train back to his base.

"Come back to see us anytime you can. Come to shul, come to lunch, come to dinner, and stay over if you want. If Lottie's in town, we can share my bedroom and you can have the guest room. Really, I mean it. You're welcome anytime."

Harry gave Rose a hug. "Thank you Rose, I will."

And then he turned to me, took my hand, and said, "I'll see you soon."

"Take care of yourself. Stay safe." I said it as casually and lightly as I could. Navigators couldn't afford to know someone was worrying about them when they went on raids. They needed to focus all their concentration on their mission.

As Harry left the station to make his way to the platform, Rose took my arm as we walked back to her place.

"Now, there's a lovely young man," she said.

"Almost half of the airman who go out on bombing raids won't survive the war."

"He's still a lovely young man."

Harry survived. Mission after mission. And every time he came to visit Rose and me at Kinloss Gardens, I liked him better and better. I found out he was exceptionally good at math, which is how he become a Bomber Command navigator. I found out when the war was over, he was going to go back to school and become an architect so he could build things instead of destroying them. When I found out his parents were Orthodox Jews who'd emigrated from Poland to Canada, I couldn't help thinking what my life would've been like if my parents had followed Harry's parents' path and gone to Toronto instead of Munich.

When Harry asked me to marry him and come live with him in Toronto when the war was over, I told him I couldn't leave until I knew for sure that my parents hadn't survived the death camps. He told me he'd wait. We could get married at the Finchley shul and I could come to Canada when I was ready. I told him if by some miracle my parents were alive, we'd have to sponsor them to come to Canada. He said of course. And then I told him if I went to live in Toronto, we'd have to come back to see Rose once a year or have her come visit us. She was my family now. He said of course. So I said yes.

We spent V-Day together in Kinloss Gardens, dancing and eating and drinking with the other Canadian airmen in town and were married at the Finchley shul several days later. We both wore our uniforms. I held a small bouquet of white calla and tulips. Rose was my witness.

The Finchley Sisterhood prepared a reception of cake and champagne, and Rose made a toast.

"To Lottie and Harry. We wish you a wonderful life together in Toronto, a life full of family and community that honours the memory of Lottie's mother and father, may they rest in peace, and the life they would have wanted for her. L'chaim. To life."

Harry borrowed a car, and we had a brief honeymoon in the Lake District, which was famous for its forests and mountains as well as its lakes. Then Harry went back to Toronto, and I waited for the list of concentration camp survivors to be posted at Bloomsbury House where all the refugee organizations were located.

After the war, Susanne wrote to say that when she was demobbed from the Air Force, she was going to try teaching. Because so many young teachers had been killed in the war there was a shortage of teachers and the government set up a program to pay for teacher training and accommodation. It turned out that teaching really suited Susanne. She had found her vocation.

Harry wrote every day, telling me what it was like to be back in Toronto, how much his parents enjoyed receiving my letters and how much they were looking forward to meeting me. It took a year for Bloomsbury House to publish the lists of people who were murdered in Auschwitz and the other camps. The day the lists were posted, I put on my mother's coat, which was no longer too big for me, and her gray cashmere scarf. I already knew I was probably going to find my parents' names on one of the lists hanging on the white cracked wall, but when I saw their names in small black print, it hit me hard. I read their names over and over again to make sure it was them. Rose was right beside me, and when I finally walked away from the wall and reached out to grab her hand, she held it tight and then took me in her arms and held me while I cried. It was over. My parents were gone. So were Susanne's parents and her little sister.

I called Harry. He told me he loved me and that he'd found a bright sunny apartment for us to live in just a few blocks away from Kensington Market. When I arrived, we'd start furnishing it together.

A few weeks later I got on one of the ships that was taking war brides to Canada. The trip across the Atlantic Ocean was rough, and we were all sick. The constant smell of vomit on my clothes reminded me of the ferry ride from Holland to Dovercourt, and all the uncertainty and anxiety I had held onto during that ferry ride came rushing back. There was a lot to be anxious about as I crossed the ocean to come to Canada. With my parents gone and Rose far away, I had to begin a new life in a new country, a new city, and create a new family. When the ship finally arrived in Halifax at Pier 21, Harry was there to meet me. He'd taken a train from Toronto to Halifax so we could travel to Toronto together. He was wearing civilian clothes—black pants, a white shirt, and a black raincoat—and I almost didn't recognize him. His curly black hair was a little longer, and he was carrying flowers. A bouquet of red roses. I'd never been given a bouquet of roses. I brought them up to my nose expecting them to have a sweet scent. They didn't. I tried not to take it as sign that life in Toronto wasn't going to be as sweet as I hoped.

On the train ride from Halifax to Toronto, Harry told me his parents were coming to meet us at the station. We'd stay at their place for a week or two while we got our own apartment ready. Thinking about living with strangers for two weeks was terrifying, and the enormity of what lay ahead of me hit me hard. Somehow, I had to find the optimism to live my best life possible in a place where I didn't know anyone but Harry. I'll be honest. It wasn't easy. But going back to school, becoming a social worker and learning how to help people heal also helped me heal. Like Susanne, I found the right profession.

My darling, precious Luisa, I don't know what you are going to find about your parents and family during your trip to Bogotá. I don't know if you are going to want to stay and make Bogotá your home again or if you're going to come back to your home in Toronto. But whatever you decide, I want you to know that you are not alone. Just like Rose loved me and was there for me, Harriet, Marty, your sisters, and I love you and are here for you. No matter what happens. No matter where you decide to make home.

Lots of love,
Nana Lottie

When Luisa finished reading the last letter, she and Harriet were quiet.

Finally Luisa said, "It's hard to imagine Nana losing her optimism. She's the most upbeat person I know."

Harriet nodded.

"What were Harry's parents like? Where they nice to Nana?"

"More than nice. They adored her and treated her like a daughter. And they respected her. They respected how clever she was and the trauma work she did with the Jewish refugees and immigrants who arrived after the war from Europe."

"Did you ever meet Rose?"

"Once. When I was ten. We went to visit her in London to celebrate her eightieth birthday. But I didn't know how close Rose and Nana Lottie had been during the war and how important Rose was to Nana Lottie."

"Did you visit Kinloss Gardens. Was it as wonderful as Nana said it was?"

"Yes."

"We should go there together some day."

Harriet gave her a big smile. "I'd love that."

"You know," Luisa said, "I think Rose was to Nana Lottie what Sister Francesca is to me. Family. When I didn't have one."

As if she knew they were talking about her, Sister Francesca stuck her head out the front door of the orphanage.

"I'm going to serve dinner in ten minutes. *Pequeña*, are you feeling well enough to eat with the rest of us?"

"Yes, I think so."

"Good. Would Harriet like to stay?"

Luisa asked her.

"*Si*," said Harriet. "*Muchas gracias.*"

"Good," said Sister Francesca. "Then go wash up and come sit down."

Harriet and Luisa got up and walked to the girls' bathroom, Luisa's fingers lightly touching Harriet's elbow, Nana's words circling in her head. "You are not alone. No matter where you decide to make home."

CHAPTER 24

The next day Daniel came to say goodbye. Harriet and Luisa waited for him on the bench outside the orphanage. He got out of the taxi with two packages in his arms and gave them an awkward wave.

Luisa laughed and got up to greet him. Daniel put down the packages to give Luisa a quick friendly hug, then picked them up again and walked over to say hello to Harriet.

"Harriet!" he said and greeted her with a kiss on her right cheek. "So nice to meet you."

"So nice to meet you too," Harriet said in Spanish.

"You speak Spanish!"

"Just a little."

"How's it going?" he asked Luisa.

"Okay." Her voice was still a little weak.

"You should sit down," he said.

Luisa sat down, and Daniel handed her one of the packages. "It's your painting of Sister Francesca. Laura wrapped it up. She said there's a note inside and she'll text you when she's back in Toronto."

"That's so nice of her."

Luisa turned to Harriet and translated.

"Fantastic," she said. "I can't wait to see it. Ask Daniel how his own painting's going."

Luisa did, and then translated back and forth while Daniel perched on a rock beside the bench and talked about his latest painting. Then he asked Harriet about the work she did at her school. Finally, he asked about Luisa. What Luisa was like as a kid.

"Determined," said Harriet. "A terrific artist and a great salsa dancer." Daniel laughed and said when she came back to Bogotá he'd take Luisa dancing.

"Well," said Harriet standing up, "I'm going to walk down the hill and buy everyone ice cream for dinner tonight."

"The kids will love that," Luisa replied.

"Tell Daniel I appreciate what a good friend he's been to you. How he was there to support you when I wasn't."

Luisa translated and Daniel got up.

"It was my pleasure."

As Harriet made her way down the hill, Daniel took Harriet's place and started to sit down on the bench.

"Be careful," said Luisa. "It's kind of wobbly."

"Okay." He eased his way down slowly and sat next to her. "I can't believe you're leaving tomorrow," he said, his voice sad.

"I know," said Luisa. "Me either. It all happened very quickly. But I have something to show you before I go."

She handed him the letter.

"It's from Beatriz. She met someone who talked to my father just before he disappeared."

Daniel opened the letter and read it slowly. Then he read it again even more slowly.

"We didn't want to believe it was true," he said. "But maybe it is. Maybe your father was one of the *falsos positivos*. How are you feeling?"

"Heartbroken. For him, for *mamá*. For Ana and me."

Luisa turned to face Daniel and put her hand on his shoulder. "You went to a very dark place with me when there wasn't anyone else I could ask. You didn't know me very well, but you went with me anyway."

Daniel reached up and placed his hand over Luisa's. They were quiet for a moment.

"I've brought you a present." Daniel reached for the second package that was leaning against the rock beside the bench. "It's my painting of the city. I just finished it."

"It's finished?! Can I see it?"

"Sure," he answered, excited to show it her.

Daniel opened the package and put the painting on his lap. It dazzled Luisa with colour. Intense, unexpected colour.

"Wow," she said. "Double wow!" Daniel grinned.

The mountains in the background were not only green they were also blue and purple. The buildings sitting below the mountains were not only pink, like the buildings in Daniel's photograph, they were also purple, red, and turquoise. And in the foreground, on top of the hill where people could take in the fabulous view of the city Daniel had painted, sat a bench. A blue bench. The blue bench at El Orfanato. Shiny and new.

"I don't know what to say. I'm a little overwhelmed," said Luisa.

"You like it?"

"It's stunning. I love it. Thank you."

Daniel was pleased. "You're welcome. So when are you coming back to Bogotá?"

"Next summer. The whole family's coming back."

"Great. I want to meet them!"

"They'll want to meet you too. Especially after they see your painting. You can take us on a tour of the street art in La Candelaria. The tour we never finished. They'd love that. So would I."

They sat together a little while longer. Luisa took a selfie of the two of them sitting on the blue bench where children make family and say goodbye to family. Then Daniel got into a taxi and went back to his life at Uniandes, and Luisa went back into the orphanage to finish packing.

That night, Luisa's last night at the orphanage, she asked Harriet to help her say goodnight to the younger kids. Since she'd gotten sick, Luisa hadn't been able to tell them a story or tuck them in. When she'd said goodbye to everyone at dinner, she'd promised to come in to tell them one more story.

"Luisa! Harriet!" the children shouted when they walked into the younger girls' room.

Harriet was a little overwhelmed at such a big welcome.

"You're kind of famous around here. Come sit down."

Harriet sat down beside Luisa on Angie's bed.

"Do you really have to go?" asked Angie.

"Yes. I need to go back to Toronto to get better."

Luisa's voice was even weaker than it was during Daniel's visit. It had been a long emotional day of goodbyes. The kids all gathered on the floor in front of Angie's bed so they could hear her.

"Can't you get better here?" asked Santiago.

"I'll get better faster if I go back to Toronto. But before I go, I'll tell you the story of when Luisa came back to El Orfanato after being away for seven years."

They all leaned forward.

"When Luisa finally finished high school, she decided she wanted to go back to the orphanage where she and Ana had lived. She wanted to see Sister Francesca again and meet all the children who were living there. She bought an airplane ticket, took a taxi to the airport, but didn't tell anyone she was leaving Toronto to go to Bogotá."

"Not even Harriet?"

"Not even Harriet."

They all gasped.

Luisa looked at Harriet. "I just told them I left Toronto to come here without telling you."

"They're as shocked as I was," said Harriet, making a surprised face and nodding at the children.

"But Luisa left Harriet a note telling her where she was going, and Harriet phoned Sister Lorena and asked if Sister Francesca could meet

Luisa at the airport and bring her back to the orphanage. She didn't want Luisa to take a taxi from the airport to El Orfanato all by herself. When Luisa arrived, Sister Lorena called her into her office and told her she wanted the children at El Orfanato to learn English. She told Luisa to call Harriet and ask her if she could stay and teach everyone English. Harriet said yes."

The kids started clapping.

"Why are they clapping?"

"I just told them about when Sister Lorena asked you if I could stay to teach English here and you said yes."

She smiled. "Right. *Sí!*" she told the kids. They laughed.

"Luisa had a lot of great days and nights at the orphanage, but her favourite was the day when the younger kids asked her to teach them how to sing "Soy Colombiano" in English. They practiced for two weeks and then performed it for everyone while Sister Francesca accompanied them on her guitar. That night Luisa could sing a song from her Bogotá life in the language of her Toronto life. That night she could be both from Bogotá and Toronto."

Luisa ended the story there.

"When are you coming back?" asked Santiago.

"Next summer."

"Will Harriet come too?"

Harriet heard her name and looked at Luisa.

"He wants to know if you'll visit when we come back next summer."

She gave the kids a big smile. "Sure."

"Okay. It's time for bed."

As the boys left, Luisa stood up, tucked each girl in and walked to the door. Harriet followed her.

Luisa turned off the lights.

"Good night, *chiquitas.*"

"Good night, Luisa!"

They went to say good night to the boys and tuck them in. As they walked out of their room, they bumped into Sophia who was waiting for Luisa.

"Could I talk to you?" she asked.

"Sure. Harriet, this is Sophia."

"Nice to meet you," said Harriet in Spanish.

Sophia shook her hand. "Nice to meet you, too," said Sophia in English. "Thanks for the ice cream." It sounded sincere. Or at least sincere enough.

"You're welcome," said Harriet. She turned to Luisa. "I've called a taxi to take me to the guest house. I'll see you tomorrow."

"Okay." Luisa gave her a quick hug goodbye and turned to Sophia. "What's up?"

"I have something to give you."

Sophia reached into the back pocket of her jeans and pulled out a red ribbon.

"It belongs to you."

Luisa took the ribbon and turned it over again and again. It was faded, frayed.

"Is this the ribbon I lost? The one my *mamá* gave me?" Luisa's voice was incredulous.

"You didn't lose it," said Sophia. "I took it and hid it under my pillow. Just before you left. I never wore it. Everyone would've known it was yours. But every night, after the lights went out, I would take it out from under my pillow and hold it. Just for a few seconds. Then I'd put it back under the pillow."

"Why did you take it?" Luisa asked. She knew the question was a little too personal and Sophia might not answer. She also knew she might not like the answer.

Sophia shrugged her shoulders. Casual. As if it were no big deal.

"I was jealous. I really wanted a family. You got one. You know, after you left, I prayed every night for a family to adopt me. I believed if I just prayed hard enough and long enough God would send me a family.

I prayed until I turned ten. That's when Sister Gabriela—she was the director then—called me into her office. She told me I needed to work as hard as I could at school so I could go to university. Now that I was ten, I wasn't ever going to be adopted. I told her, no, that wasn't true. I could still get adopted because you were adopted after you turned ten. Sister Gabriela said you were the only child she'd ever known who'd been adopted at ten. It rarely happened. I know she was trying to look out for me, but it really hurt. If you could be adopted, why not me? What was wrong with me?"

"Of course, it hurt. But nothing was wrong with you. Nothing *is* wrong with you. You deserve a home just like everyone else."

"I'm sorry I took your ribbon," Sophia said, contrite, looking past Luisa towards the younger girls' room.

Luisa looked down at the washed-out ribbon clutched tightly in her hand. She was holding the ribbon her *mamá* had held in her own hands before she tied it around Luisa's ponytail.

"Thanks for returning it. I've missed it."

"Is it okay for me to keep the grammar book?"

"Sure." Luisa reached out to give Sophia a hug goodbye. She let her, kind of.

Luisa went back to Claudia's room. She was busy studying but looked up when she came in.

"I have something for you," Luisa said with a smile.

She walked over to the bed and lifted the grey blanket.

"Your red blanket!"

"You know about my blanket?"

Every morning, when Luisa made her bed, she had made sure to hide it underneath the gray one so Claudia wouldn't see it. She didn't want to show it off.

Claudia laughed. "I've had my eye on it for a long time."

"Well, tomorrow it's yours."

"Thank you! So, I have some news." Her eyes glimmered with excitement.

"What?"

"I had coffee with Alejandro yesterday."

Luisa's heart flip flopped.

"How was it?" She tried to be generous.

"Wonderful."

"I'm glad." She was. But she was also jealous. Fortunately, Claudia didn't pick it up.

"It was easier than I thought," said Claudia. "But it wouldn't have ever happened if you hadn't told me to go say hello to him at the clinic. The only reason I went to see him is because you told me to. You were confident that he liked me. Your confidence gave me confidence."

She hugged Luisa, and Luisa hugged her back. Pleased. Genuinely pleased she'd done something to help Claudia.

The next morning, Luisa got up early. There was just one thing left to do. Say goodbye to Sister Francesca.

She headed over to the kitchen carefully carrying her portrait of Sister Francesca with both hands. Sister Francesca was making toast.

"Hello *pequeña*! How are you this morning? Do you want some toast?"

"No thanks. I still don't have much of an appetite." The smell of toasted bread actually made her feel a little nauseous.

Sister Francesca took a good look at Luisa and said, "You look a little pale, you better sit down."

Luisa sat down at the small table in the corner with the painting on her lap.

"What's that?"

"It's a painting. It's not finished yet. But I wanted you to see what it looks like so far." Luisa unwrapped it carefully and held it up so Sister Francesca could see it.

"Is that me?"

"Yes."

"But my breasts are gigantic! So are my hands and feet!"

"That's because you worked so hard to take care of the little girl in the picture."

She looked carefully at the little girl who still needed a face.

"You held her close when she was upset, cared for her when she was sick, and walked down and up a crazy steep hill to buy her and the other children good, fresh food to eat. You also welcomed her back to the orphanage, tried to teach her about patience, and loved her with your big, big heart. Even when she disappointed you. You are the little girl's Colombian mother."

Sister Francesca came over and gave Luisa a hug, struggling not to cry.

"I'm happy to be your Colombian mother."

They hugged for a long time. Grateful to be in each other's lives.

Sister Francesca let go first. "So when will you finish up my painting?"

"I'll bring it with me when we come back and visit next summer. But before I go, there are two things I want to tell you. The first is I asked Harriet to go the bank for me and buy some pesos." Luisa took a white envelope out of her knapsack. "This is for a new television."

"*Pequeña*, you shouldn't spend your money on a television for us. You're going to university in the fall. You'll need it."

"Don't worry. I'll find a job this summer to help pay for university. I want to leave the children with something special."

Sister Francesca took the envelope. "That's very generous. Thank you."

"Okay, the second thing." Luisa took a deep breath. "I've wanted to tell you this for a while but was too afraid. Did you know Harriet and Jonathan aren't married anymore?"

"Yes."

"How did you find out?"

"The girls were talking about it."

"Did they also talk about Harriet's partner Marty?"

"Yes."

"So you know. I wanted to tell you myself, but I was afraid. I know how important the Church is to you and I know what the Church thinks of homosexuality. I didn't want it to come between us. But Sister Lorena told me she believes everyone is a child of God no matter who they love. She can accept Harriet and Marty for who they are. Maybe you can too."

"You know, *pequeña*, I didn't go to a liberal school like Sister Lorena. My teachers were traditional, and my beliefs are traditional. Including my beliefs about marriage. But I try not to judge people. Harriet's created a beautiful life for you and Ana and Clare. She loves you and has worked hard to give you everything you need. Marty's helped her. They are good people, and I think you're lucky to have them in your life."

It wasn't exactly what Luisa hoped to hear, but it was close enough. She gave Sister Francesca another hug.

"I'll miss you," she said.

"I'll miss you too, *pequeña*. Take care of yourself and Ana."

"I will. I always do."

The taxi dropped Luisa and Harriet off at the international terminal close to the Air Canada counter. They printed off their boarding passes, checked their luggage, then headed off to the Juan Valdez coffee shop.

While Harriet waited for her ten bags of coffee to be ground (gifts for the Globals), Luisa sat at a little table in front of the shop sipping a café con leche. Her last Colombian café con leche for a while. By the time Harriet paid for the coffee, it was time to go to the gate. They got there just as people were beginning to board. The flight was easy. No turbulence, no unexpected bad weather. As they started the descent into Toronto, the pilot came on the intercom and told everyone there were clear skies ahead. He expected a smooth landing.

As Harriet and Luisa tightened their seatbelts, Luisa turned to Harriet and said, "Thank you for coming to Bogotá to take care of me and help me find my strength again."

"Of course."

"You know, I've been thinking. Nana, you, and I, we have a shared legacy. A legacy of survival. Nana Lottie survived Nazi Germany because someone she didn't know took her in. And because of that you felt compelled to adopt Ana and me. And when I came face to face with the violence of my parents' deaths, you came to Bogotá and faced it with me. Nana, you, and me, we have all survived violence. We will share that legacy forever."

Harriet reached over, hugged Luisa the best she could with her seat belt on and gave her a kiss on the cheek.

"Forever," she said, taking her hand, happy.

The landing wasn't as smooth as the pilot promised. The wheels of the plane hit the ground with big bump, and Harriet and Luisa lurched forward and backward while the plane sped down the runway to the gate. As it began to slow down, they both took a big breath. Everything was fine. In a few minutes the plane would stop, they'd get out, go through customs to the luggage carousel, and then out the door where Ana, Clare, and Marty were waiting for them.

"Are you ready to go home?" asked Harriet. "I mean to your Toronto home?"

"Yes," said Luisa. "I'm ready."

EPILOGUE

It took almost three weeks for Luisa to fully recover from the pneumonia she caught in Bogotá, but as soon as she felt well enough, she went to visit Nana Lottie. They met in her room at the retirement residence, and Nana had dressed up for the visit. She was wearing a hot pink tank top with a matching cardigan sweater and black dress pants. No eyeshadow, mascara, or rouge, but her signature hot pink lipstick had been perfectly applied. Maureen had helped her get ready. Nana looked eighty-two, not 102.

"My precious darling girl. How wonderful to see you!" Nana took both of Luisa's hands in her own and held them tightly, excited to see Luisa again.

"It's wonderful to see you, too, Nana."

"So? How was it?"

"It was hard. It's still hard."

"I understand," she said squeezing both of Luisa's hands.

"I've changed. I don't feel like myself. It's like I don't know who I am anymore. Do you know what I mean?"

Nana nodded slowly. "The first time I felt that way was in England. Being on my own, taking care of Mother Ross, trying to find work for my parents. I wasn't the person I was when I lived with my parents in Germany. And you know what? I never found that person again. That self was gone. But I built a new self."

"I think I'm going to have to build a new self too."

Nana nodded seriously.

"Nana, do you think we could read your letters together? I have so many questions I want to ask. So much I want to tell you. Would that be okay, or would it be too tiring? Too painful?"

"I don't know," Nana said taking away her hands and shaking her head. "I don't like to talk about the past."

"I know, Nana. You never talk about Germany or England. But I'm feeling a little lost. I need to know I'm not always going to feel this way."

Nana took Luisa's hands again. They were cold.

"Okay," she said. "Let's try and see how it goes."

For the rest of the spring and summer Luisa went to visit Nana Lottie so they could re-read her letters to Luisa and talk. Early on, Luisa asked Nana if she ever went back to Munich.

"No. The Munich I loved as a child didn't exist after the war. I never wanted to go back. After the war I would've been happy to make Kinloss Gardens my home and spend my life living close to Rose, but when I married Harry, I needed to make Toronto home. So, I guess you can say I've had three homes."

"How long did it take for Toronto to feel like home?"

"A long time. At first it was just a place I was going to because Harry lived there. It was Harry's home. But when I became pregnant with Harriet, Toronto became the place I was going to raise my family. That's when it started feeling more like home."

"After we lost *mamá*, El Orfanato was my home. When Harriet and Jonathan adopted us, Toronto was this strange place I had to live in for a while because that's where they lived. It was their home, not mine. But now I want to try to build two homes. One here, one in Bogotá."

"That's exciting."

"I hope so. If you had three homes, maybe I can have two. Maybe it will take pressure off both places needing to be everything home is supposed to be. There are things I love about my home in Bogotá and things I don't love. It's the same here. I'm going to try to enjoy what I love in both places and try to change the things I don't love."

"Like what?"

"In Bogotá, the dismal lack of health care for poor families. I want to change that. Here, I want to change the way people think about transnational adoption. I've been doing a lot of reading about transnational adoption since I've been back. And even though I understand why Harriet wanted to adopt us, I don't think it was the right thing to do. And I'd like to talk to people about it, but it's a hard thing to talk about. Most people here think it's absolutely the right thing to do. Like Anita."

"Anita?"

"Anita who runs Global Family, the adoption agency Harriet and Jonathan worked with to adopt us. Anyway, whenever someone who is thinking about adopting a child from another country asks Anita if it's better for children to be adopted by families living in their birth countries, she tells them off. She gets very loud and righteous and says, 'Thousands of children are growing up in orphanages all over the world. Children who need a home should get a home. Wherever it is.' But it's more complicated than that. While no one likes to admit it, transnational adoption is a way of supplying wanna-be parents in rich countries with children from poor countries. When poor parents have to send their children to an orphanage because they can't take care of them and parents from rich countries go to those countries to adopt those children because they *can* afford to take care of them, we're separated from our biological families. We're displaced to a culture that's not our own. We grow up in a family that's White when we're not. A family that doesn't always understand the racism we face in our lives."

When Luisa finally stopped, she could see Nana was very upset. Very, very upset. Her eyes filled with pain and suddenly she looked a lot older. 102, not eighty-two.

"Have you told Harriet how you feel?" she asked.

"No, but I want to. When I find the right moment."

"It's going to be hard for her to hear what you want to say." Nana sat back in her chair. Luisa sat back in hers to give them both a little space.

"I know. But when she came to Bogotá to help me recover, I had a chance to tell Harriet a few things about being adopted that were hard for her to hear. She managed. She did more than manage. She did very well. And now we're a little closer than we were before because she understands the way we became a family is more complicated than she thought."

Nana's face cleared a bit.

"Well, if you're closer now than you were before, I'm happy."

"Nana, did you stay in touch with the family in England that took you in?"

"The Rosses? A little, mostly at the beginning of the war. I'd write the occasional letter, ask Mrs. Ross how the family was doing and talk about my work for the Air Force. But by the time I left England, we'd lost touch."

"Did that make you sad?"

"No, they never became my family. I didn't need a family. I had a mother and a father who needed my help to get out of Germany. And when that became impossible, they needed my help to stay alive in the camp in France."

"Until they were taken away."

She nodded, her face suddenly filled with grief.

Luisa took her hand. "So much loss."

Nana nodded again. "But when I get too sad thinking about how they died, how needlessly they died, I remember my mother's last words to me at the train station. 'You have been an exceptional daughter,' she said. 'Write as often as you can. We love you.' I take comfort knowing she thought I was an exceptional daughter and that my parents loved me. I take comfort in that I did write and found a way to send money to help them in France. I did what I could. And then after they died, I did what I could to live a life that would make them proud, make them happy."

Nana stopped for a moment and squeezed Luisa's hand.

"Life can begin again in a new place."

Luisa squeezed back. "Yes, Nana. I know it can. Even if it isn't easy."

***

That spring Luisa continued working on Sister Francesca's portrait and made time to hang out with Carolina and Paola from El Orfanato. On Saturday mornings their adoptive parents drove them over to Harriet's house and they'd paint together and write letters in Spanish to Sister Francesca about their lives in Toronto. Although Paola had been the one who didn't want to leave El Orfanato, she was adjusting to life with her new family more easily than Carolina. She liked her teacher and had made some friends at school. Carolina was struggling to find a place for herself. But at least she had Luisa to talk to and didn't have to carry her feelings of not fitting in all by herself. Luisa understood exactly what Carolina was going through.

Luisa finally finished Sister Francesca's portrait in June and began working on the painting of her father again. When it was finished, she started on a series of ten portraits called El Orfanato to auction off at the fundraiser she and Harriet had begun to plan for the health centre she was planning to set up in memory of her parents. Luisa's two favourite paintings in the series were Sister Francesca playing her guitar and Sister Lorena standing in front of the map in her office—the map with all the pins.

In July Sophia used some of her Global Family Scholarship money to study English in Toronto before starting pharmacy school in the fall. She stayed with Luisa's family, sharing Luisa's room while Ana was at music camp. Given how much animosity Sophia had felt towards Luisa at El Orfanato, they got along better than Luisa thought they would. As Luisa had suspected, Sophia was gifted at learning languages, and when she arrived back in Bogotá six weeks later, her English was so good that Sister Lorena asked to her to begin Luisa's English classes again.

As promised, at the end of the summer Harriet took the whole family to Bogotá and Daniel spent every day of their trip showing them the places he loved best. Everyone had a great time, and when they left, Luisa knew that when she returned, she'd still have a friend in Bogotá she could depend on for help if she needed it. And Daniel had a family he could stay with when he came to Toronto.

While she was in Bogotá, Luisa also spent time with Sister Francesca and Claudia. Claudia and Alejandro had started seeing each other and were beginning to develop a relationship. When Claudia finally told Alejandro she was worried his parents might think a girl with no family and no money wasn't good enough for him, he told her his parents weren't that narrow minded. And even if they were, what his parents thought didn't matter. What mattered was that she was as passionate about nursing as he was about being a doctor. She'd always understand the demands of his work, and he'd always understand the demands of hers. They were well matched. Claudia was ecstatic.

During Daniel's tour of the street murals in La Candelaria, Luisa asked if he would donate some of his photos to the fundraiser. He said yes immediately, and suggested he go on a photo shoot in Ciudad Bolívar during Día de los Reyes Magos so he could bring back photos of people marching in Father Álvarez's parade. Many of the kids who'd been adopted from El Orfanato would have memories of the parade, and their parents would want to buy a photo for them to keep their memories alive. Luisa thought it was a brilliant idea. In addition to selling the twenty-five prints Daniel had made, Luisa created greeting cards of all the photos and sold them in packs of five for fifty dollars each.

Luisa scheduled the art auction on a Sunday afternoon, the day before her nineteenth birthday. Almost exactly a year since her first visit to Father Álvarez. The goal was to raise $10,000. Carolina and Paola's adoptive parents, who ran a successful clothing store, had pledged to match whatever was made at the auction. To thank them, Luisa started on a painting of Carolina and Paola writing letters to Sister Francesca. She painted them both in red t-shirts, just like the ones in the painting she'd done when she was seven.

Harriet invited her principal and every single teacher at her school to the fundraiser for the health centre and challenged them to each bring three more people with them. Luisa had decided to name the centre after her *mamá* and *papá*. The Rodríguez Family Health Centre would be a place where the pain of being taken away from Bogotá as a child could be turned into something that would help other children.

Harriet decided to launch a school-wide fundraising project for the health centre, and for the rest of the year Luisa and Harriet spent time together planning fundraising events the school could host. Having a common goal helped them connect in a new way. While neither of them could change the years of anger, sadness, and loneliness Luisa had lived through after being adopted, raising money for the health centre helped them build on the closeness they'd found in Bogotá. It was on the way home from one of the school fundraisers that Luisa found the right moment to talk to Harriet about her feelings around transnational adoption.

"You know," said Harriet after she heard Luisa out, "There's a new vice principal at the school who adopted two brothers from Costa Rica ten years ago. She feels the same way you do. While she didn't understand this when she adopted the boys, she now believes transnational adoption in Costa Rica has delayed social reform. I asked her how she makes sense of it all, and she said, 'When I look at things up close right in front of me, I can feel my own personal joy of living with my children. But when I move back a bit, I can see the injustice of parents having to give up their children to keep them alive and healthy. The joy and the injustice live side by side.' What do you think of that?"

Luisa gave herself a few seconds to think about it.

"I think I can live with that," she said. "I like that she owns the injustice. The harm that's been done. Once you own the harm you can begin to do something about it. Like we are."

On the day of the fundraiser, the family transformed Harriet's living room into an art gallery. Marty and Luisa moved all the furniture into the middle of the room so Luisa could hang her paintings and Daniel's photos on the walls. Both Laura and Diego had sent Luisa pieces to auction off. Laura had packed her paintings and Diego's sculptures very carefully and sent them to Harriet's house. They arrived in perfect condition.

Luisa and Harriet invited all the Globals to the fundraiser. Luisa also sent an invitation to everyone from her Latin American studies and Spanish classes, and to Eli.

Luisa met Eli on the first day of her biology class at the University of Toronto. Taking a biology class was the first step to getting into medical school, but the class was held in a building on campus Luisa had never been to before. On the first day, she walked in late. Two hundred heads turned towards the door to look at her. The professor was lecturing at the bottom of the auditorium to a class sitting in rows above him. He was not happy.

"You're ten minutes late," he said.

"I know. I'm sorry."

"And you let the door slam. I lost my train of thought."

"I'm sorry. It won't happen again."

"Good. Find a seat."

Luisa looked up. The room was packed. There wasn't an empty seat anywhere. Then someone in the back with piercings, tats, and a short haircut stood up.

"There's one here," they said, confident.

"Thanks," Luisa said, sending a grateful nod.

The professor picked up where he'd left off, and Luisa headed up the stairs to the empty seat beside her savior. It was in the middle of the back row, so she had to step over people's feet and knapsacks. A few gave her a long-suffering look as she passed them. When she finally settled into her seat, Luisa leaned over and quietly thanked her rescuer.

"I had trouble finding the room," she whispered.

They nodded, eyes on their laptop screen, taking notes. "Me too."

Luisa pulled out a pen and notebook from her knapsack and her cell phone.

Eli shook their head.

"No cell phones."

"Oh."

"They're distracting." They nodded towards the professor.

Luisa put it back. "He's easily distracted."

They smiled, just a little, without taking their eyes off the screen.

"We're going through the syllabus." They turned their laptop to face Luisa so she could follow along.

"Thanks. I didn't know I needed to bring my laptop."

"Everything's online."

Luisa looked at the course description for Biology 1. Evolution, inheritance, cell theory, introductory biochemistry, biodiversity, ecology. Heavy.

By the time the class ended she'd written out ten pages of notes. She only understood about half of what she wrote. Less than half. People began packing up. Eli shut down their laptop, put on their navy-blue hoody and got up to go. There was a button on the front. It said, "they/them." Luisa made a mental note to use the right pronouns.

"Hey, thanks for helping me out."

"No problem."

"I'm Luisa."

"Eli."

"Nice to meet you."

"You, too."

"So" Luisa asked. "Are you majoring in biology?"

"No. English and gender studies. This is my compulsory science course. You?"

"Right now, Spanish and Latin American studies. But I need to take two half courses in biology so I can transfer into physiology next year. That will give me the prerequisites for med school. I'm going to build a health centre in Bogotá. That's where I'm from."

"Cool. So, you speak Spanish?" They raised their eyebrows, interested.

"Yeah, but with a *gringa* accent. When people in Colombia ask me where I'm from, and I say Bogotá, they laugh. They think I'm joking."

"That's annoying."

"Very."

"What did you think of the class?" Eli asked.

"Actually, I'm a little lost. I didn't take biology in high school."

"Me either. It's like learning a whole new language."

"Totally. And a quiz every week?!" She shook her head, remembering how hard Claudia had to study for her weekly biochem tests.

"I know. Really stressful."

"Maybe we could study together," Luisa suggested.

Eli nodded and handed her their phone. "That'd be good."

Luisa added her number to their contacts and handed it back. "It's under R. My last name is Rodríguez."

"Thanks. I'll text you later."

"Okay."

Eli made their way back across the row of seats that was now empty. Luisa packed up and went to apologize to Professor Ryan for being late. There were two other people waiting to talk to him. While she waited, she discreetly sized him up. He was tall, White, probably in his sixties, dressed in black pants and a white dress shirt, which he wore open at the neck. One-on-one he seemed friendlier. The student talking to him was finished. It was her turn.

"Good morning. Hi. I'm Luisa Gómez Rodríguez Silver. I just wanted to apologize for being late and disturbing you. I got lost trying to find the room."

"Apology accepted. Thanks for staying behind and explaining. How did you like the first class?"

He was definitely friendlier one-on-one, Luisa thought.

"To be honest, pretty challenging. I didn't take biology in high school. But I'm going to work hard at it."

"Make sure you to go all the tutorials."

"Who runs the tutorials?"

"I run one of them, but my teaching assistants run the rest. They'll go over all the material I've covered in the lecture, and you can ask them questions if there's something you don't understand. You can also email them in between classes."

"Is there any way I can be in your group? I really need to do well. I'm planning to go to medical school."

He hesitated, and Luisa could tell he was going to say no. He couldn't pick and choose who was placed into his group. It wasn't fair.

"Last winter, when I was volunteering at an orphanage in Bogotá, I found out that my birth mother died of pneumonia. She couldn't afford to see a doctor or buy antibiotics. I'm planning to build a family health centre in Ciudad Bolívar. That's where my sister and I were born. That whole plan starts today. With your class. I need to be in your tutorial group."

It was bold, thought Luisa, but maybe it would work.

Professor Ryan was impressed and looked around to see if there was anyone around listening. There wasn't.

"Okay. I'll move you to my section. Just don't tell anyone."

"I won't. Thanks so much."

Luisa showed up early to the second biology class that week and looked for Eli. They were sitting near the front of the auditorium, on the aisle. On the seat beside them there was a black knapsack with a rainbow keychain attached to the zipper of the bottom pocket.

"Hi. Can I sit there?"

"Yeah, I was saving it for you." They removed the knapsack and put it under their seat. Luisa sat down, then looked up to nod at Professor Ryan who was setting up his laptop at the front of the auditorium. He nodded back.

"How's it going?" Eli asked.

"I'm still adjusting to being back in school. And sharing a bedroom with my sister. She was away most of the summer."

"Older or younger?"

"Younger."

"Just one sister?"

"No, two. The second younger sister has her own room, but it's tiny. What about you? Siblings?"

"A sister. Older. She's in university in Vancouver."

"My adoptive father lives in Vancouver."

"It's beautiful there. Except—"

"It rains a lot."

"Yeah."

"Are you from Toronto?" Luisa asked.

"Yeah."

"Are you living at home?"

"No. I'm living in a queer house with three other people."

"How do you like it?"

"I'm adjusting."

"Yeah."

"So, you live with . . ."

"My adoptive mother Harriet, my birth sister Ana, my adoptive sister Clare, and Marty. My mother's partner. They identify as non-binary."

"So, you live in a queer house too."

"Totally."

"Cool. How long have Harriet and Marty been together?" Eli asked, keen to talk about them.

"Six years."

"So, you grew up with them."

"Yeah."

"Are you going to Queer Orientation Week?"

"There's a Queer Orientation Week?" Luisa asked.

"Yeah. Next week. You should come to the poetry slam. I'm going to perform."

"When is it?"

"Next Tuesday night. We could meet for dinner around six, get ready for the quiz, and then go over together."

"Sounds great." Luisa smiled, quietly thrilled.

The queer poetry slam was held at Tony's, a café on campus that had a stage and a bar. While Eli went to get them beers, Luisa looked for a table. She found one in the back and took in the scene. The event had attracted about fifty people. Most of the audience was White, but there were a few people of colour there too.

Eli found Luisa and handed her a beer. "Here you go."

"Thanks."

"No problem. Have you ever been to a poetry slam before?"

"No. How does it work?"

"People sign up to perform a poem they've written. At the beginning of the slam, the emcee chooses people from the audience to be judges. If it's a big slam, there are five judges. But tonight, there are only three. Most slams have three rounds. But some only have one. In the first round everyone who's signed up performs. After every performance each of the judges gives the performer a score between zero and ten. If there's only one round, the performer with the highest score wins. If there are three rounds, the performers with the highest scores go to the next round."

"What's happening tonight?"

"One round."

"How many people are performing?"

"Eight."

"Have you signed up?"

"Yeah."

"Do you perform often?"

"No. This is only my second time. My first time was in high school. But I want to push myself. If I'm going to be a writer, I have to get used to performing."

"Are you nervous?"

"Very."

"I'm sure you're going to be great."

"Thanks. I don't care about the score I get. I just care about getting up there and giving it a try again."

The emcee came out, welcomed everyone, and chose three judges. Then the first performer took the stage. She was a young Latina woman named Gina. Her poem was a testament to her aunt, the first person she came out to as a lesbian. When she started performing, Luisa could tell Gina had performed the piece before. She used a lot of Spanish words, and Luisa was thrilled to discover she understood every single one of them. When Gina used a phrase the audience really liked, they clapped and snapped their fingers in appreciation. When she finished, the applause was generous.

"Seems like a friendly crowd," said Luisa.

Eli nodded.

Two young men went next. A Black performer named Anthony rapped about homophobia in his high school using Jamaican patois. Then William, who was White, did a piece about the pain of not being out to his Christian family.

Eli was next. They grabbed a last sip of beer and made their way up to the stage.

"Hi. My name is Eli, and I want to perform a piece I wrote when I started transitioning in my last year of high school." The crowd clapped and cheered to encourage Eli on.

"Thanks. My piece is called 'Dear Mom and Dad.'
Dear Mom and Dad:
My name is Eli now.
Dear Mom and Dad:
Please call me Eli.

Dear Mom and Dad:
My pronoun's they now.
Dear Mom and Dad:
Please call me they.

Dear Mom and Dad:
I've turned eighteen now.
Dear Mom and Dad:
I'm starting T.

Dear Mom and Dad:
I feel so good now.
Dear Mom and Dad:
I'm finding me.

Dear Mom and Dad:
So no more talk now.
Dear Mom and Dad:
I've started T.

Thank you."

The crowd stood up and made a lot of noise. Eli smiled, nodded, and made their way back to their table. Luisa was on her feet with everyone else. When Eli reached the table, she gave them a big hug.

"That was amazing."

They hugged her back. "Thanks, I'm glad you liked it."

"How do you feel?"

"Pretty good."

"Wait, here come the judges' comments." They sat down.

All the judges praised Eli's piece and told them to keep writing. They got one nine and two eights, but only because their piece was less than a minute. If it had been longer, they would've had a higher score. Eli was happy.

After the slam Eli and Luisa met twice a week to study biology and go out for a beer. They became friends, and a week before the fundraiser, Eli came over and helped Clare and Luisa cook. They made ten big pots of chili—vegetarian and chicken—and 225 empanadas, enough for everyone to have three.

At the fundraiser, Ana performed two songs before the auction and two after. As a special surprise for Luisa's birthday, she sang "Soy Colombiano," which made Luisa's heart pound the same way it did the first time she'd heard Sister Francesca play it again. Luisa couldn't believe Ana had taken the time to learn the song and sing it in Spanish. When Luisa asked her who had helped her, she told her Harriet had brought Carolina over to the house while Luisa was at school to teach her all the words and the melody.

At the end of the afternoon, Ana and Luisa counted up the money they had raised and announced the total: $12,250. Twenty-four thousand, five hundred dollars with the matching gift from Carolina and Paola's parents. Enough money to put a down payment on the land they'd need to build the health centre.

After cleaning up, the family sat down to eat leftover chili and empanadas for dinner. Carolina and Paola and their parents joined them. Eli also stayed, and Luisa felt, for the first time since Carlos had left, she had a good friend in Toronto. With just enough chemistry on both sides to make Luisa think that one day, maybe, she and Eli might be more than friends.

Nana Lottie came over for dessert, and when she arrived, Harriet brought out some champagne and the *ponqué* she and Ana had made using Sister Francesca's recipe. It tasted just like the one Sister Francesca had made. As everyone finished up their last bites of cake, Luisa held up her glass of champagne and made a toast.

"When I was in Bogotá, my friend Daniel told me, 'You can't change what needs to be changed unless you understand how it happened.' Here's to understanding our past and changing the future. Here's to the Rodríguez Family Health Centre. *Salud,*" she exclaimed, joyful.

"*Salud,*" they all repeated, sharing Luisa's joy.

"L'chaim," said Nana Lottie, tears in her eyes, lifting her glass of champagne. "To life."

"L'chaim," Luisa repeated, clinking glasses first with Nana Lottie and then with Harriet who was standing beside Nana with her hand on Nana's shoulder.

"Wait, don't move," said Clare. "I want to get a picture of the three of you."

Luisa turned to face Clare who was positioning her phone to take a picture and clinked glasses once more time with Harriet.

"Okay, got it," said Clare.

That picture was the last picture taken of Luisa, Nana, and Harriet. A few weeks later, Nana fell and broke her hip. While the surgeon thought Nana could survive the surgery needed to repair her hip, she died before he could operate. Luisa printed the photo Clare had taken and found a lovely silver frame to place it in. The picture sat on her desk, reminding her of the first time her people in Toronto came together to honour her *mamá* and *papá* by raising money for their health centre.

The night after the fundraiser, Luisa couldn't sleep. Her mind was spinning with memories of all the excellent moments of the day: the food, the music, the love in the room. An idea for a new portrait popped into her head. She got out of bed and walked downstairs to the den where she kept her art supplies. She stretched out a new canvas, pulled out a sketch pencil, and started drawing lines across the canvas. Hands appeared. First Nana's hands, then her own hands. Huge, beautiful hands interlaced together. Every night for the next few weeks Luisa returned to the portrait and painted them sitting in the armchairs in Nana's living room, holding hands, talking about their lives in Munich, Brighton, and Bogotá. Luisa painted the light gray cashmere scarf Nana's mother had given her and placed it loosely around Nana's shoulders. Then she gave herself a curly black ponytail tied with the red ribbon her *mamá* gave her. No longer old and faded, the ribbon was bright red, just like it was when her *mamá* tied it around her ponytail for the first time. As Luisa painted, she imagined Nana's mother's hands packing her cashmere scarf into Nana's suitcase and then her *mamá's* hands sitting lightly on Luisa's shoulders after pulling her ponytail tight.

Luisa hung the portrait in the living room in Harriet's house. But one day, she would take it back to Bogotá and hang it in the health centre. Alongside portraits of her *mamá* and *papá*.

The End

ACKNOWLEDGEMENTS

Land Acknowledgement

I wrote this story while working, teaching, and living in the city of Toronto on the traditional land of the Huron-Wendat, Anishnabeg, Chippewa, Haudenosaunee, Seneca, and Mississaugas of the Credit. Today, this meeting place is still the home to many diverse First Nations, Inuit, and Métis peoples from across Turtle Island. Toronto, whose name originates from the Mohawk word *Tkaronto*, meaning "the place in the water where the trees are standing," is covered by Treaty 13, signed with the Mississaugas of the Credit, and the Williams Treaties, signed with multiple Mississauga and Chippewa bands.

At the University of Toronto, my students and I believe that "we are all treaty people" and that all people have treaty rights and responsibilities. We are beginning to learn about the role settler-colonialism has played in the immensely violent histories that have taken place against Indigenous peoples on their lands. And we carry a commitment to engage in reconciliation work to build better relationships with Indigenous peoples from across Turtle Island.

Other Acknowledgements and Thanks

For their important feedback and support during the writing of this novel, I want to thank Basil Abu Sido, Jorge Arcila, Terry Armstrong,

Jeysa Caridad, Emma Dryden, Carolyn Flynn, Doug Friesen, benjamin lee hicks, Blair Hurley, Margot Huycke, Karen Kaffko, Sharon Jennings, Brian Lam, Allan Luke, Audrey Lowitz, Ken Murray, Karleen Pendleton Jiménez, Beatriz Pizano, Jenny Salisbury, Rob Simon, and Jocelyn Wickett.

To publish this story, I worked with editor Kerry Fast, book designer Gerardo Faelnar and visual artist benjamin lee hicks. I am deeply grateful for their superb work. I am also grateful to Gezel Zozobrado for her support around managing this project.

Finally, deep gratitude goes to Martha Hen, Blair Hurley, Karleen Pendleton Jiménez, Mary Ellen MacLean, and Diane Samuels who gave generously of their time to review and comment on the novel.

Further Reading, Listening and Viewing

Transnational/Transracial Adoption

Boluda, Anna, dir. and prod. *Queer Spawn*. New York: Anna Boluda, 2005. Documentary.

Bonkowski, Basia. *Jesse's World: A Story of Adoption and the Global Family*. Milsons Point (Sydney): Random House Australia, 2005.

Demby, Gene, and Shereen M. Meraji, hosts. "Transracial Adoptees on Their Racial Identity and Sense of Self." *Code Switch*. National Public Radio, October 13, 2018. Audio podcast episode. https://www.npr.org/2018/10/13/657201204/code-switch-transracial-adoptees-on-their-racial-identity-and-sense-of-self

Opper, Nicole, dir. and prod. *Off and Running: An American Coming of Age Story*. New York: Nicole Opper Productions, 2009. Documentary.

Register, Cheri. *Beyond Good Intentions: A Mother Reflects on Raising Internationally Adopted Children*. St. Paul, MN: Yeong and Yeong, 2005.

Trenka, Jane Jeong. *Fugitive Visions: An Adoptee's Return to Korea*. St. Paul, MN: Borealis Books, 2009.

Trenka, Jane Jeong. *The Language of Blood*. St. Paul, MN: Borealis Books, 2005.

Trenka, Jane Jeong, Julie Chinyere Oparah, and Sun Yung Shin, eds. *Outsiders Within: Writing on Transracial Adoption*. Cambridge: South End Press, 2006.

Kindertransport

Harris, Mark Jonathan, dir., and Deborah Oppenheimer, prod. *Into the Arms of Strangers: Stories of the Kindertransport*. Sabine Films and the United States Holocaust Museum, 2000. Documentary.

Harris, Mark Jonathan, and Deborah Oppenheimer, eds. *Into the Arms of Strangers: Stories of the Kindertransport*. London: Bloomsbury, 2000.

Samuels, Diane. *Diane Samuels'* Kindertransport: *The Author's Guide to the Play*. London: Nick Hearn Books, 2014.

Samuels, Diane. *Kindertransport*. London: Nick Hearn Books, 1995. Play.

British Women's Forces in the Second World War

Barrett, Duncan, and Nuala Calvi. *The Girls Who Went to War*. London: HarperElement, 2015.

Photo credit: Stephanie Romero

Tara Goldstein is a writer, playwright, theatre creator and Artistic Director of Gailey Road Productions, an independent theatre company where research meets theatre and theatre meets research. Raised in Montreal, Tara currently lives in Toronto with her wife Margot and calls Australia her second home.